What Reviewers
Gill McK

Falling Star

"Angst, conflict, sex and humor. [*Falling Star*] has all of this and more packed into a tightly written and believable romance. …McKnight has penned a sweet and tender romance, balancing the intimacy and sexual tension just right. The conflict is well drawn, and she adds a great dose of humor to make this novel a light and easy read."—*Curve* Magazine

Green Eyed Monster

"When an unlikely cast of characters sets out for a lesbian romance in Gill McKnight's *Green Eyed Monster*, anything can happen, and it does! In this speedy read, McKnight succeeds in tantalizing with explosive sex and a bit of bondage; tormenting with sexual frustration and intense longing; tickling your fancy and funny bone; and touching a place where good and evil battle it out. With love vs. money at odds, readers ponder which will win, thanks to McKnight keeping the stakes high and the action palpable."—*JustAboutWrite*

By the Author

Falling Star

Green Eyed Monster

Erosistible

Goldenseal

GOLDENSEAL

by
Gill McKnight

2009

GOLDENSEAL

ISBN 10:1-60282-115-1
ISBN 13: 978-1-60282-115-6

THIS TRADE PAPERBACK ORIGINAL IS PUBLISHED BY
BOLD STROKES BOOKS, INC.
P.O. BOX 249
VALLEY FALLS, NY 12185

FIRST BOLD STROKES PRINTING: SEPTEMBER 2009

CREDITS
EDITORS: CINDY CRESAP AND STACIA SEAMAN
PRODUCTION DESIGN: STACIA SEAMAN
COVER DESIGN BY SHERI (GRAPHICARTIST2020@HOTMAIL.COM)

Acknowledgments

Once again, a big thanks to my main team, Cate, Kristin, Effey, Rae, and Ruth for keeping it fun. X

Dedication

For Ali Bell. And her big, big heart. Love and kisses.

CHAPTER ONE

Oh no, I don't need a chaperone! No way. Not here. Just tell me where in the valley I can't go, north, south, east or west, and I'll keep out of the way."

Amy Fortune was angry and adamant, underscoring her words with a furious glare at Leone Garoul, her ex-girlfriend and supposed chaperone around Little Dip Valley. Amy wanted it understood she was not going to comply. She had practically grown up in Little Dip Valley. Amy was as good as adopted into the Garoul family that owned it. She did not need an escort to go and work in the forest or mountains.

"Hey, I don't want to babysit you either, but Mom's got a point," Leone responded with a big, annoying grin. "It's hunting season in Little Dip, and you could get hurt out there. I'll just drop by your cabin each morning and take you to a safe place. You can toddle off with your paint box and draw plants to your heart's content, and we'll all relax knowing you'll return in one piece."

Amy glowered at the open taunt. She had no idea what Leone's game was, but she was not playing. Amy was a long way removed from the gullible teenager who years ago had left Little Dip to study art in Europe. A lot had changed and Leone had best remember that.

"Amy, it's only because it's a family hunting week." Marie Garoul, Leone's mother, tried to soothe the standoff. As Connie's loving partner, Marie had practically raised Amy. Marie would always be family to her. Now Amy saw Marie struggle valiantly to maintain peace between her and Leone. "We don't want you accidentally stumbling into a shooting alley. Fantastic as it is to have you back home with us, we have to make sure you're kept safe. We don't want our new botanical illustrator coming to any harm, now do we?"

Amy did not miss the irony of her words. She was here because they had already lost an illustrator. Connie Fortune, an artist of great renown. Amy's aunt and Marie's loving partner had taken seriously ill and Amy had stepped in at the last minute to replace her.

The Garoul almanac was an eagerly awaited volume of botanical and medicinal interest. It was scheduled for release at the end of the year and now was in jeopardy due to Connie's illness. Amy was prepared to scour the valley floor for the specimens still to be represented alongside Marie's text. But she was not agreeing to Leone Garoul escorting her every step of the way. That had not been in the small print when she signed up. In fact, it was a recent and very annoying change of plan.

"What say we organize something else so you know where to go and where to avoid. Maybe a daily alert?" Marie looked hopefully from Leone and back to Amy.

The storm clouds were gathering already and Amy had only just arrived. She turned to Marie, deliberately ignoring Leone. "I'm still a little jet-lagged, Marie. Could we discuss it later, after you've shown me where Aunt Connie left off? I need to see the work you want me to do."

"Of course, but first you need to eat. We can go over to the office later and look at the work." Marie smiled gently.

Amy was tired after her journey. She had barely unpacked before paying a quick call to see Marie, anxious for the latest news on Connie. Now, two hours into her visit, here she was, embroiled in an embryonic argument with Leone, Marie's eldest daughter and a former thorn in Amy's side. *No, she's not a thorn; she's a whole damn cactus field.*

Marie's kindness mollified her slightly; she had neither the inclination nor the energy to enter into a silly argument with Leone at this time—or any other time, for that matter. Amy was not a stranger to Little Dip. She did not need to be led about the place on a short leash, and she particularly did not need Leone Garoul anywhere near her.

Marie pointed through the throng of family members milling around the main camping compound. "I think the cook is almost ready to start serving."

"You're right, I am hungry." Amy relaxed at Marie's measured tones. "And I want to catch Uncle Claude before he starts doling out the food or I'll never get near him." She turned to find her adopted uncle, as expected, stationed over the grill. "And there's the man himself."

With a cheerful good-bye wave to Marie and a total blanking of Leone she made her way past the Garoul party crowd to say hello.

"Can I assume that was an example of 'How not to do it'?" Marie said dryly as soon as Amy was out of earshot. "You do know it's impossible to bodyguard someone who doesn't want to cooperate, Leone? You'd better back down and give Amy some room."

"She hasn't changed one little bit. Still obstinate and pigheaded…" Leone murmured back. Her eyes were glued to Amy as she ambled across the picnic area toward Claude, waving hello and swapping greetings with everyone she met.

"Oh? I think she has. I think you're looking at a very sophisticated young woman. One who will keep you on your toes. However you do it, just make sure she comes to no harm. We owe Connie that much."

Leone listened to her mother's remarks as her eyes devoured every movement Amy made. Her mother need not have worried. Leone was prepared. She was more than ready, and she had waited a long, long time for Amy Fortune to come back to Little Dip.

❖

The outdoor eating area of the Garoul holiday compound was dominated by a huge barbeque and fire pit. These were surrounded by a variety of long wooden tables and benches capable of seating the whole clan if the occasion called for it. Dozens of men and women from the Garoul family relaxed around the tables. They had come from near and far for the start of the hunting season and now sat chatting and sipping beer, catching up with family gossip and shop talk as they waited for the food to grill. The atmosphere was happy and buzzing. This was one of the more popular family gatherings and was always well attended.

"Amy," a voice called her, and she glanced up and waved energetically at a huge bearded man who stood guard over an obviously beloved barbeque grill.

"Hey, Claude," she greeted him back, "something smells good. What's on the menu for tonight?"

"Meat." Amy shook her head at his ancient tease at her venture into teenage vegetarianism. Claude had a long memory and a soft humor. Every barbeque she received the same teasing response; Claude liked his routine. She grinned mischievously at him as he pointed to a cooler.

"Amy, hon, could ya fetch me another brewski?"

She selected his favorite brand and one for herself, and wandered back to where he sweated over the grill.

"Ah, you're a lifesaver, hon." He wiped the sweat off his brow and took a deep swallow from his beer. "Settling in okay?"

"Yes. But it's odd staying in Connie's cabin and not having her around. Though I expect Marie will keep me so busy I won't have time to get too maudlin. And I'll be able to visit Connie soon, apparently."

"Sure." He gave her a warm grin. "She'll be fine. Just needs a rest is all. Trust Marie on this. And it's great you're here to cover her workload for her so she can get a break," he added, sounding a little too upbeat. Amy caught the forced joviality and understood his attempts to ease her worry. He was a good man; she had enormous affection for him. Claude would always be family to her. She cracked the cap on her beer and smiled up into his beaming face, florid from the grill like a big bearded pumpkin.

"Yes. She will be okay," she murmured, more to reassure herself.

It would have been so much better if she'd had the chance

to see Connie first, but Marie's call had come out of the blue. By the time Amy had flown in from Heathrow, Connie had already been whisked away for treatment. The retreat Marie found for her insisted on a several week isolation period for initial assessment and orientation before family or friends could visit. To Amy it sounded extreme but she also knew Marie only wanted the best for Connie; she loved her dearly. So Amy relaxed and hoped the weeks would fly by. She knew if she immersed herself in the work she'd come to do it would. Time always slipped away from her when she was painting.

"Marie is going to show me where Connie left off. Have you seen any of her plant illustrations yet, Claude?" She watched him flip the enormous venison steaks. The Garouls were big on meat.

"Nope, not yet. Though Leone said they were fantastic."

Amy stiffened slightly and then forced her shoulders to relax at the mention of Leone's name. She had better get used to it here in Leone's home valley.

Leone Garoul is ancient history, she reminded herself, *as defunct as the Roman Empire, and anything you have to do with her will all end in ruins.* She was not going to let Leone get under her skin now that Amy had returned to Little Dip, not even their earlier run-in over Leone's self-assigned babysitting duties. Amy had practically grown up in this valley; she did not need someone to show her around.

"Connie's got a worldwide reputation now. And I hear you aren't two steps behind her." Claude poked at the sizzling meat.

"Oh, I've got a long way to go before I could touch Connie's reputation." Nevertheless, she was pleased he'd followed her success in Europe.

She cast a swift glance across to where Leone had been standing with her mother. Marie was now talking with another family member. Leone had moved away.

"How're you liking London?" Claude asked.

"I'm loving it. And Barcelona, and Athens, and Bucharest. I'm loving Europe, period."

"You're doing swell. But it's good you've come back home to

do some prestigious work here, too. Not that you're forgotten, but it does no harm to have your name on one of Marie's almanacs. Keeps your profile high in the U.S. market." Like most of the Garouls, he was employed in the family's publishing business. Claude headed up marketing and promotions for Garoul Press at its Oregon home office. Marie, an acclaimed author and expert on herbalism and First Nation medicines, had recently stood down as Editor in Chief to make way for her eldest daughter, Leone. Though she still presided over the boardroom.

"Yes, you're right. I need to keep a toehold here, too." Amy had spent the last several years studying and working abroad. She loved Europe for its multilayered vibrancy, history, and culture. Each job took her somewhere different, and while for some it might be a rather lonely, nomadic way of life, it suited her perfectly. The only true sense of home she could ever remember had been her aunt Connie and this valley. For years she had been reluctant to return to it. Somehow it had always seemed right to keep moving on, to the next city, contract, pinprick in the map.

Marie trudged over to join them, looking appreciatively at the grill and its contents.

"Are we nearly ready to serve some of that up?" she asked.

"We're about ready for round one." With one final flip Claude bellowed, "Paulie," over his shoulder into the family throng.

A tall teenager peeled away and came over.

"Paulie, I'm sure you don't remember her, but this is Amy, Connie's niece. She's come to stay for a few weeks and help Marie with the almanac," Claude said while transferring a steak to a nearby plate. Paulie smiled shyly down at Amy. He looked to be in his mid teens, and was easily over six feet tall.

"Oh my God, it's little Paulie." Amy was flabbergasted. "You were just starting school last time I saw you. Look at you now, you're enormous." She wasn't sure why she needed to point that out; all the Garouls loomed over her compact five foot four inches. They were all very tall and dark, and even when they married shorter, fairer people, the offspring were undeniably Garoul in stature and coloring.

Paulie blushed and laughed good-naturedly. "I'm fourteen now. I was already at school when you left. And I do remember you, Amy. You and Leone took me to the fairgrounds a few times." His blush deepened. He was at that sweet but gawky self-conscious age.

"Here, first bite goes to the hunter." Claude handed him a plate brimful with bloody steak.

Amy felt a little queasy looking at it. All that heat blasting off the massive grill and Claude still hadn't cooked the damn meat through.

"Paulie provided tonight's dinner," Claude stated proudly. "He came a little earlier in the week with me and got his first kill last night."

Paulie blushed even more and was immediately surrounded by the rest of his family slapping his back and congratulating him profusely. They all gathered around the grill now that it was time for the food to be dished out.

"Congratulations, Paulie. Good for you." Amy added her praise knowing how much hunting and fishing mattered to the Garouls. It was a big deal when their youngsters followed in the family footsteps.

"Mmm, could I have mine really well done, Claude?" she asked anxiously as she watched him fill the line of plates. Part of her would always be that teenage wannabe vegetarian.

"Yup. I can do that. Go and sit, and I'll send it over when it's ready."

"I'll bring it to you." A silken voice came from right behind her. She spun around and found herself swallowed by Leone's dark, enigmatic gaze. Amy stepped back, finding Leone much too close for comfort. The small smile playing across her lips told Amy she was well aware of the effect she was having. An awkward silence hung between them, allowing Amy's disquiet to simmer slowly. She found Leone smug and arrogant.

"Back there." Leone indicated the area with a nod.

"Pardon?" Amy asked coldly.

"I'm sitting back there. With Jori and Elicia," Leone stated. "Go on over and I'll bring your steak when it's ready."

It was a badly disguised order and Amy bristled. She wanted to refuse except that she was genuinely friendly with Leone's younger brother, Jori, and was dying to meet his new girlfriend. Lord knew she had heard enough about the wonderful Elicia in all Jori's e-mails and telephone calls to be more than curious. It would have been her natural choice to share his company for the evening. Now she was warring a childish impulse to sit elsewhere simply because she did not want to be near Leone.

Her rational, mature side won—but barely. Without another word she peeled away to Jori's table. She really did want to sit with him and meet the lauded Elicia, despite Leone's presence. Reluctantly, she decided the smart thing was to steel herself and get this first evening with Leone over and done with. It might be for the better to set her boundaries early.

On approaching the table Amy noticed Jori had mooched off to join the long line at the grill, leaving a young Hispanic woman with beautiful brown eyes and long dark hair sitting on her own.

"Hi, I'm Amy." She smiled and extended a welcoming hand. "I'm a family friend, but I guess odds are anyone under six foot is probably only visiting."

The woman burst out laughing and shook her hand. "I already figured you weren't a Garoul with that blond hair. I'm Elicia. I'm here with Jori, and it's nice to meet someone nearer my own height in this valley of the giants."

Amy climbed into the bench opposite, shucking off her jacket. Elicia seemed fun; she could see why Jori had fallen for this pretty woman with warm, laughing eyes.

"You're Connie's niece. I've met her a few times. What a lovely woman. I do hope she gets better soon," Elicia continued as Amy settled in so that they faced each other across the wooden table.

"Thank you. She will. It's nice to meet you too, Elicia. Are you the fishin' huntin' type, or are you up here for a week of relaxing?"

"Oh, I'm planning on reading a pile of books this big." She indicated her waist. "Jori says you're here to work. You're a botanical illustrator like your aunt?"

"Yes, that and wildlife illustration."

"You must be in your element here. It's gorgeous. I could hardly believe it when Jori told me his family owned the whole valley. It's like owning your own holiday resort. Imagine just packing up and coming here every time you want to chill out, or hunt, or hike, or whatever."

"It's fantastic the way they maintain it." Amy was happy to find another convert. Very few outsiders knew of this valley. You had to be invited by a Garoul to even find the damned place, and that only happened when you were as good as one of the family. It was obvious Elicia and Jori must be in a serious relationship if he'd asked her along on a hunting break. For the Garouls the hunting vacations were tantamount to a holy pilgrimage. In fact, Jori's increasing mention of his new girlfriend in his e-mails had alerted Amy that something major was happening for him. She was close to Jori and regarded him with the warmth and affection she would have for a brother of her own—if she'd had any siblings.

"Just look at all these little holiday cabins waiting for visitors." Amy looked fondly around the compound as she spoke. It was very picturesque—a little log cabin village right out of a fairy tale.

Her gaze fell on Leone, who was still in the line chatting with her brother. As if sensing Amy's eyes on her, she looked up and winked. Amy turned away sharply and continued talking to Elicia.

"When I was younger this place was packed with kids all summer. We used to run wild. It was the best time ever. It's nice to know the little Garouls still come and meet up every year for a summer camp." She smiled happily at her memories. "It's an ideal way to keep family connections strong generation after generation."

"And you were the only little non-Garoul?"

"Yes. I've always been a sort of honorary cousin. Connie has lived out here as long as I can remember, and I visited every school holiday. I loved it here." Her smile widened. "I'm so looking forward to hiking around the valley with my work pack, sniffing out plants and birds to sketch."

"How do you do that? I mean, do you just sit down with your paints and stuff and draw a flower?"

"Not really. First I do detailed field sketches with color swatches. But I also use my camera to catalogue—" A deep chuckle interrupted her.

"Hey, you two, Claude sent us over with these. Typical…sitting in the middle of a forest and you both expect waiter service."

Amy swiveled in her seat and looked up into the twinkling eyes of Jori Garoul. He stood behind her with a full plate in each hand.

"Jori," she cried as he leaned down to kiss her cheek warmly. She gave him a quick peck and a big hug back.

"Amy, darling. It's great to see you again. I got your last e-mail. Hey, those photos of Venice were amazing." He moved to sit beside Elicia, delivering her plate as he spoke. "We're so gonna go there someday. Take a year out and just travel. Venice, Rome, Paris. Do the whole deal." He smiled at Elicia, openly including her in his dreams of Europe.

"I got tons more photos of Italy. I'll bore you both to tears someday and show you every single one…" Her sentence died away as she noticed Leone poised directly behind her carrying another set of plates. Their eyes locked momentarily before Amy suddenly became very interested in her paper napkin. She shifted in her seat as Jori and Elicia shared their food. Leone placed the plates on the table before squeezing her long frame onto the bench beside Amy. She ended up sitting much too close, unfazed by Amy's clumsy sideways shuffling to make more space between them.

"Here." Leone pushed a plate toward Amy, unaware of any awkwardness or else choosing to ignore it. Amy was uncertain which, and felt even more unsettled.

"I'm sorry for the earlier misunderstanding, Amy." Leone flashed a big smile and launched into conversation as if they were the best of friends. "Your hair's gotten really long. And you lost a stack of weight," she continued as they prepared to eat. "It's been a long time, hasn't it?"

Amy was disgusted that her frosty vibes were totally wasted on Leone's thick skin. Taking a new tack, she looked at Leone as if she were insane.

"Yes, it has. Six years, eight months, and fifteen days," she threw out flippantly, ignoring the rest of Leone's statement. It was none of Leone's business what her hair, or metabolism, had been up to these past years.

Leone's coal black eyes twinkled back at her. "Twenty-one days." Her grin widened even further.

Amy blinked back confounded. *Has she really been counting the days?* She glanced questioningly into those unfathomable eyes, and deep within caught the slightest teasing glint. Immediately Amy slammed shut, tight as a refrigerator door. All her thoughts and feelings sealed away, cooling right down to zero.

"Well, I guess you keep count better than me," she said snippily, wanting to convey her annoyance but not alert Jori and Elicia that there was something amiss.

Amy knew before she arrived she would have to work alongside Leone Garoul. She had schooled herself on the flight over to be civil, no matter what the circumstances. She was here on a mission on behalf of Connie and at the anxious request of Marie, who was not only Connie's partner, but co-author, too, as well as publisher. This was an important project, and Amy was a professional. If Leone was going to be her editor, then she would just have to cope with it and not let any murderous feelings for her ex-girlfriend get in the way.

She decided the best thing was to ignore Leone for the rest of the meal. Mind made up, she cut into her steak but was more than a little perturbed to find it still quite bloody. Sighing, she plucked at her bread instead, plopping a cherry tomato into her mouth.

Leone looked over, happily tucking into her own. "Under-done?"

"A little. I told Claude to make sure mine was cooked through, but I don't think he knows what that means."

"Do you want me to take it back and tell him to incinerate it?"

"To be honest, I'm not that interested now. I'm happy enough with the salad," Amy said truthfully. Leone reached over and took her abandoned steak, piling it on top of the massive one already on her plate. Amy looked at her aghast.

"What?" Leone asked, cutting into it. "You said you didn't want it."

"I'd forgotten what a big stuffer you are. How the hell you keep your figure with the amount you pack away beats me." Amy shook her head in genuine mystery, all intentions to ignore Leone forgotten in the sight of such happy gluttony.

"That's because I am a wild woman of the woods, and you always had the metabolism of a marshmallow," Leone mumbled around an enormous mouthful. Amy stared at her, mortally offended. It was as if the years had all melted away to nothing and she was once again looking at the smug, exasperating teenager who'd been her first love.

Don't you dare try to take me back there as if nothing ever happened. She glared at Leone, who smiled gracefully back and continued to wolf her food. Basking in the hot, angry stare as if it were sunshine.

CHAPTER TWO

S o." Elicia pushed her empty plate away. "Paulie's actually the youngest Garoul here? This is his first hunting weekend and he's just supplied us with dinner? Talk about a natural."

"Yeah, he's just turned fourteen and this is his first big hunting trip. He's so proud of that deer." Leone smiled, happy for him. "Next year he'll be joined by his sister Adele and their cousin Celina. The girls will be old enough to learn to hunt by then. In fact, there's a whole slew coming up in the next few years. Before you know it this place will be overrun with teenagers, just like the mall back home."

"I suppose if your family owns a whole valley it's silly for everybody not to use it for rest and relaxation." Elicia nodded thoughtfully. "Or hunting vacations."

"To come here and learn to hunt, the kids have to be in their teens. No small children are allowed on hunting breaks like this. Instead the little 'uns arrive in the summer. Kind of like summer camp, except it's all Garoul kids and you get to know all your cousins," Jori told her, clearly proud of the wonderful simplicity of the Garoul vacation system.

Elicia, vainly trying to stifle a yawn, snuggled up against him. He wrapped his arm around her and pulled her in tighter.

"Sorry, we've been traveling all day and just arrived about an hour ago. I'm exhausted," she said to Leone and Amy.

"You drove down from Seattle?" Amy asked. Behind her the music started again. The party was warming up, with an accordion and fiddle playing boisterous old French migrant tunes passed down from musician to musician over the generations. Soon singing would start with hearty ballads and folksongs from their homeland, sung in the old langue d'oc dialect. The Garouls clung proudly to their ancient French heritage, even though over the last few centuries they had dispersed across the Americas as far apart as Rio de Janeiro and Iqaluit. This diaspora only served to enrich annual get-togethers such as this one. Garouls had come from all over to attend it.

"Yeah, with stops and such it still took a little over eight hours." Jori was yawning, too. "Come on. I can see you're nodding off. Let's call it a night." He held out his hand and hauled Elicia to her feet.

"We'll stay and dance another night," she said and let him lead her away toward their cabin. "Amy," she called over her shoulder, "can I go hiking with you sometime and watch you work? I promise not to get in the way."

"Sure. I'll catch you over the next few days and we'll plan something, okay?" With a friendly wave they said good night.

"She's lovely, isn't she?" Amy smiled after them. "Jori talks about her all the time on the phone and in his e-mails." Her thoughts were out before she remembered she didn't want to make small talk with Leone. She grabbed her coat and bag and was about to leave to find Marie.

Leone kept talking at her nonstop, as if anxious to keep her there. "Yes, Elicia's lovely. Jori tells me he keeps in touch with you all the time. Finish your beer. Would you like more salad?"

"Hey, did you two get enough to eat?" Marie appeared before them, taking the seat just vacated by Jori and Elicia.

"Lots," Amy answered and sat back down now that Marie had found her.

Marie looked around her. "Did Jori and Elicia retire early? The dancing's just about to start."

"They had a long drive down and were exhausted. I hope you gave them a cabin set well back." Leone winked at her mother.

Marie smiled excitedly. "Oh, I catered for their privacy. Jori gave me strict instructions. This is the fifth time I've met her, you know," she told Amy. "He always makes sure she's around when I go to visit him in Seattle. He's very smitten. I wouldn't be surprised if they made an important announcement this week."

"Do you think they'll get engaged?" Amy, forever the romantic, was agog. "Wow."

"And this is the best time for Jori to do it," Leone stated matter-of-factly.

Amy turned to her. "Why? Because you're all here to give your blessings, so to speak?"

Leone looked over to Marie. They shrugged in unison. Amy hid a smile at the shared characteristic. At some stage while growing up Leone had subconsciously adopted Marie's posture and movements. It added to the other physical similarities between mother and daughter. Both were tall and lean, with long dark hair, tanned complexion, and burning black eyes. Their heritage, a mixture of old migrant French and native Nez Perce, shone from them; from all of the Garouls, truth be told. They were a handsome breed that could trace their ancestry back not only to the actual ship that brought their founder to the New World, but beyond to murky, ancient origins in the Gevaudan region of France.

"Well, it means she gets to meet most of us in one go. Though I suppose it can be a bit daunting as there are so many Garouls here for the hunting," Leone answered. Just over fifty family members had descended on the valley for this particular week.

"Before it starts to get too frantic, can I show you Connie's illustrations now?" Marie asked.

"Please, I'd love to see them. Oh, and I have a gift for you." Amy opened her bag and pulled out a thick hardback. "Here, it's the contract I did in Madeira last year."

Marie read the cover. "*Island of Eternal Spring: The Garden of the Atlantic*. Thank you, Amy. What a beautiful book." Immediately she began riffling through the pages. Botanical illustration was her passion, next to herbalism and natural medicine. Leone craned her neck to see, too, but Amy was on her feet, determined her time spent with her was now done. She wanted to head off with Marie to look at Connie's work and suck in some fresh air. Sitting beside Leone had been stifling in a way she hadn't fully appreciated until she'd moved away.

Marie stood, cradling her new gift, and accompanied Amy around a circle of energetic polka dancers. They headed for the largest cabin in the compound.

Smoke curled from its stout stone chimney. The porch was chock full of potted plants and gardening tools. Rubber boots, fishing poles, and comfortable wooden furniture all cluttered the small space. Lanterns and candle stubs sat on a battered wooden table, and bunches of dried herbs hung from the uprights, giving the cabin a year-round lived-in feeling as opposed to its smaller, vacation time neighbors.

Amy smiled in total contentment as she mounted the steps. It was a rare sentiment for her these days. Cliché or not, this cabin, Marie's home, reminded her of some of the happiest days of her childhood. As she entered directly into the main living room, waves of emotion swamped her, triggered first by smell. The spiciness of burning apple wood, baking pies, and faded incense tickled at her nose and memories. It was clear hardly anything had changed. The same threadbare couch covered with the thick Wallowa blankets stood in the center of the room opposite the stone fireplace. Beside each armrest a cut-off section of tree trunk served as a small table. Amy knew from childhood experience each weighed a ton, and the left-hand one was slightly lopsided, so pens and oranges always rolled off it. Marie's favorite old reading lamp still sat there along with a stack of books. The other side table still held the tin ashtray Leone won at the Summer Fair a million years ago. Battered and faded with ash burns and time, it was hard to make out the garish etching of Mount Hood. Leone had been so proud to bring it home to her mother.

It was like a punch in the guts, a time shift in Amy's reality. Mixed with the fond memories of childhood was that last, stinging blow. A memory that changed Amy's path forever, taking her out of this valley, and far away. She was immediately transported back nearly seven years to the last time she entered this cabin and the pain that had accompanied that final visit. Leone had abandoned her.

It was as simple as that. And now she was back in the valley, and Leone was all over her, as suffocating as a heavy, wet blanket. But this time it was Amy who didn't need Leone.

Marie moved off toward the kitchen, but Amy hesitated. An oil painting of a moonlit night over Little Dip Valley hung on the chimneybreast. She recognized the palette intimately. Drawn to the canvas, her gaze slid over each brushstroke, as familiar to her as Connie's handwriting or the laugh lines on her face. If she were to touch the surface it would talk to her like Braille. But what would it say? *Oh, Connie, I wish you were here tonight. Everything is so emotional, so hard.*

"Here." Marie handed her a steaming mug of pungent herbs and hot water. "It'll lift your headache."

"How did you know I had the start of a headache?" She gratefully took the drink.

"Your left eye squints a little, and you get a tiny crease right between your eyebrows." Marie smiled. "Come through to the office and I'll show you Connie's latest artwork." She nodded to a far door.

Amy nursed her cup and followed Marie to the back room that had been her office for as long as Amy could remember. One wall was faced with a built-in floor-to-ceiling bookcase, full of Marie's reference manuals. Any other free wall space was covered with botanical paintings and watercolors of the valley. Painted in soft, spring colors, the room had a calm ambience laced with warm practicality, reflecting the work ethos of its owner. Amy knew it would be a lovely space to work in. It hummed with quiet energy.

In her opinion the only curiously jarring note was the Bosch triptych of The Garden of Earthly Delights hanging over Marie's desk. Full of hell and damnation, despair and cruel intentions, it had always hung there and Amy had always hated it. As a child she imagined a top-secret safe hidden behind it. Her young, inventive imagination could think of no other reason a beautiful person like Marie would have such an ugly thing hanging in her home.

Marie's computer sat snug on an antique desk of rich mahogany and tooled leather. A second sturdy table, handmade in cedar wood, sat under the window where it would catch the best of the daylight. It was strewn with various papers and folios. Marie flipped one open to reveal a stack of watercolor illustrations. Amy stepped forward; the artwork was Connie's.

"We need a handful of seasonal insets now that September's here. And maybe a little touch-up of two existing plates…" Marie shuffled through the stack and carefully lifted out a page, sliding it toward Amy. "This…and this." She set a second page beside the first.

Amy's eyes lingered on one, then the other.

"They're exquisite," she murmured. "Some of her best work has come about these last few years. I love her new technique. She's an absolute master."

"Yes, but it's come at a cost. She burned herself out on this project—"

"Didn't you see the breakdown coming?" Amy heard the accusation in her voice and winced inwardly. She did not want to condemn or accuse. She knew beyond all doubt Marie loved Connie and would do anything for her. She also knew she was being childish and selfish. "I'm sorry, Marie, I'm just grumpy and still a little jet-lagged. I know you took care of her. I don't know why I snapped."

A cool hand settled on her forearm. "How's the headache?"

Ruefully, she admitted, "It's gone. I can't even use it as an excuse."

The hand shook her arm gently. "You don't need an excuse. You love Connie, and you're worried sick. We all are. This came out of nowhere. Nobody and nothing could have prevented it. But she's in the best possible place and you'll get to see her soon."

They stood side by side looking at the illustrations laid out before them. The colors swam with translucence even in the drab artificial light. Marie's arm wrapped around Amy's shoulders reassuringly, offering support at a time of great stress.

"The best thing you can do right now is throw yourself into finishing her work. She was so relieved to know you'd agreed to fly in and take over. It took a great load off her mind." The embrace tightened into an affectionate hug.

"When can I get to see her, or even talk to her?"

"We'll visit the retreat in a couple of weeks. But no communication until then. It's one of the rules. She's suffering from complete mental exhaustion and it's a slow process recharging those batteries."

Amy reached out again to finger an edge of the vellum. "It will be nearly impossible to touch these up, especially with wet on wet. There's no way it will scan if I dampen the paper again. I know I learned my trade at Connie's elbow and our styles may look similar, but to a trained eye we're a world apart. And frankly, at two hundred LPI, maybe even a layman could tell the difference. What kind of retouching did you have in mind anyway?" She frowned; the work was perfect as it was. Why did Marie want to jeopardize it for a few extra embellishments?

"I'd hope at two hundred lines per inch a myopic chimp could pick up the style differences…but it's just a few lines mostly on the outer edges. Could you add them in dry? It's just a tiny little oversight, but it has to be done. The rest are a series of close-ups of autumnal foliage for text insets. Those will be all yours to do."

"Marie, you know I can't go in and touch up these illustrations. I'll ruin them. Even with the best effort in the world, the color strengths wouldn't match, and I really don't want to play around with Connie's work." She lifted an illustration of goldenseal for them both to admire. "I mean, how can anyone improve on this?"

Marie simply shook her head. "Let's leave it to the editorial meeting tomorrow, okay? What about your own work schedule? I guess you'll want to do field sketches, but I'm not sure where you'll find all the plant specimens on your to-do list. You may have to root around for the rarer ones."

"Ah, but that's half the fun."

"What's half the fun?" Leone strolled into the small office, and immediately Amy felt claustrophobic.

"Rooting around for the specimens on Amy's list," Marie answered her.

"I'll need to know what you're after and where you intend to look." Leone sounded bossy again. Her chin jutted as it did when she was determined to get her own way. Amy recognized the look of old and her hackles rose in response.

"What do you mean you need to know? I can manage my own workload." Her tone was frosty as she realized they had come full circle back to the babysitting argument. She might have known Leone wouldn't give up.

"I need to know so I can make sure you're not wandering around out there like a sitting duck." Exasperation crept into Leone's voice, making Amy stiffen all the more. They were in a face-off and Marie stepped forward to break the impasse.

"I'm inviting the both of you to dinner tomorrow evening so we can discuss exactly what's needed now that Connie is resting." She attempted to pull the conversation back into the professional arena and neutral territory. "Amy, the e-mail I sent you with the list of the required plants, it's lengthy. Are you happy to continue with the existing deadline?"

"Yes. I've seen the list, and I'll start field research first thing tomorrow. It's an easily attainable deadline…if there are no unforeseen hindrances." She shot a hard look at Leone before sidestepping for the door. "Thanks for the dinner invitation, Marie."

Marie accompanied her as far as the porch. "It's great to see you back in Little Dip, Amy. I wish with all my heart it was under different circumstances."

Amy gave a small, sad smile. "We all do, Marie. I'll see you tomorrow evening." With a final wave Amy trudged back to the party only to hear accompanying footsteps crunching alongside her. She halted and looked with indignant surprise at Leone, who had popped up beside her, seemingly content to dog her every move this evening.

"What is it now?" she asked, her patience wearing thin.

"What's what?"

"Why are you following me?"

"I'm not. I'm joining the party." Leone nodded toward the revelers. "You wanna dance?" Leone raised her eyebrows questioningly. Amy looked at her as if she had grown two heads.

Both brainless. Shaking her own head in amazement, she turned toward the trail to her cabin.

"No. I'm going to bed. I need a good night's rest."

"Okay." Leone turned with her.

"What are you doing?"

"I'm going to walk you to your cabin. It's late," she responded gallantly.

"No, you're not. I know the way there in the dark. I've done it a thousand times."

"Mom said I was to look out for you—"

"I don't need a babysitter, as you so elegantly put it. Go pester someone else."

"Nope. I've got to pester you. Mom told me to." Leone sounded even more determined now that Amy was in a defiant mood.

"Oh please yourself, freak." Amy stomped off, leaving her escort behind. It took mere moments before Leone's longer stride caught up with her, and together they walked away from the lights and music into the heart of the forest.

"So," Leone struck up a friendly chatter. "How was Venice? I saw the photos. You seemed very impressed with it."

Amy frowned heavily. "You saw the photos? The photos I sent Jori?"

"Yup, and the ones you sent to cousin Andre and Connie, too. I follow everything you do, you know. It's fascinating. All those places you visit. I go nowhere much, so I'm very envious. But then you always wanted to trav—"

"You follow what I do?" Amy was appalled. "Well, stop it. Don't follow me or any of the things I do. If I wanted you to know then I'd e-mail you, too!" Her words rang out harsh into the still night air. She felt incredibly indignant. She didn't want any part of her life exposed to Leone Garoul.

"Hey, I'm not snooping. It's just general family conversation. Sheesh, do you really think I'd spy on you? You're not that freakin' interesting."

"Well, if I'm not freakin' interesting, stop freakin' following me."

"I'm not freakin' following you. I'm escorting you."

"I've spent half my life here; there's no way I need an escort. And I don't believe for one moment that Marie meant for you to walk me home. I know these woods like the back of my hand—*oof*." She was flat on her back looking at the stars through the forest canopy, her foot tangled in an upraised tree root. Leone's smug face loomed into her celestial vision.

"The back of your hand needs to give your feet a clue." A hand was offered to help her up. "Imagine that, someone's put a forty-foot tree there since your last visit." Leone tutted.

Amy swatted the hand aside and scrambled to her feet, furiously wiping herself down. "I would have seen it but for your annoying yammering. Now go back and let me make my own way home in relative safety. The only dangerous thing around here is you."

"Nope. I'm doing what Mom says and that's that. You don't like it, then take it up with her tomorrow night at dinner." Leone continued to stroll beside her as Amy fumed. "You got a bit of dirt right there. On your backside…" she murmured, smiling as Amy heatedly dusted her bottom.

After several yards of silent huffing from Amy, Leone tried her hand at light conversation again.

"I like your accent. You're all British now."

"It's a mixture from living in London so long. The English think I sound American."

"Mmm, it's nice though. Go on…say 'nappies' and 'dustbin.'"

"Shut up, idiot."

"Say, 'Why thank you, Your Majesty.'"

"Stop it. You're not clever."

"Can ya curtsy at the same time?"

"I'm warning you."

"Okay, sorry. But you sound good."

"I'm not a bleeding car engine." Amy snapped. She knew Leone was baiting her and had no time for it. They'd played all the games they were ever going to play a long, long time ago.

"'Bleeding'—I love it." Leone chuckled. Amy snorted in annoyance and picked up her pace. The sooner she was back at Connie's cabin and devoid of her "escort," the better.

CHAPTER THREE

They moved on silently. The nocturnal calls of the forest wrapped Amy in a long forgotten, but now familiar comfort. The crunch of footsteps and huff of soft breath was the only contribution the women made to the night.

They rounded one last bend and the cabin's dark outline loomed into sight. Amy was about to open her mouth to dismiss Leone when a hollow, melancholy howl rent the night air around them. She froze.

"Wolves. It's been years since I heard them call," Amy whispered, awestruck.

"Someone's feeling lonesome." Leone lifted her face to the wind and smiled.

Amy shuffled her feet, a little unnerved. The howling was reminiscent of many childhood nights spent in the valley, but it still unsettled her as if she were a kid all over again. She'd always found the plaintive calls mournful and scary, whereas Leone and the other little Garouls had always been comforted. Now she was bounced back to summer nights and enormous eiderdown beds with five little sleepy heads in a row. Four dark as tar, and her own white blond curls drifting over the pillows. She would lay listening wide-eyed and fearful while the rest smiled sleepily as if hearing secret lullabies in the eerie howling. Leone always slept beside her and would reach for her hand, holding it tightly until Amy eventually fell asleep with her nose buried in her shoulder.

"You should leave a light on in the window," Leone said

glancing at the cape of trees wrapped tightly around the small, isolated dwelling. In some places there was barely two yards of clearance between the cabin walls and nearby cedars.

"Why? I told you I know the way." Amy stood on the porch steps; the added height drew her eyes level with Leone's. "Will you be okay getting back home? You know not to leave the path or talk to strangers?" She smiled syrup sweet.

"Very funny. But now that I've delivered grandma to her cottage I'll try to get back without being eaten by the big, bad wolf," Leone deadpanned back.

Another distant howl wavered over the treetops. Again Amy tensed, and looked anxiously in the direction she imagined it came from.

Leone smiled. Amy was facing the wrong way. She had never quite mastered the acoustics of the valley. Cocking her head, she took a chance.

"Any chance of a nightcap before I head back?"

She could see it was on the tip of Amy's tongue to say no, but the chilling serenade had unnerved her. Leone pushed a little more. "What's the harm in one drink? It's getting chilly out here. It will warm me all the way home."

"Okay." Amy turned abruptly and pushed open the door. "I suppose one of us has to act adult."

Behind her Leone bounded up the steps as eager as a stray dog offered a meal. Her eyes devoured every square inch of Amy's back. Every line and curve, every indent and rise, all measurements were calculated and stored away for recall later. Then she would lie in bed and think of each spoken word, each gesture. The angry flash of hazel eyes, and that smile… Amy's sweet smile, so rarely, if ever, turned on her. Not that it mattered. Amy Fortune was back in the valley, and that was enough.

Together they entered Connie's cabin. It was really only one large space. A square living room with a countertop that separated off the small kitchen. Behind that, a door that led into Connie's north-facing studio, her pride and joy and the reason the rest of her living quarters were so cramped. The fireplace was the central focus of this main room. Pulled up before it, a cozy couch, draped with clashing tartans and woolen blankets, promised snug winter evenings before a blazing fire.

Every wall was filled with either artwork or shelves wedged full of books. Connie's entire collection of albums and almanacs, lexicons and references, folios and compendiums adorned the room. A myriad of colored spines and embossed leather decorated her simple walls. Thick and thin they stood side by side, bewitching in their symmetry and richness, sentries to Connie's life, loves, and passions. To the right a galley ladder led up to a railed platform that acted as the bedroom. The bathroom was housed directly under this.

Amy loved the small, intimate cabin. Every pore in her body knew it as home. A sanctuary where she had flourished and grown unhindered into the young woman and artist she was today. Earlier that afternoon she had unpacked on the small bed platform above, tidying her things away. Next she had brewed tea and sat on the settee before the cold ashes in the hearth and simply cried. She missed Connie so much and was terrified this place would never again be filled with her laughter and warmth.

Now, on returning from this evening's entertainment, she was surprised to find her fear of its emptiness no longer existed. Leone's presence seemed to dispel the eerie sense of loneliness. But it was more than just another body in the room. It was the unexpected feeling of companionship and comfort that disconcerted her. Almost as if the room itself had been molded for them. Built to their dimensions. It wrapped around them as warm and comforting as the woolen blankets flung across the couch.

"It's cold in here. If you're going to sit up a little longer I can light a fire. It'll be roaring away in no time." Leone's eyebrows rose in question. Secretly she wanted to sit before this fireplace sharing a nightcap with Amy and talking nicely to each other for once. She watched Amy puttering around in the kitchen looking for glasses, cracking open her duty-free booze. The lamplight blazed a halo around her crazily curled hair. It was tied back, but still untamable. Leone's fingers itched to run through it, to snag and snarl it in great fistfuls, and crush the cool silkiness into the heart of her palms. She forced her gaze away and poked at the burned-out embers, waiting for permission to bring them back to life so they could both relax before a cozy fire. She desperately needed some time alone with Amy.

"Well, if it will only take a moment to light." Amy frowned; this was getting far too chummy. Leaving Leone to nimbly build the beginnings of a fire, Amy dug out two heavy crystal tumblers, adding a generous dash of cognac to each. She glanced over at Leone. Her fine, bronzed features glowed with the blazing kindling as she gently fed the flames. Once again Amy was struck by the easy familiarity of it all, and it perturbed her. She didn't want these feelings. They were the kind she knew could become addictive, and she was never going to snare herself like that again. Never going to be hurt like that again.

Leone perched on the edge of the couch as Amy joined her with their drinks.

"Here."

"Thanks." Leone took an appreciative sip. "Mmm, good cognac." They settled back and watched the flames steadily grow. It was a strangely restful end to an emotionally tense evening.

"So," Leone finally broke through her reverie, "can I see the rest of the Italian photos?"

Amy looked over in surprise. "There are hundreds of them."

Leone shrugged. "I'd love to look at them. It would be great to see even a few and have a blow-by-blow commentary." With the fire warming the room and the nightcap warming her belly, she was loath to leave the little cabin and prepared to try every ploy possible to prolong her time there. She knew Amy had a weakness. Like every artist, she liked to share imagery and discuss ideas. Leone shamelessly played on this now. "Especially the ones about Italian architecture?" She raised her eyebrows in question. "I love soffits and spandrels." Soffits and spandrels were the only architectural terms Leone knew, apart from door. But it was worth a try.

"Mmm." Amy squinted at her suspiciously, but Leone could see her wavering.

"Okay." Amy caved. "We can look at some, but there are too many photos for one sitting. I'll show you Florence and Sorrento. You've already seen the best of the Venice ones." She stood to fetch her laptop.

"What was your favorite city?" Leone asked.

"Oh, that's hard as they were all so special in different ways. But if I had to choose I'd say Sorrento. It was absolutely beautiful."

Amy came back and settled in beside Leone, flicking on the computer. As the light bounced off the screen onto their faces Leone took the opportunity to scoot a little closer until her shoulder and thigh pressed along the length of Amy's. At first Amy stiffened, but stealing a look out of the side of her eye she could see all Leone's concentration focused on the first of her photographs. She decided she was being far too paranoid and forced herself to relax. Although Leone had annoyed her repeatedly tonight, there had been nothing sexually suggestive in her behavior. Leone was just clumsy around Amy's boundaries. It was something Amy would correct later; she had no energy left for another round of "back off" tonight. As she fully intended to avoid Leone while she did her fieldwork, there would be even less opportunity for Amy to feel this bugged.

Leone felt the slight shift in the Amy's muscles; a sneak peek out of the corner of her eye checked Amy's profile and saw that her physical closeness had been deemed acceptable. She smiled encouragingly at the screen without actually focusing on it; all her attention was on the parts of her body pressing up against Amy's warmth.

"Okay." Amy found her starting point. "The Basilica di Santa Maria del Fiore. Wait 'til you see the spandrels on this baby."

For the next twenty minutes Amy rattled through her slideshow with Leone making informed comments like, "Wow, so that's Vesuvius?" and "Aren't the streets narrow?" and "Look at that donkey with the hat." Until—

"Who's that?"

"That's my friend Katherine. She went on vacation with me," Amy explained.

"Friend?"

"Yes."

"A friend you go on vacation with?"

"Yes, sort of." Amy pulled up another album.

"Sort of?"

"Mmm."

This was greeted in cold silence as the screen slid through another few frames of Katherine doing this and that, and standing here and there, in and around Sorrento—much to Leone's displeasure.

"I didn't see her in Florence?" Leone tried to sound casual.

"No, she went home before then. I traveled there by myself," Amy murmured, concentrating on her next selection.

"Oh, so you broke up?"

"Huh?"

"Went separate ways, I mean...not broke up. Traveled... separate ways. Apart. Parted."

"What are you babbling about? Katherine only had a week's holiday."

"Pity," Leone said flatly, glaring at the digital Katherine. Just then the battery light flashed and a warning message displayed.

"That will have to do until I recharge." Amy snapped shut the laptop and set it to one side. She leaned back into her seat to find Leone had not moved an inch; they were still co-joined along shoulder, arm, and thigh, squeezed into one-third of the entire couch length.

"So...do you think Katherine will miss you while you're over here?" Leone asked, out of the blue.

"What? She can e-mail me, or telephone if she needs to. Look, I'm tired and I need to get to bed." Amy wriggled out of her cramped corner onto her feet, signaling the end of the evening. Leone sat on for a moment, unwilling to move.

"Good night, Leone," Amy said bluntly, prompting Leone to reluctantly stand.

She managed a polite reply. "Good night, Amy. Thanks for the nightcap and the photo show." A look of consideration crossed her face before she suddenly reached out and swamped Amy in a good-bye bear hug.

It took several seconds for Amy's benumbed mind to register what the hell was happening. Leone had moved with the speed of a cobra, grabbing her by the shoulders and slamming her into her chest. Amy's synapses exploded with a million alarms, alerts, and klaxons as her nose was buried in Leone's sweatshirt and the arms circling her squeezed the air out of her lungs. Then Leone's hands began to roam across her back, the broad flat of her palms brushing and circling the planes of Amy's ribs and shoulders, tracing her spine, hesitating just above the flare of her hips.

Leone breathed her in, her hair, her skin. She adored this scent. It had been so long, so achingly long since she had last held Amy. So she just held on, breathing her, stroking her, memorizing by touch. Greedy, because she knew it would all be over in a microsecond. The moment Amy recovered from her surprise enough to push her away, she would have to let go.

Flustered, Amy grabbed Leone by the upper arms and stepped back out of range. The ferocity of Leone's hug scared her. It stirred up feelings she was not prepared to look at yet—if ever. Leone gazed down at her, eyes black and intense with unspoken questions. Amy felt blindsided, fooled. Right up until Leone had lunged, Amy had no inkling there was any emotional residue in Leone aside from deliberately annoying her. But now she could feel it, an undercurrent of desire as strong and solid as the floor she stood on, as the walls surrounding her, as the heartbeat she'd been crushed against. And she didn't know what to do, where to place it, what to think. She only knew she needed to protect herself, and immediately.

"Stop grabbing at me. We're not teenagers anymore," Amy snapped angrily, sounding harsher than intended in her struggle to regain control. "Look, Leone, I don't know what weird nonsense you have in your head about us, but forget it. Okay?"

"It was just a good-night hug," Leone bit back, her tan cheeks bloomed with heat, eyes flashing defensively.

"It was a good-night grope, and you know it." Amy was not letting her get away with anything. "I'm here to work on the almanac and then spend time with Connie. You don't figure in my plans. So go. Just go. Go on, get out of here. Go."

She was too angry and embarrassed to look Leone in the face as she ushered her toward the door.

Reluctantly, Leone let herself be scooted along. Every molecule of her body screamed at her to gather Amy up and hold on to her forever. That this was all wrong. But she accepted she'd moved too fast and overstepped the mark. Now she backpedaled onto the porch where Amy quickly closed the door with a terse good night.

❖

Shivering with errant emotion and frustration, Leone stepped onto the trail and headed back to the Garoul compound. At least she had managed to cover as much of Amy as possible before being swatted off. Leone's scent now clung to her. It might help.

When she entered the clearing all was quiet. The celebrations had ended early, as tomorrow the hunting would begin in earnest. In one bound she mounted the steps to her mother's porch and sat heavily on a wooden chair. She struck a match and shuffled through the candle stubs on the table, lighting only the green ones. Then she sat back and contemplated the moon. In a few days it would be heavy and full.

Leone listened to the soft shift of leaves in the night air. Beyond that she could hear the sounds of the forest waking, the rustling of undergrowth as small nocturnal creatures scurried about their activities. Deeper still she could make out the movements of their hunters, the pad of paw, the sweep of wings. Her ear caught the soft calls of night.

Scent was stronger as well; the richness of earth, sap, and bark all sang out to her. Before her the warming scents of myrtle and verbena began to waft up from the candles. Next came the subtler musk undertones released by the heat of the flame. But best of all, on the flesh of her palms, brushed across her lips, cheek, and chin was the smell of Amy. Leone was saturated with her. Her scent, her heat—her woman and mate. She looked deep into flickering candles, the molten wax puddling in green pools at their base.

"Amy Amelia Fortune." She breathed her wish into the flame.

CHAPTER FOUR

Birdsong. Amy opened her eyes to delightful birdsong.

Home. She smiled up at the wooden beams above the sleeping platform and stretched luxuriously. Home sweet home sweet home. *God, how I've missed waking up to Little Dip birdsong.*

Her energy levels skyrocketed to the top of her skull and burst right through it. With a surge of momentum she kicked back the blankets and started her day.

She took a light breakfast of muesli and coffee out to the small bench table on the porch where she sat soaking up the early morning sunlight and forest greenery, excited to be back, savoring her first morning.

Every school vacation she could ever remember had been spent at Connie's cabin. The whole valley had been her adventure park. Her Treasure Island and Neverland all rolled into one. With the other young Garouls she had fought pirates, shot robbers, hunted pretend bears and tigers, and rescued princesses all summer long. Well, okay, so she'd always been the princess, tied to a tree yowling for a hero. And of course, the hero had always been Leone. None of the others ever managed to get there to save her quick enough. It was always Leone who leapt into the center of the evil villain's den; the evil villain was always played by cousin Andre. They would clash wooden swords or shoot water pistols or do kung fu, whatever the favorite weapon of the week was, until finally Andre would lie writhing in theatrical death throes. Then Leone would free her princess and drag her away by the hand back to their secret hidey-hole. She smiled at her drift back to childhood games. Today, walking through the woods would be like a trip back in time.

Amy cleared up her breakfast dishes and was soon stuffing her backpack with the makings of a little picnic. This was a workday. She would hike down to a bend in the river where she knew one of her target plants grew and get a start on her inset work.

As an afterthought she had grabbed Connie's rod and fishing box, deciding an entire day by the water would not be complete without a little fly fishing and maybe a nice fat trout for the grill. If she still had the knack?

All packed and ready, Amy paused on the top porch step to draw in a deep lungful of clean mountain air, then tucking a wayward corkscrew of hair behind her ear she stepped off onto the hard-packed dirt track. The shoulder straps of her backpack were once more shrugged into position and she checked the camera slung around her neck. In less than two minutes the forest trail had swallowed her.

With a cheerful step she headed for the Silverthread, the slow, meandering river that wove through the heart of the valley. It was going to be an exceptionally warm day for the time of year. Even at this early hour she could feel it on her skin, warming her bones as she moved in and out of the tree shadows. Her smile grew wider as she looked out for that first glimmer of silver water peeping through the trees.

Oplopanax horridus, or devil's club to the layman, was a fantastic medicinal plant to the initiated. As kids racing around the forest wrapped up in one game or another, it had always been one to avoid, its sharp thorns an irritant to tender skin. Amy grinned as she remembered the vile tea infused from its bark forced on all the children at the first sign of a sniff or cough. Her boots crunched along the trail to where she hoped devil's club still grew. It was set back a little from the river in a moist and shady patch, ideal conditions for it. And if she had remembered right she'd be only half a mile from one of Connie's favorite steelhead fishing holes.

❖

Leone stood and stretched. She was cramped from falling asleep in the porch chair. She blinked and noted her green candles had all burned down and sputtered out. That was good.

With a lazy scratch to her sides she went indoors and headed for the shower. After she had washed and changed she'd head back up to Amy's and sort out her schedule for the day. Tell her what parts of the valley were out of bounds, and try to smooth some of the feathers she had ruffled last night. Yes, she had a fine line to walk, but Amy was under her care whether she liked it or not. As far as Leone was concerned she was supervising Amy's visit, and she intended to take full advantage of her position to manipulate any romantic odds in her favor.

Jori was on his porch sipping coffee, heels hitched on the rail, looking perfectly at ease with the world when Leone passed by on her way to Amy's.

"Hey, Leone," he called. She glanced up and he raised a coffee cup along with his eyebrows in silent offer. Leone did a ninety-degree turn and headed purposefully toward him. He had some explaining to do.

As she approached he eased upright in his seat, aware she was not targeting the coffee but him. His feet were planted on the floor, and he was sitting bolt upright by the time she reached the porch.

"What's up, sis?" he asked.

"Who the hell is Katherine?" Leone demanded.

❖

Amy snapped shut her watercolor pan and looked over her loose-leaf sketches. She had drawn about thirty different plant parts she especially wanted to concentrate on. After she'd finished her detailed pencil drawings she had gone back in with her watercolors, mixing the colors as accurately as possible and applying tonal washes onto each sketch. Her swatch key on the edge of the page gave the tonal code for each mix. Together with her photos she could balance her paint palette back at Connie's studio. Satisfied with her early morning work, Amy stashed away her sketch block and camera. Her stomach was rumbling with hunger and it felt like the perfect time to head on down to the river. She'd find a nice flat rock, open her coffee flask, and treat herself to a cheese sandwich.

Amy was thrilled when her rusty navigation brought her out not ten yards from Connie's fishing spot. It lay midway between two lazy river bends where the water ran a little slower and shallower. A platform of wide stepping-stones cut across the riverbed. The largest was as big as a queen-sized bed and had in turn been a pirate ship, a whitewater raft, and a treasure island in her childhood games. It was a magnificent rock for all sorts of reasons. Close by, deep, cool pools were tucked in under the bank side where steelhead trout rested and fed. Connie had taught her to stand high and dry on this huge, flat stone and wait patiently for hours, casting her line over and over, waiting for that one fish to see her fly and leap. Then the hunter became the prey, and sport and supper were reeled in as one.

Amy sat on the riverbank munching her sandwich, scanning the surface for telltales to its underwater secrets, deciding where she would position herself and where she would cast. She brushed the crumbs off her fingers onto the legs of her jeans and flipped open Connie's tackle box.

Hmm. She looked thoughtfully at the flies pinned in colorful, feathery rows. Chronimid number 14. *Let's try the red one. If that sucks we can go for the green.*

Already her stomach was fluttering with excitement.

Leone's long strides ate up the trail to Connie's cabin. She was much more satisfied with life now that Jori had assured her that the English girl in Amy's photos was her housemate and nothing more. In fact, he confirmed there was no love interest whatsoever on Amy's current horizon. That was all Leone needed to know for the sun to shine, the birds to sing, and the world to turn in total harmony. Much more relaxed now, she looked forward to spending the day with Amy.

"Yo, Amy?" Leone rata-tat-tatted on the porch post as she cleared the steps in one bound. "Wake-up call."

Without hesitating she pushed at the door. It swung open. She'd have to get Amy into the habit of locking it. That would be a standoff in itself. It seemed Amy was still as obstinate as ever, always ready to butt heads over the least little thing. Leone stepped inside and immediately noticed how quiet it was.

"Amy?" she asked the emptiness. "Damn it. I told you I'd visit every day and tell you where it's safe to go," she exploded in exasperation.

She strode back out onto the porch and stood stock still, head tilted to the air. And waited. The only movement was the breeze, stirring long strands of her hair across her eyes. It didn't matter— she wasn't using them. They were closed.

"Damn her. Mulish, thick-skulled woman," she murmured to the trees. Then, whipping her head around to the right, she was off the porch in one loping stride and thundering down the trail that led to the Silverthread.

❖

Two easy fish later, one around three pounds and the other maybe a six pounder, and Amy tidied away her tackle. There was little point fishing on, for though there were plenty for the taking, the refrigerator at the cabin was small and couldn't really store much more than these two. She was due at Marie's for dinner that night. Maybe she'd take the larger one as a present and cook the smaller one tomorrow. It would do her for a couple of meals. After cleaning out the fish she laid them on the bank by her backpack. With a sigh of satisfaction she stretched out the kinks in her shoulders. Her casting was still a little stiff and rusty. Not that it mattered. If she'd opened her pants pocket today the fish would have jumped right on in.

By midday it was warm enough for her to feel overheated in her long-sleeved fleece shirt. Glancing down at the pure water bubbling past her toes and then up at the sharp sunlight over the tree-lined lip of the valley, Amy made an impulsive decision. *I'm going to have a quick dip.* Partly because she was hot and the water sang seductively, partly as homage to the many times she had splashed about and swum in this river. As a kid she'd learned to swim downstream in the creek, with the overhanging rock and the old rope swing. Amy peeled off her clothes and dumped them on the riverbank with the rest of her belongings and in bra and panties stepped gingerly into the water.

"Oh, sweet mother of God," she squeaked. It was freezing! With a deep breath she bobbed down to immerse herself up to the chin, one, two, three times.

All right, that's enough childhood nostalgia. I'm outta here. Quickly she scampered back and rummaged through her bag for the towel she always carried. Too often she got soaked on field trips. A warm pair of socks was another mandatory item hidden away in a side pocket. Her little hip flask was yet another. Little luxuries like these could make even the foulest, wettest job almost bearable.

The sunshine on her pebbled skin was soothing, brushing away the chill. It was possibly one of the last fine days before the weather turned with a wintry vengeance. Amy took the towel over to the stepping-stones and spread it out on the big central rock and lay down to dry off in the sun's rays. She had been up and about very early and so far it had been a wonderful day, but now she felt tired. *I suppose I'm still jet-lagged. Perhaps a little catnap is in order.*

An afternoon snooze would be a lovely addition to her first full day here. And to top it all off she was having dinner at Marie's later, always a culinary delight. She settled down on her belly, resting her head on her arms, and with a happy smile let the bubbling water sing her a lullaby.

❖

Amy wasn't sure what woke her. She was surprised to be in such a deep sleep. Her eyes popped open and she felt chilled even though the sun still shone warmly. She lifted her head and scanned the tree line hugging the riverside. The birdsong had stopped, and an eerie quiet had descended. Was that what had awoken her? The unnatural silence?

Something drifted into her peripheral vision, dark velvet slinking through the shadows before being swallowed by the forest. She squinted, trying to focus on its fluidity, a liquid whisper that melted from tree to tree. It was nothing more than a penumbra, as vague as a watermark on the surrounding gloom. No sooner had she caught it than it dissolved away into nothingness. She rose onto her knees to look harder but all was now uniform darkness. Nevertheless, she was left with a strong residue of unease. It coated her tongue and cramped her stomach but she had no evidence for her physical discomfort. Tentative birdcalls began to fill the quiet. The ominous pause in nature seemed to flutter, then lurch hesitantly back into the everyday life of the forest.

Amy gave one last sweeping glance along the riverbank. It was then she noticed her fish. Her trout lay several feet away from where she'd left them. How long had she been asleep? She stood, as if that would give her a better perspective on events. Towel in hand, she padded across the stepping-stones to the bank. As she approached she noticed the rapidly drying paw prints circling the fish. They were massive, and clawed, and made every fine hair on her already goose-bumped flesh stand on end. She watched aghast as the prints slowly dissipated before her eyes with the heat of the sun. A rustle in the nearby undergrowth shook her out of her stupor and galvanized her into action. She dropped her towel and hurriedly grabbed at her clothes, deciding it was best to get dressed and go as quickly as possible.

"Been fishing?" Leone emerged from the tree line just several yards upstream from where Amy stood.

Startled, Amy spun around angrily. *As if this wasn't creepy enough, now I've got a peeper ogling me from the woods.*

"Do you mind?" she barked scrabbling to cover her semi-nudity with the towel.

Leone blinked and flushed hotly. She turned away to give Amy her privacy, but not before taking in the gentle sway of lace cupped breasts as Amy bent for the towel, or the russet curls nestling under a soft, rounded belly. The damp translucency of Amy's underwear hid little. Saliva flooded Leone's mouth and she swallowed hard. Her stomach tightened as a primal power shifted, bearing down heavily on her chest and belly. Her nostrils quivered lifting a succulent scent from the air. It felt so unnatural to turn away from this woman, but she wanted Amy to feel as comfortable as possible around her. It was important if Leone was to get anywhere near her.

"Okay, you can turn around now."

Leone did so, slowly. Amy was fully dressed, stuffing her towel back into her backpack and gathering her gear together. She seemed flustered and upset. She glanced up as Leone turned to her.

"Thank you." She gave curt approval of Leone's manners, and then nodded toward the fish. "Something's been at them."

"What do you mean? Has an animal been sniffing around your fish?" Leone stiffened, but her voice remained casual and light.

"I didn't see it. I was sleeping." Amy indicated the big river rock she had sunbathed on. "But whatever it was it had big feet."

"Like a duck?" Leone asked flippantly, masking her concern in banter.

"No! Not a duck…huge feet." Amy held her hands out about two foot apart in the proverbial bragging fisherman pose. Leone's eyebrows rose. "Come and see for yourself." Amy pointed to the dried out marks around her fish.

Leone approached and looked at the damp, rapidly drying smudges. They looked like nothing but told her everything.

"Oh my God. It's an Oregon Duck, all right. From the size of those splotches, it looks like the linebacker."

"You're such a smart-ass. They've all dried up, but I'm telling you they were big…with claws. Maybe bears?"

"Nah, they're all playing for Chicago."

"Again, you are so not funny. This is serious."

"Yes, it is. What are you doing out here anyway? I thought we'd agreed I'd drop by in the morning and tell you where the hunting was so you'd be safe from the ducks and the bears with the big feet."

"We did not agree on any such thing. I'm seeing Marie tonight and telling her to get you off my back. You're like a melanoma." Amy scowled in discomfort. Leone knew catching Amy in her underwear had not been the best of moves. She needed to fix it somehow, and fast.

"Anyway, this area is safe." Amy continued to harangue her, and with great aplomb went on to list all the reasons she did not need Leone glued to her throughout the day. "It has never been hunted; it's for fishing only. It's near a quick trail home. Plus, it's one of the places I knew I'd find the first specimen on Marie's list."

"You started already?" Leone made sure she sounded impressed. "Good for you." As she spoke she stooped to collect the fishing pole and tackle box. If she was helpful she reasoned she could walk back with Amy rather than leave her alone again. To make certain, she scooped up the fish, too, letting them dangle at her side from the joint line through their gills.

"Yes. Remember the devil's club up on the slope? The one Jori fell into when he was eight or nine? Well, it's still there, bristling away as evil as ever." Amy rambled on happily now that she was on a favorite topic. She grabbed at her backpack, her annoyance forgotten as she began to regale Leone with her news. "I got some great sketches. It looks so pretty in the fall, and it's no longer toxic this time of year either. I'm going to tell Marie where it is in case she wants to harvest it."

Leone listened happily to Amy's lilting voice as they strolled alongside each other. Before joining the riverbank trail she took a last narrowed eyed look at the woodland on the far side of the Silverthread. There was nothing she could pick up on.

"…and then I caught the other one nearly five minutes later. I swear if the cabin had a freezer I could have filled it." Amy had moved on to her fishing stories. Leone smiled, sharing in the excitement of a good day's fishing.

CHAPTER FIVE

And you're sure there are no bears or other man-eating monsters in the valley?" Amy's voice was filled with concern.

"If I told you there were huge, man-eating, really monstrous bears would you let me escort you everywhere?"

"No. I would just have to carry a gun and be worried and intimidated and my work would suffer and your deadline would go belly up."

"Okay. Definitely, no bears."

"Well, wolves, then? There are wolves all over the place."

"The wolves are too high up. And too shy to come this far down to the Silverthread. Nope, it was just a beaver or something sniffing around your fish. You probably scared him off before he could steal one."

"Beaver?" Amy guffawed. Leone was being ridiculous. "No way would a beaver leave such big prints. I saw them, remember? You aren't going to make me change my mind. I know what I saw. It had to be at least as big as a bear."

"Well, all you have as evidence are some dried-out splashes and two unmolested trout. It's hard to believe Godzilla's on a rampage."

"Bite me, Garoul. Something with great big paws was on that riverbank poking at my fish."

"Look, let's be rational. A great big, ferocious animal would just take the fish and run. Right?"

"Yes, I suppose so." Amy frowned. "I have a feeling I'm about to be rationalized out of my 'big bad bear' theory."

"I think a heron or beaver or something like that came after your fish and you surprised it before it could drag these big beauties away." Leone held up the beauties in question. "It makes the most sense. Think about it."

"Pfft. Heron?" Amy snorted again. "Perhaps it was Big Bird? If only there were some discarded yellow feathers to prove your theory…or I'd heard the alphabet song."

"Okay, you win. It's a big bad, killer bear and you need a bodyguard." Leone sneaked in her knockout blow.

"No. Maybe you're right. It was probably just a thieving beaver or some such." Amy hastily U-turned on prowling carnivores if it meant she was going to be railroaded into having an escort.

Leone smiled and let her. All she needed was a fix on Amy's whereabouts and she could easily keep a discreet eye on her. It was better than locking antlers with her every morning over where she could and could not go. It could all be done on the quiet and Amy would be none the wiser.

They continued to enjoy the walk back. The afternoon sun was fading away, and Amy felt cold as they moved into the shadowed side of the valley. Damp underwear didn't help her chill factor, either. She gave an involuntary shiver.

"You're cold. Could I make you a nice pot of tea when we get home? Maybe you could show me your field sketches?" Leone tried to wrangle an invite.

"I'm not cold." Amy remembered the drink they'd shared last night. She didn't want to encourage that sort of scenario again.

"It's just so I can get a feel for how your work will complement Marie's text." Leone shamelessly played her editor's card.

Amy hesitated. She loved talking about botanical illustration, and could yak about it for hours on end. So what if Leone wanted to be the one she spent time yakking to? Leone was her editor, after all. It was right that they should talk about these things.

"Well, okay, if it's to do with work. But no hugging," she warned.

Leone defended her good-night squeezing. "I was just saying good night."

"Keep your hands to yourself." Amy was adamant there would be no replay.

They turned the final bend and the cabin lay before them.

"Okay, no hugs," Leone said. "But can I see the sketches? I need an overview."

"Fine. Just let me change into something warm and dry first." Together they mounted the steps to Connie's cabin.

"Better yet, go and grab a hot shower and I'll light a fire. You can bank it up to keep the cabin toasty while you're at Marie's for dinner. How does that sound?" Leone pushed her luck now that she was through the door.

Amy felt shivery every time she moved out of the direct sunlight. Now that she was indoors, a full chill settled on her bones. A warm fire and hot cup of tea sounded really good.

"You've got a deal. It is cold in here."

❖

With hot water pouring down her body and all the chill and cramps of the afternoon washing away with the suds, Amy was glad her world was returning to normal after her earlier scare. As annoying as Leone's teasing could be, Amy was comforted by the plain common sense hidden in it. Amy didn't want hungry bears, or wolves, or even cougars, lurking nearby as she sunbathed, so part of her was more than willing to listen to Leone's more acceptable theories. The alternative was to admit she did need someone watching out for her as she worked. And that someone would doubtless be Leone. And that would never do.

❖

Leone quickly lit a small fire and put the kettle on the stove to boil. She hunted along the cluttered mantelpiece for Connie's battered old wooden box. Lifting the lid released a myriad of pungent aromas from the various incenses and essential oils stored in it. The rich mixture was overpowering but also curiously warm and welcoming. Leone found the small incense cone she was after, and placing it on the hearth, lit it. Thin strands of smoke curled into the air. Some escaped straight up the chimney; others wound their way through the cabin, draping it with a spicy tang.

The kettle bubbled and she moved back into the kitchen to prepare a pot of tea. She sorted through the various containers lined along a shelf and finally wandered over to the bathroom door.

"What flavor tea are you in the mood for? I got mint, chamomile, or maybe some ginger would warm you up?" she called through to Amy.

"Yes, ginger sounds good. I'll only be a few more minutes."

Amy felt the stiffness melt out of her bones. Part of her muscular tension she put down to being damp and cold after her swim. The rest was due to her earlier fright. Imagined or not, she found the entire experience unsettling. Not so much the fishy footprints as the horrible feeling she'd had gazing into the eerily silent woods. She could have sworn a wave of utter malignancy had flooded from the forest, chilling her more than the cool afternoon air ever could.

Now, in the warmth and safety of her cabin, with Leone puttering about in the kitchen, she put all her strange sensations down to re-acclimatizing to the valley and its wildlife. She was being ridiculous. Nevertheless, she was glad of Leone's company. Amy felt silly at being spooked at shadows, and it was good of Leone to hang around until she felt more settled. She knew there was more to this visit than Leone wanting to look at her sketches. Leone had seen she'd been unnerved and wanted her artist rested and reassured. Amy appreciated the kindness.

The bathroom was fogged up and Amy opened a window to let a blast of fresh air into the tiny room. The wooden edge rasped and caught across the badly weathered windowsill. Amy frowned; the wood surround was gouged and splintered and almost jamming the window shut. Connie was usually on top of the constant maintenance a home like this demanded. She'd have to ask Marie which of the

Garouls were responsible for doing odd jobs on the cabins and get them to come out. The window needed serviced badly.

Amy threw on some clean sweats and opened the door into the cozy living room with its crackling fire. Leone was clattering cups and spoons in the kitchen; a pot of tea sat brewing on the countertop. Amy's heart lurched at the happy domesticity of the scene. She was suffused with a feeling of contentment, as if she'd just arrived home. Confused at the sudden rush of emotion she gulped a deep breath of…of…

"Oh my God. What's that smell?"

"You don't like it?" Leone looked up anxiously.

"No. What is it?"

"Scullcap." She sounded a little dejected.

"What crap?"

"Scull*cap*. Shake the water out of your ears. Connie told me to burn it."

"What the hell for? It smells like feet—"

"It does not smell like feet. It's a nice smell."

"Satan's feet. Why the hell are you stinking up my cabin?"

Leone frowned at the question. "Mmm…termites. It's a natural termite deterrent." She brought over two steaming mugs of ginger tea.

"Termites? Here? In Connie's cabin? And that smell chases them away how?"

"I don't know how," Leone snipped back, very unhappy with the topic of conversation. "It just does."

"Maybe they think Satan's coming," Amy groused, sinking onto the couch. "Okay, I give up. I'm too tired and you're too ridiculous to argue with."

She reached for her mug, her nose wrinkling in disgust. "Can you turn it off now? I'm sure the termites have all absconded. In fact, I might not be far behind them. Wouldn't it be better to get in pest control?"

"Nope, Connie told me what to do. We just sit here and let the incense burn out, nice and easy. So stop your yammering and drink your tea." Leone joined her on the couch looking relieved the conversation was over. As usual she sat too close, almost shoulder to shoulder and hip to hip. Amy glanced at her with a small frown; Leone seemed oblivious that she was eating up the prescribed space for a normal seating arrangement. Amy decided to let it go. This time she was prepared for any sudden hugging.

After a few moments of fire gazing and tea sipping Leone turned and asked, "So, can I see your devil's club sketches?"

"Mmm, yes." Thoroughly relaxed and content, Amy went to collect her folder and camera from her backpack. When she returned to the couch she sat in the same place she'd just vacated without a second thought, unfazed that she was wedged so close to Leone's long, lean body.

Right up until dinnertime they browsed through the sketches and then the photos, discussing the merits of each, happily sipping tea, crushed into the corner of the couch, as the little cone of incense burned away.

The wonderful aroma of beef curry greeted them as they entered Marie's cabin.

"Perfect timing, you two. It's ready for the table. Leone, uncork the wine please," Marie called from the kitchen. In a few minutes they were sitting at the dining table enjoying a robust Pinot Noir with their meal.

"So, you had a good day in the field?" Marie asked.

Amy nodded enthusiastically. "*Oplopanax horridus.* The very first one on your list, and I knew exactly where to find it."

"She remembered the clump Jori fell into years ago." Leone chuckled.

"Oh, Lord, what a day that was. Poor Jori. Talk about learning the hard way." Marie shook her head at the memory, a rueful smile on her lips.

"The initial sketches are fantastic," Leone said.

Marie looked hopefully at the bag Amy had brought with her. "I don't suppose you brought them with you?"

"No. But I'll call by and show you the ones Leone and I singled out. I plan to start in Connie's studio tomorrow. But if the weather's good then I'll go out again and paint later at night."

"What's next on the list?" Marie asked.

"Um, next is *Prunus emarginata.* I can find bitter cherry most places along the river. After that it's *Hyoscyamus niger*. Black henbane, I didn't know that grew here. It's a poisonous weed isn't it?"

"Yes. You'll find it higher up near the south ridge, close to the logging track," Marie said.

"It's way up there?"

"Mmm, about a half mile or so back from the road before it bends around Big Jack." Marie mentioned a particularly large tree used as a local waypoint.

"I'll take you up there tomorrow if the weather holds," Leone said.

"No need, I can go myself now that I know where to look."

"I'd rather Leone went with you. It's a long hard hike, and I'm sure she can help carry something," Marie said.

"All I take is my backpack. I hardly need a sherpa."

"Well," Leone pointed out, "what if you fell or something? Or that panda came after you again? It's a long way out."

"What panda?" Marie looked inquisitively at Leone.

"Ignore her. She's teasing me because I thought I saw something in the woods today."

"Something in the woods?" Marie was immediately concerned.

"Oh, it was nothing, just a spooky feeling. But something was sniffing around my fish. Leone assures me it was a small animal with big feet." Amy caught the look between Leone and her mother. Worried they would gang up on her about needing a chaperone, she moved quickly on to another of her morning activities. "You should have seen the fish I caught, Marie." She held her hands up, about two feet apart. "He was a whopper. This big."

"Yeah." Leone snorted derisively. "Like it was ever that big."

"He was so. He had to be seven pounds at least. Maybe even closer to eight. I'll bring him over for your dinner tomorrow," Amy said.

"More like five, maybe six pounds." Leone pointed out the discrepancy and was primly ignored.

"It's a deal. You deliver, and I'll broil it with rosemary and garlic lemon for supper." Marie was very happy at the offer of a hefty trout. "Now, are you sure Leone can't be of use tomorrow?"

"I could drive you up to the logging road and halve the hike time?" Leone pushed.

"No, thanks. The light up there's good. I can head out early if the weather's fine and have plenty of time to set up. Believe me, I'll work faster without you looking over my shoulder." Amy was adamant on retaining control over all aspects of her work environment. "I don't need a guide. I know these mountains and valley well, remember?"

Marie shared a dubious glance with Leone but conceded. Leone looked as if she would argue on, but took her mother's lead and stayed silent.

"Okay. Now that that's sorted," Marie defused the conversation, "how about we look at the illustrations I'd like you to complete for Connie? Let's discuss it over coffee and I'll show you exactly what we need."

Amy knew this was the crux of the dinner invitation, the editorial chat. She was already more than a little concerned at retouching Connie's work. From what she had previously seen the illustrations were superb and definitely didn't need her to do anything other than admire them.

Marie returned from the kitchen with a pot of coffee in one hand and a pie dish in the other.

"I thought we could all take a slice and sit by the fire."

They retired to the fireside, each with a plate of pie and coffee. Marie and Amy shared the couch while Leone took the overstuffed armchair.

"Okay," Marie began. "We've called you in at Connie's suggestion as she is currently incapacitated and we have a tight deadline for this work." She reached for the portfolio already sitting on the side table and extracted the two illustrations she had shown Amy last evening.

"This one is goldenseal, growth above ground. And this one is its root ball." She next produced a slip of paper with several black curlicue marks scrawled across it. "And these are the marks Connie hasn't managed to incorporate."

Amy frowned in confusion. "What are these? They have no relevance to the plant."

"It's a sort of an embellishment Connie adapted for the Garoul Press Almanac. The marks are much smaller than this, of course. Very unobtrusive. These are not to scale," Marie explained confidently.

Amy's brow knit over the separate papers. "Why on earth would she augment goldenseal with marks that didn't apply to the botanical accuracy of the illustration?"

"Kind of like a certifier?" Leone leaned forward in her chair. "Like a signature for Connie's work. It's traditional for our artists to include them, but before Connie could finish these two illustrations she became ill. The marks that go with these particular illustrations still need to be added. Some squiggles belong to one, the rest to the other."

"It was agreed from the start that Connie wouldn't use her recognized signature but a series of marks we use for cataloging and other indices." Marie supported Leone's words.

"But she would have added any marks, superfluous or otherwise, at the same time she did the illustration. I told you last night, to go back into these could warp the paper." Amy squinted over Connie's work, still not happy with the explanation. "And Connie uses a lightweight hot press paper. It could cockle and scan incorrectly if I were to tamper with it. I can't understand why she didn't add these…marks as she painted. Was she interrupted?"

There was an uneasy silence between the Garoul women. Amy glanced up from her inspection to find them exchanging another look. *What are they not telling me?*

"Well," Marie said hesitantly, "neither Leone nor I are artists, and I certainly don't know all the ins and outs of Connie's work methods. We don't use certifiers on every illustration, but these two definitely need them. So, you're saying you can't do it?"

"I'm saying the chances of destroying Connie's work are too high to risk it. I can do the insets for you, but as far as touching up Connie's existing work? I think you need to leave these extra marks out or else get your designer to add them in digitally after they've been scanned. If an illustration is damaged at this point it will seriously threaten your deadline." Amy was blunt in her assessment. What they were asking her to do was crazy.

"Oh dear. Well, you know best, Amy. We need to keep on track. The deadline is too close to take any chances. If Connie's work were damaged we'd really be in trouble. Let's push on with your list of insets. How do things look now, Leone?"

"Despite losing Connie we're not too far behind schedule. Amy has less than five weeks to deliver thirteen insets. I know that's tight, but the plants are already here in the valley and in season. All Amy has to do is find them. Your last copy edits are done, Mom. The text is ready for proofing." Leone looked over at Amy. "I'll be proofing in Mom's back office for the next few weeks. Until we get to the reprographic stage, then I'm back in the city to oversee the move to film."

"Do you still print in Vancouver?" Amy asked, full of interest. The Garouls ran a print house too, north of the border.

"Yes, Garoul Print is still up there. I'll fly up and approve the proof copy in late October. The almanac has priority and the presses are already booked up for us. We should be on time for our release early next year."

They all nodded in agreement. It was a tight but doable schedule.

"Would you mind if I took these with me?" Amy indicated the portfolio with Connie's work. "As a reference to her more recent styling. It might come in handy later when I begin my own work."

"Of course." Marie happily handed the folder over.

"Thanks. It's late and I need an early start tomorrow." Amy collected her coat from the hook by the door, calling over her shoulder, "I'll drop by tomorrow sometime with the trout and my devil's club sketches. With any luck I'll be able to show you the henbane ones, too." She was buttoning her coat when Leone rose to pull hers on, too. "For heavens sake, Leone. I don't need an escort tonight. Marie, tell her I don't need any help to find my own goddamned front door." She pulled her flashlight out of her pocket to prove her point.

"I'm sure Amy will be okay, Leone. Look, she's even got a flashlight." Marie put a restraining hand on Leone's arm.

Leone shrugged. "Okay. Good night, Amy. Maybe I'll catch you tomorrow." She settled back in to her chair. "Call me and I'll give you a lift up to the logging road."

"For the last time, I don't need a lift." Amy was unable to hide her exasperation. Embarrassed at her outburst, she turned to Marie. "Thank you for dinner. It was fantastic."

She collected Connie's folio and said good-bye, stepping out into the crisp night air surprised to get away from Leone without more of a fuss. Maybe a full belly and a warm seat by the fire had damped down her hero reflex.

❖

Amy was glad of the walk home alone. It gave her time to stargaze as she gathered her thoughts. And she had plenty to think about tonight, Connie's illustrations being foremost in her mind. She knew instinctively Connie would never misrepresent a specimen she was illustrating.

Connie had been her teacher from an early age, when Amy had first displayed an interest in art and nature. It was not that surprising. Amy came from an artistic family. Connie was already a recognized wildlife artist, and Amy's English father was as famed for his abstracts as he was for his drinking. Both her parents preferred to view reality through the bottom of a rose-tinted bourbon glass. If Connie hadn't been there for her, giving her all the love, care, and attention a young child needed... Amy shuddered to think how miserable her life could have been.

As it was, she whiled away her childhood years at an upstate

New York boarding school, yearning for the holidays when she could escape to Little Dip and see her beloved aunt Connie. Amy was always fearful that maybe one year her parents would decide to drag her off on vacation with them. But it never happened. The dreaded year never came.

By the time she was in her late teens her father was in an early grave, bequeathing his daughter his artistic genes and Anglo American citizenship. At least with her British passport she could freely live and work in Europe. Her mother, Connie's sister, was on her third marriage and had moved to Argentina. Amy rarely saw her now, and it didn't seem to bother either of them. They orbited each other like distant planets.

In contrast, Amy was a satellite to her aunt's life. No matter how far her wanderings took her, Connie had always been her constant. Between telephone calls and e-mail they kept up with each other's lives. Frequently, they'd meet in exciting European cities and tour the galleries and art shows together.

Amy kept a tight hold of those she loved. Besides Connie, many of the Garoul family kept her in the loop regarding Little Dip and all its news. It was important for her to know that home, Connie's home, was always there for her. Then came the frightening phone call from Marie, and Amy's world had splintered apart, the needled shards penetrating to her core. Connie was ill, hospitalized. And now Amy was back in the valley trying to complete her work and understand what the hell was going on.

Signatures and catalogue certifiers, my ass. No way would Connie add erroneous marks to her work. I'm going to check this out for myself. Connie simply doesn't work like that. And she knew just where to look—Connie's own library. Her shelves held every book she had ever contributed to, as well as a vast selection reflecting her own private interests. That would be Amy's starting point.

CHAPTER SIX

Connie's book collection was impressive. It was a bibliophile's paradise and had more than tripled in size in the time Amy had been away. Connie's range of interests seemed to have expanded with it, the primary themes being the natural world, botany, art, and the esoteric. Amy wondered how many Connie had actually contributed to, or were these merely a reflection of her reading preferences?

She went directly to the shelves she knew housed Connie's earlier work for the Garoul Press, and in particular the older almanacs. Connie's working partnership with Marie spanned over two decades. Amy pulled out a few at random,1988 and 1997. They were large leather bound volumes of an irregular size, slightly larger than quarto. The almanacs were produced to a bastard size.

These babies must be expensive to churn out. Amy suspected they were created for a specialized clientele rather than the general public. Ultimately, they were for a collector's niche market and had to cost a small fortune.

For good measure Amy also selected a third, more recent book Connie had worked on, but not for Garoul Press. The comparison might prove useful.

Comfortable on the couch, she slowly began to browse the first of the almanacs. The pages were matte and thick, creamy to the touch, and oozed luxury through her fingertips. The tactile lusciousness, combined with the exquisite world of Connie's artistry, totally immersed her. Before her eyes petals rippled in a soft breeze, grasses flowed across paper, leaves rattled and crunched, and the turn of each page wafted her with an imagined floral bouquet. Engrossed, she sat for over an hour drifting through Connie's delicate world, lost to the time and motion of this one… until she saw it.

A mark.

A series of sigils, to be exact, embedded in *Angelica sylvestris*. Angelica, a favorite herb of hers; Amy had drawn it many times, root and stem, bloom and seed head. So often, in fact, that she immediately noticed the adventitious lines and swirls in the illustration. If she hadn't already known this specimen inside out, and had a professional interest in its representation, the markings would have been almost undetectable.

Most of the markings were applied to parts of the plant, but a few floated through the background and were the easiest to pick out. Quickly Amy flipped forward a few pages and concentrated on *Cnicus benedictus*, or blessed thistle, a plant she was unfamiliar with. There was nothing. Did that mean there were no marks there or that they couldn't be seen with a layman's eye? Had she only noticed the angelica markings because she happened to know every last whisker of the herb?

Sighing, she sat back. This would need a lot more investigation than a quick look. And what did the marks mean? She'd have to find that out, too. She was certain they made no reference whatsoever to Connie's artistic signature, or any cataloguing system Amy knew of. Certain now that there was more going on than either Leone or Marie were prepared to tell her, she set the almanacs aside and stretched.

Why were these markings endorsed by the Garoul Press, and did they have anything to do with Connie's collapse? Amy placed the almanacs on Connie's desk. She would need to go through all of them with a fine-toothed comb. She picked up her third and final selection and glanced at the spine. *Witchery for Wooers*. The publisher was The Wiccan Wheel.

With a wry smile she opened it. She hadn't known Connie contributed to books like this. It looked rustic and quaint. It had probably been a fun project to work on. There were few full-page illustrations inside, but two of them, renditions of a yew and a gingko tree, she easily recognized as Connie's work. Here her usual signature was employed, making the Garoul sigils seem even more suspect.

Well-worn and loved, the pages spilled open in her hands, easily cascading from beginning to end. This was more a friend than a book. Amy was content to casually dip in, halting here and there to cast an idle eye over amulets, charms, scrying spells, and love potions. There were chapters with recipes for fragrant oils, herbal sachets, and incense cakes. Even one on magical candle making, with scents and dyes, and the inevitable candle spells.

Green is for Venus.
Musk, Ambergris, and Myrtle her scent.
Burn through to first hour of sunrise.
Call your love 'til candle's spent.

Gently she closed the covers with a smile. She had to admit it was a charming book. She would have been proud to contribute artwork to something as delicately fashioned as this. An editing coup and marketing masterpiece, it vibrated with positivity and promise. It would make a lovely gift, and was beautiful to browse through.

But I can't see anyone actually believing in this stuff, never mind practicing any of it to woo a lover. I mean, lighting green candles to Venus and calling people to you...how daft can you get?

She headed wearily to the bathroom. It had been an intriguing day, full of ups and downs. Her first working day back in Little Dip was, objectively, a success. She had found and recorded her first specimen, fit in some brilliant fishing, and had a lovely dinner at Marie's. The editing problem with the extraneous markings she knew would make sense once she properly understood what was going on.

The only real blight had been the animal lurking in the woods, and the fact that it had been bold enough to sniff out the fish. That alarmed her, though her initial feelings of unease had now numbed.

No harm had come to her; she had just been spooked. Nevertheless, she was left with a vague feeling of disquiet she could not consciously identify.

As she brushed her teeth, her mind wandered back to the more comforting moments of the day. Surprisingly, she found herself thinking of the time spent with Leone, laughing and joking as they strolled home from the river, or sipping ginger tea before a log fire mulling over her morning's work. Even dinner at Marie's had been fun. Sitting around a table with Leone and Marie sharing good food, good wine, and good conversation. A surge of old emotion, old memory, broke to the surface, flooding her with bittersweet nostalgia. Immediately, she forced it down and sealed it shut, entombing it deep within. She rinsed and spat its residue into the basin along with the toothpaste. She knew where this softening of her heart would lead, and she knew she didn't want to go there. She had no love left for Leone Garoul. Not anymore. With one long, stern stare in to the mirror she turned away to prepare for bed.

Soft, yellow lamplight spilled from the cabin window. Outside, yards from her door, Leone settled under the cedar trees waiting for the lights to douse and the cabin to plunge into darkness.

Ten minutes later the cabin's lights went out. Its sole inhabitant now settled for the night, Leone focused steadfastly on Amy's darkened windows. All was still. Immobile in the shadows, she waited a further hour before turning away and melting into night, as soft as a velvet shadow.

CHAPTER SEVEN

A beautiful dawn chorus greeted Amy on her second morning. Before she could even blink herself awake, a smile was on her face.

This place is magical. I always wake up happy here. She kicked the quilt to the foot of the bed and quickly padded down the ladder to start her day.

Soon she was washed and fed, and almost out the door when she thought to bring a scarf. The daily forecast promised chill northerly winds. She fumbled in the small dresser by the door. Connie also favored scarves for the cooler fall weather. Amy scrabbled through a nest of knotted silk and wool, trying to extract one from the jumble. Her fingers brushed against cool metal near the back of the drawer. Carefully, she pulled away swathes of colorful fabric to expose the metallic gleam of a Ruger. Amy held the Bearcat revolver in her hand, frowning. She peered further into the drawer and found an opened box of bullets.

Gingerly she set the box of bullets on the dresser and examined her find. It was not a hunting gun. Connie had always declared she was a fisher, not a hunter. She had never cared much for guns and weaponry, so why did she have a firearm tucked away in her cabin?

Amy remembered the claw marks around her fish and the ill ease she had felt. Had Connie not felt safe? Perhaps the gun had always been lying neglected at the back of the drawer? A token to American household security out here in the middle of nowhere?

Pushing the weapon and its accompanying bullets back where she'd found them, Amy let it go. She had enough to get on with today. She tied a silk scarf around her neck and headed out to work.

She took the high trail that led north to the logging road and Big Jack. It was a very long hike and Marie was right, it would take her most of the day to make it up there, never mind all the way back before dark. But Amy had a plan. If she got high enough, soon enough, she was sure she could locate areas where the growing conditions suited henbane perfectly. There was no real need to go all the way to Big Jack. As far as she was concerned, if the plant grew happily in one part of the valley there was no reason it couldn't grow in other suitable areas, too. All she had to do was find the nearest one. Simple. She knew the soil was lighter and well drained higher up the valley walls, and with the amount of seed black henbane produced, she wouldn't be surprised if it was rife in any clearing it could find.

Her hunch was right. A few hours later and she literally struck pay dirt. The first thing she dug out from the side pocket of her backpack was a pair of disposable gloves. All parts of this weed were toxic and she didn't want to inadvertently absorb anything as she examined the specimens for her model plant.

Her selection made, she set to work quickly with her camera. The day was still young and the light good, but the forecast was for heavy cloud cover by midday. She should be finished here and back home in time to call on Marie with the trout long before she lost the best of the light.

After supper she planned to spend the rest of the evening in Connie's studio, working on the henbane and the devil's club sketches. Then she'd treat herself to a big cognac and some more almanac investigation. Her work schedule for the next few weeks was perfect, if she lucked out with the weather.

Time flew when Amy became absorbed in her work. She was coming to the end of her series of sketches when a sudden cold sensation, like ice water trickling down her spine, ripped her focus apart. The effect on her system was immediate. She stiffened, her skin chilled, and the small hairs on her arms stood to attention. Silence filled the small clearing.

When did the birds stop singing? She raised her head, listening… to nothing. Even the breeze seemed to drop away and abandon her. It was back. The shadow was back. She knew it. She could feel it, dark and predatory, circling in the forest behind her. Slowly inching to the tree line, fixing on her like a target! *Stop being silly. All you're doing is scaring the crap out of yourself. Just pack up nice and slow, and head home.* She was more or less done anyway.

All the while scolding herself for her excessive imagination, but still unable to shake her unease, Amy packed up in double quick time. The silence from the surrounding woods was unnerving. She needed to get moving and she'd hear the birds soon enough. Probably an eagle overhead had made them all hush up.

Backpack on her shoulders, she now had the awkward decision of which way to go. The route she had come by would take her straight into the silent forest. Although she felt a little calmer now, and her skin had stopped crawling, she was reluctant to do that. The other option was to go a little higher up and connect with the logging road. Then she could double back along it to where it eventually met up with the main route to the Garoul compound. It was by far the longest way home, but she had time today. Her gut instinct told her that was the way to go.

As she strode quickly in that direction the woodland around her came back to life, making her doubt her earlier fears. Once again she felt silly and blamed her ripe imagination for her turmoil. Still, it was an uphill slog and she refused to slacken her pace. She wanted to be home. She kidded herself it was so she could get an earlier start in the studio, but her feet were moving far faster than was necessary and she had no intention of slowing down.

❖

Elicia pulled the Jeep over to the edge of the dirt road and let the engine idle. She stuck her head out the window. "Hey. Need a lift anywhere?" she called over to Leone.

Leone shifted and strolled over to the vehicle. She had been propped against Big Jack for quite some time now and her patience was wearing thin.

"Nah, thanks. I'm just out for a stroll and thought I'd drop by and visit the big fella." She nodded toward the tree but her gaze flitted along the tree-lined track, expecting something or someone to appear any moment.

"Some stroll. Sure you don't want a lift back? I'm heading into town. I can easily drop you somewhere closer to home?"

Leone smiled and shrugged. "I'll be okay. It's early yet and I'll have plenty of time for the hike back. Think I'll hang out here for a while. Thanks for the offer though." She returned to the tree and her slouching. "Have fun in Lost Creek. Be sure to spend all Jori's money."

"Oh, I'm fantastic with his plastic," Elicia joked back as she pulled away.

Less than half a mile from the logging road Amy's skin began to prickle again. The muted sounds of the forest once more fell away. *Shit. I can do without this right now. There's a bear out there. I know there is. I don't care what Leone says, there's a big, hungry bear, and he's got my scent. Eau de poopoopants—*

She was tired and ill humored from the uphill hike. Now she was frightened as well. Around her the only sound was the rustle of wiregrass. She had never felt so alone. Part of her wished she had taken Leone up on her offer to help. It seemed like a damned good idea now.

The terrain changed and she found herself on a slight incline heading down toward the logging road. In the distance she could hear a motor engine slowly chug along the rugged track. Relieved at the sound of human activity, she picked up her trot, taking advantage of the downhill roll. Out of the corner of her eye a stealthy shadow began to sway and flit, always edging away from her full vision.

Unlike yesterday at the river, she decided not to waste any time trying to focus on whatever was out there. It moved parallel to her only to fall back out of her eye line, as if challenging her to stop and look. She could feel it, if not quite catch it, flitting from tree to tree in the shadow of the deeper forest. It was there; she could sense it stalking her…off to her right, playing with her.

Keep your breathing regular and your feet flapping. Don't let whatever it is know you know it's there. Maybe it'll shy away when you get on the logging trail. Please, please, please.

Her panic was sounding suspiciously like a prayer. By the time the trees thinned out enough to see the dirt road a hundred yards ahead she was practically a convert. The engine noise she'd heard earlier was louder now. It felt imperative to wave down the vehicle as it churned along the track. Only then would she feel safe.

She broke into a wobbly run, dodging low branches and hooked roots. She swerved around bushes, leapt over low clumps of undergrowth. All she could hear was the ragged rasp of her breathing and the thump of her heart. She had no idea what was going on around her. Forward momentum became her entire universe. She burst through the tree line and leapt an overgrown drainage ditch. Gravel and dirt rattled as she skidded to a halt, puffing and sweating. Anxiously she gazed down the road for the first sight of the vehicle. It sounded so close it had to be almost upon her. Where was it? Had she missed it? God, no!

Beep!

Amy nearly leapt out of her clammy skin. She spun around to find Elicia driving up right behind her. Shocked, she stared through the windshield at the bemused driver. The horn blare faded and Amy realized the birds were twittering, the breezes blew, and forest life had returned to normal. The arrival of another person had magically removed whatever threat she had felt. Her shoulders relaxed as Elicia vacated the car and came around the hood to join her.

"You okay, Amy? Were you lost?" Concern flooded her voice and she placed a comforting hand to Amy's forearm.

"Mmm, yes. I got a little disorientated and stumbled onto the logging road. Where are you heading, Elicia? Could I grab a lift a little further along the track?" she part lied. She didn't want to share her fright with Elicia. She'd think she was crazy being spooked by shadows.

"Sure you can. I'm on an errand run to Lost Creek. To be honest

I wanted to get out of the valley for a while. I'm taking Marie's books back to the library, and I need a few odds and ends from the pharmacy. Hey, come with me?"

Amy brushed loose curls off her flushed face with shaky hands. "You know, I'd love to visit Lost Creek. I haven't been there for years." She made up her mind to spend time with Elicia. It would be fun, and a much needed break from the oppressive atmosphere she'd just experienced. "It never was the friendliest of places when I was young. I wonder if it's changed any?"

"Well, jump in and let's go and find out."

Amy dumped her backpack on the rear seat and clambered into the passenger side as Elicia slid in behind the wheel. Suddenly she was looking forward to spending some more time with Elicia. Amy found her upbeat and cheerful company.

As the Jeep moved off Amy threw a last surreptitious glance at the surrounding forest. There was nothing. No weird feelings or sensations—nothing. Her earlier unease was already melting away, leaving her feeling embarrassed at her semi-hysteria. For two days in a row, first Leone, and now Elicia, had come along and saved her from a panic attack.

What was wrong with her? Was she imagining these things? Was she manifesting her anxieties about the project, or about Connie, or maybe even returning to Little Dip into some sort of phantom menace? *I need to either get a grip, or get therapy. This foolishness has to stop right now.*

The Jeep gathered a little more speed and crunched along the dirt road, throwing up plumes of dust, taking her away from her troubled thoughts and on to a welcome distraction. Hopefully, a quick trip outside the valley would help put all these jumbled feelings into perspective.

❖

Leone sat leaning against Big Jack, daydreaming at clouds with bunny ears, watching ants struggle with dead bugs, sullenly throwing pebbles at a larger stone. She waited with growing impatience.

Amy had sidestepped her again. She was obstinate, and mulish, and maddening, and ignored everything Leone told her to do. She had given Amy too much freedom. She had failed to make her understand who was the boss here in the valley. But that would soon change.

It was time for these games to stop. Time for Leone to make a few things crystal clear to a certain Amy Ameila Fortune.

CHAPTER EIGHT

Listening to local radio and chatting happily to each other, Amy and Elicia rumbled down the forest lanes. Finally, they emerged onto an asphalt surface that wound down the mountainside into the small town of Lost Creek.

"What do you think of Little Dip?" Amy asked, curious if Elicia was enjoying her valley vacation.

"I love it. I can see why Jori comes here every chance he gets."

"And it's not too daunting, meeting most of his family all at once?"

Elicia gave an awkward smile. "Well, I'm a little overwhelmed… but coping. I just didn't expect them to be so nice. They have a real family connection thing going on, and they are all so kind. They made me feel incredibly welcome…" Her words trailed off uncomfortably, and she blushed. She seemed either embarrassed or surprised at the quality of feelings she felt for Jori's family. "Hey, can I still go out with you on a field trip?"

"Sure. What about tomorrow morning?" Amy allowed the quick change in subject. She realized this was a big vacation for Elicia in so many ways and wondered once more at Marie's prediction that Jori would announce his engagement before the week was out. She could feel ambivalence from Elicia, as if she knew she was on some sort of cusp this week. It must be stressful. "But be warned, I start early."

"I'm there. Just tell me where and when. I'd love to see the valley through your eyes."

"Okay, it's a deal. I'll make you love it even more. You're talking to the converted." Amy put Elicia's ill ease down to Garoul overload. They were a big boisterous clan that seemed to swallow newcomers whole. "As a kid I spent every moment I could here. I've been known to hide in trees rather than go back after the holidays. I think I'm duly adopted."

"I can see why. And your aunt living here makes it even more like home. I suppose that makes it easier for you and Leone, seeing as how Marie is already like family to you."

"Huh?"

"I mean Marie's already as good as a mother-in-law."

"Oh no. No, no. Leone and I are not like that." Amy was flustered, and sat up straighter in her seat.

"God, I'm sorry. That idiot Jori gave me the impression you were a couple."

"Well, yes, we were once, but it was ages ago when we were in our teens. It's all dead and buried now." Amy tried to sound breezy. She didn't want Elicia to feel awkward about bringing up her teenage romance with Leone.

"But everything's okay now. You're friends," Elicia stated rather than asked. "Please don't think I'm usually this nosy. I really did get the wrong end of things from Jori. For an educated guy he can be such an idiot sometimes." Elicia concentrated on the road as they entered Lost Creek's one and only shopping street.

"Don't apologize. His sister is the exact same," Amy said. "Sometimes Leone acts so weird, standing there looking at me with that crazy glint in her eye, like I have all the answers to her secret questions." Amy gazed around her as they crawled along the main drag that passed as Lost Creek's town center. "God, this place hasn't changed one iota. Still the same old one-dog town."

Lost Creek had a total population of a little over eight hundred. Even that was declining as young people moved away to the larger towns to raise their families and work closer to the area's major industries.

Elicia and Amy parked before the town library. It was a pleasing, sturdy affair, fashioned out of an old stable-house. The gray and white wood-framed building had been preserved from the turn of the century by the kind beneficence of a past mayor, bequeathed at a time when the little logging town had much more affluence.

"Okay, first on the list is to return Marie's books. Hey, this has to be the cutest library I've ever seen. If there was such a thing as library porn, this would be the centerfold." Elicia looked impressed with the quaint public building.

Amy laughed. "Yeah, the whole town's picturesque. If only the townsfolk realized it and maintained it better, they'd have a proper little tourist trap."

Amy looked around her. Apart from the library there were three other shabby storefronts. One was Johnston's general store. It limped along selling newspapers and overpricing the items people ran out of, like coffee and cigarettes. Then there was the pharmacist with the part-time dental practice upstairs, and beside that was Barney's, the local bar; and that was about it for Lost Creek.

The library only survived due to a combination of conservation and county funding, but it was an ongoing battle. Connie had told Amy years ago that the Garouls privately supported it with a small annual grant paid through the local county office. Not many townsfolk knew this, and if they did they wouldn't be impressed. They cared little for the Garouls. Lost Creek and Little Dip were not easy neighbors.

They pushed open the swing door and entered the hushed interior. It was light and airy with the cool-toned outside color scheme continuing on through. Inside, the gray and white were complemented with raw pine shelving. The entire library was smaller than Amy remembered, but just as cozy and welcoming.

I wonder who the librarian is these days. Miss Crosier must be at least a hundred and ninety by now if she's still kicking around. Amy recalled the formidable lady who had ruled these shelves with stern authority for as long as she could remember. On the rare occasions when she and Leone had visited as kids, accompanied by either Marie or Connie, Miss Crosier's shushes had sent chills down their spines. Terrified, they ducked heads and giggled quietly, bright eyed with guilt and mirth.

Her question was answered almost immediately when a tall, silver-haired gentleman appeared behind the counter from a back office.

"Good morning. May I help you?" he said.

"Hi." Elicia stepped up, setting her bag on the countertop. "I'm returning these books for Marie Garoul."

"Thank you." He opened the plastic bag and removed the books one by one. Every movement was delicate and relaxed, showing he was at ease with his work and environment. "But you young ladies are not Garouls, are you? If you don't mind me asking, that is?" He smiled at them charmingly.

"No. We're visiting for the weekend. Well, I am. Amy will be staying on a few weeks longer." Elicia indicated Amy.

"Amy?" He looked over questioningly. "Would you be Connie's niece?"

"Yes. Yes, I am," Amy said. "You know my aunt?"

"Connie's a good friend. Let me introduce myself. I'm Virgil Bloomsy, town librarian and a self-confessed avid ornithologist. I simply adore your aunt's books, whether they're on botany or birds. In fact, we have a considerable collection of her work under Natural History." He beamed at her. "My budget is very limited, so Connie kindly contributes from her own library. She donates her surplus author's copies. It's a great boon to our resources."

Amy's interest was immediately piqued, and she decided then and there to take a quick look at this collection and see if there was anything of interest. Virgil continued to smile at them. He held out his hand and shook Elicia's, then Amy's warmly.

"It's a pleasure to meet you both. Give my best regards to your aunt when you see her. I understand she has been unwell."

"I will." Amy shifted a little uncomfortably. She didn't want to discuss Connie's illness, not even with a friend.

As if sensing her discomfort, Virgil rushed to make amends. "If you see something you'd like to take with you, I can issue a temporary pass. Please, feel free to browse to your heart's content.

I'll be here if you need me." With another reassuring smile he retreated into his office.

"Would you mind if I stayed here and had a quick look around while you did the rest of your errands?" Amy asked Elicia.

"No, not at all. I'll call back in, say…twenty minutes?" Elicia sounded pleased at the idea. "Maybe we can grab a coffee somewhere before we head back." With a little wave she headed for the door.

Amy wandered down to the Natural History section at the back of the small library. After several minutes' browsing she came to the conclusion there was nothing here that was not duplicated on Connie's own bookshelves. Connie had simply done as Virgil had stated, passed on her surplus author's stock to the town library. No wonder he was happy. With Connie's international reputation, if she kept endorsing his library like this, eventually he would end up with a unique collection and a center of study for her work.

Slowly meandering back to the front desk, she hesitated by the General Interest section, surprised that there was an entire shelf on code breaking, word puzzles, and other conundrums. She pulled a few down and flicked through the pages. *Now this might be interesting.* She eventually selected a basic introduction to ciphers and their history and took it up to Virgil's counter. He appeared out of his office almost immediately.

"Found something?" He went to his computer and punched a few keys.

"Is it okay if I borrow this one?" She set it down before him.

"Of course you can. I'll use the same address details for Connie, but I'll need your full name for the temporary ticket."

"Amy Amelia Fortune."

"You're as well known as your aunt," he said. Amy smiled back easily.

"Well, not quite. I'm based in Europe and the competition there is fierce. But I do get my fair share of intriguing commissions."

"I loved your book on Elizabethan gardens. Connie told me it was actually a televised series in Britain, and your illustrations were used for the opening credits."

"Yes. That was very special. I loved working on that project."

She was pleased he knew of it, and equally pleased Connie was proud of it, too.

"Do you study codes and ciphers for relaxation?" he asked as he entered the book's details beside her name.

"Not really. It's something that's beginning to interest me, and this book looked like an easy starting point. You have quite a few back there."

"Yes. It's an interest of my own, and being the librarian I have the luxury of ordering the books I like, as well as the few requests I get for the latest best sellers. I think of it as a perk."

"How long have you been here?"

"Nearly a year now."

"Good grief. Miss Crosier hung in there."

"No, no." He laughed. "Miss Crosier passed away quite a few years ago. After she retired another lady took over, but she left very suddenly. Then I applied for the post." The door swung open as Elicia returned.

"Hey, good timing. You get what you want?" She noted the book in Amy's hand.

"Yes, and you?"

"Yeah, let's go grab that coffee." They took their leave of the kindly Mr. Bloomsy and went out into the sharp fall day. The sky was electric blue, and the small town lay huddled in a horseshoe of snow-capped peaks and dark green forests.

"The car's open. Why not dump your book with my messages? Mmm, is there a place around here to get a coffee?" Elicia looked up and down the street, not seeing anywhere obvious.

Amy opened the back door and placed her book on the rear seat.

"There's a little booth section at the back of Johnston's store. It's not the best but it's better than nothing," she called over her shoulder. As she pulled back, her coat sleeve brushed against Elicia's pharmacy bag, tipping the contents. Amy quickly scooped them back into the paper sack, but not before she noticed the home pregnancy kit. She set the sack upright and closed the car door. Elicia was a few paces ahead, leading the way to Johnston's.

It's none of my business. But I hope if she is pregnant it's what she and Jori want. Amy hurried to catch up, deciding to forget what she had inadvertently seen.

❖

"I don't know what sucks most. The coffee or the service," Elicia muttered into the cup that had been slammed down in front of her only moments ago. Both women had jumped in their seats as Norman Johnston served them with abrupt and surly rudeness.

"The service…you can always sweeten the coffee," Amy mumbled back, mopping up the coffee spill with her own tissues. The paper napkin dispenser was empty.

Elicia shuddered at her first mouthful. "This is stone cold. Is yours?" Amy took a small sip and nodded.

"I'm taking these back." Elicia lifted their drinks and headed for the counter. She returned minutes later with two steaming mugs and an angry face.

"That has got to be the rudest man on the planet. If I hadn't watched his every move I swear he would have spat in our drinks. Why the hell he isn't bankrupt I'll never know," she ranted. "What gives? They were just as stuck-up at the pharmacy. You'd think they didn't want my money."

"It's always been like this. Once they find you're from the valley they treat you like you kicked their dog, or sideswiped their truck, or ran away with their wife, wallet, rifle, God knows what."

"Well, why the hell is that?"

"History mostly. They just hate the Garouls. They sort of blame the family for the town's decline. But I think it's more like envy or scapegoating."

"What have the Garouls ever done to this pokey little place?"

"Nothing. The problems began after the war, when many of the young men who left to fight didn't return to logging. I suppose there were new and better opportunities opening up in the late forties. In fact, the timber industry in this area slid into decline. There were simply better resources and easier access farther north."

Elicia looked at her. "I still don't get it. What has the decline of logging got to do with the Garouls?"

"Basically, the town believed Little Dip should be opened up for public logging. It had plentiful premium timber that the family managed for itself. Still does. Sylvie Garoul, Marie and Claude's mother, said no. And she was right to. It would have made no difference to the commercial climate of the time and possibly taken away Garoul autonomy in the valley forever."

"The Garouls always seem to have a woman in charge."

"Yes, they believe in matriarchy, all right. Hallelujah." Amy smiled as Elicia snorted into her coffee.

"Boy, these people can hold a grudge. All that was over sixty years ago."

"Well, every so often it bubbles up again over some other issue. Connie told me it was tourism this time. There's some funding available for promoting hunting and fishing businesses. Some townsfolk thought they could benefit by providing accommodation for visiting hunters. But the best access to Silverthread is through Little Dip and Marie refused right of way down to the river, or any hunting on Garoul property. She wants to keep it strictly for family use. Hence the dark stares. The Garouls own the prime land around here outright. Have for generations, and they won't give up an inch of it. And frankly, it sticks in some people's craws. End of story. And I'm afraid there's no way I'm drinking this cup of scalding mud."

"I would understand local opinion better if the valley was neglected, but it's carefully managed and the Garouls use it all the time." Elicia also pushed her untouched drink away and stood to leave. "Guess it explains the bad service and shitty attitude. But there's no excuse for this coffee. Come on, let's head back. I think I've had enough of Lost Creek hospitality."

CHAPTER NINE

Amy was tired by the time she said good-bye to Elicia and wandered up the trail to Connie's cabin. She desperately needed a shower, and some lunch, in that order. Then she needed to set up Connie's studio for the work she planned to do later. What she didn't need was Leone Garoul sitting on her porch step scowling. *Yet here she is.*

Her unwelcome visitor sat with her elbows on her knees, viciously shredding leaves from a twig as she watched Amy approach. Amy immediately scowled back, too tired to assume haughty disinterest. Leone flung the denuded twig away and strode over to meet her.

"Where were you this morning?" she demanded.

"What do you mean, where was I? I was working, and then I went into town with Elicia," Amy replied hotly. How dare Leone address her like this. What was her freakin' problem?

"Working? I waited for hours up at Big Jack. You never showed." Leone's voice was tight with held back anger.

"I was further down the ridge. I never said I was going to Big Jack, and I sure as hell didn't ask you to meet me there. In fact, I remember saying the exact opposite." Amy was too tired to hold back anything, especially her annoyance at Leone's high-handedness.

Leone glared at her, face thunderous. "You know it's dangerous to be wandering around the valley alone. You need to tell me what—"

"I don't want another goddamn shadow. You refuse to listen. I said I didn't need your company and I still don't."

"I'm only trying to—"

"You're trying to monitor every freakin' move I make is what you're trying to do. And it's suffocating." With that Amy pushed past Leone onto the porch. Wearily she dropped her backpack onto the wooden planks. She was about to open the door when rough hands grabbed her and spun her around.

"You need to tell me your plans. This is no joke." Leone's jaw was tight.

Amy knew Leone was on the verge of losing her temper, but she didn't care. Leone Garoul was nothing to her. She jerked her arm to try to free it but Leone's fingers tightened painfully.

"Let me go." Amy tugged again. "Now."

Instead Leone backed her up against the cabin wall, pinning her with her body. The height difference was intimidating, the cabin rough and uncomfortable against her back. Amy froze. She recognized this move from before…when they were young…when they were lovers. Leone would reach for her bottom, squeezing and massaging, then hoist her up in one quick, effortless lift. Amy would wrap her legs around Leone's waist and be kissed, and caressed, and fucked up against whatever wall, tree, vehicle, they happened to be standing by.

She also recognized the hungry glint in Leone's dark eyes. It was an old look—half forgotten. Remembered only in vague, hot, troublesome dreams that left Amy feeling lost and adrift for days afterward. A look that said *I want you, I'll have you, you're mine*. Amy knew that look could swallow her whole. It had chewed her up and spat her out before.

She felt Leone's hands on her hips, ready to lift her, ready to settle her onto Leone's waist, ready to carry them straight back into the past.

"No." Amy pushed at solid shoulders, trying to gain an inch of room to slide out and get away. "No. I don't want this."

A deep growl rumbled in Leone's throat. Her hands drifted

over the curve of Amy's buttocks and rested there, warm and heavy through the denim. Slowly she lowered her head, the growl fading away to a reverberation in her chest. Amy twisted her face away from the oncoming kiss. Leone's breath blazed across her cheek, hot and excited. Their faces were close. Too close.

"For God's sake, what are you doing? I told you I'm not interested," Amy snapped, panicking. She had no control here. She knew where they were heading and was terrified. She couldn't go there, couldn't go back.

Leone stilled. Carefully she released her grip on Amy, but she didn't step back, not one inch. Amy had to wriggle out past her, brushing up against her to escape. Heat poured off Leone like a furnace. Amy could feel her entire body tense as she squeezed slowly past her; Leone hummed like a charged bomb.

Free of her, Amy turned away and ran shaking hands through her tangled hair, her face flushed.

"Don't ever touch me like that again. We're through. You had your chance years ago and you walked away."

"I didn't want to." Leone's voice was thick and hard.

"But you did. And now it's history."

"It doesn't have—"

"It does. I called you and asked why you left so suddenly, and you said you wanted to be where you were more than with me. Well, now it's my turn to feel like that." Amy took a deep breath. "I came here to do a job. That's all. Let's concentrate on that, not the past. I don't want to keep looking over my shoulder, Leone. I want to move on with my life."

With that she walked through the door, slamming it shut behind her. She was upset, stunned, confused. Tears filled her eyes. She didn't need this on top of the day she'd had. She didn't need Leone Garoul back in her life...not like that. It amazed her that after all these years she should feel such a strong sexual pull for her. And it scared her that her teenage hurt still pulsed so close to the surface, covering every inch of her, threading through her skin like a network of poisoned veins.

Outside Leone stared sullenly at the closed door. Her temper had made her move too soon. But she didn't regret it. She savored it. Amy swamped her senses. Her tongue tingled with Amy's scent.

"Look where moving on with your life brought you," she murmured to the wood planking. "Right back to me."

❖

Amy changed into sweats and made a light lunch before digging her library book out of her backpack. Her anger at Leone's overbearing behavior began to dissipate. In a cold, rational light she realized that Leone was as much captive of their past as she was. It had poured from her since that first night when she had pulled Amy into that boa constrictor hug, intense, suffocating, stealing all the air between them.

Amy didn't want this vacuum. All she needed to do was keep a calm head and keep Leone at a safe distance, and she could get through this. In fact, they both could. It was hormones, and…and history. And closure. Yes, they were both seeking closure. They were both raw, even after all this time. Red raw. The sexual connection was still there, strong as ever. It had not diminished. But that didn't mean they had to act on it either. She couldn't afford to be sidetracked with this nostalgic nonsense. There was an important job to do. Brimful of new resolve, she stood and moved to the studio. She had paper to stretch and a studio to set up.

Connie's studio was one large north-facing room. It got great light for most of the day, but a clever lighting system using Daylight North bulbs allowed for late night working. Connie liked to paint past midnight and into the small hours. They both found it a satisfying and relaxing way to end the day. And there was nothing more delightful for Amy than taking her field sketches and digital images and translating them into a detailed illustration.

After soaking the art paper in cold water, she fixed the edges to one of Connie's drawing boards with gummed tape. The unusual proportions required for her insets reminded her of the bastardized page size of all the Garoul's almanacs. *Why is that? I must ask Marie more about it at supper*. Amy thoughtfully crunched on the cherry candy Connie left all over her workplace. There had to be a good reason to offset the expense of nonstandard paper sizing. Amy had a lot of questions for Marie this evening.

❖

Work done, Amy began rinsing her hands clean in the sink when she noticed a colorful cloth draped over a small table at the back of the studio. She wandered over and lifted a corner. With a frown she pulled it completely away. Underneath was a compact workbench complete with a vise. It was littered with saws, borax, tongs, and hammers. There was even a small smelter. Connie must have been experimenting with metals. Strange, she'd never mentioned it. There were no books about it in her library either, that Amy could recall. Amy knew Connie would read everything she could get her hands on if a new interest engaged her. But there was no information on precious metals or jewelry making on her shelves, and this equipment was expensive, so she was doing more than dabbling.

Once again Amy sorely missed Connie, if only to sit down and have an illuminating conversation with her. She was sure there was a reasonable explanation for all the little mysteries that seemed to be piling up all around her. She was missing something obvious and probably very trivial. Something that would make her feel like an idiot the moment it was revealed in all its glory.

Amy replaced the cloth and returned to the kitchen. She collected the trout she'd promised Marie. It would be nice to relax with her this evening and share a glass of wine. She still had a million questions about Garoul Press and the nature of Connie's work within it. Perhaps a one-to-one chat with Marie might shed a little more light.

❖

Marie hugged her warmly when she arrived, gift in hand.

"My goodness, this is a big fella. There'll be plenty for supper, and unless Leone joins us, leftovers for tomorrow's lunch." She took the wrapped fish to the kitchen to prepare it for the broiler.

"You should have seen the fight he put up." Amy followed her, relaying a blow-by-blow account of her fishing exploits.

She grabbed her usual seat by the kitchen counter and sat and watched Marie's movements as she put together supper. Marie looked tired. There were dark rings under her eyes, and now that Amy noticed, she was a little disheveled. Her clothes were crumpled, her long hair needed combing, and her hands were covered with deep scratches that disappeared under her cuffs.

"Marie? Are you okay? You've got some nasty scratches there."

"Oh, they're nothing. I was out foraging in the undergrowth and got cut. I got back here too late to clean up."

Amy felt guilty. "I'll look after dinner. You go jump in the shower." But already Marie was shaking her head.

"I'll have a long soak in the tub later." She gave Amy a pleasant smile but her eyes were flat with sadness and exhaustion. "I'm okay, Amy. Just tired. Fetch me the creamer, dear. It's in the fridge. Top shelf."

Amy did as she was asked, knowing that any further questions would not be welcomed. But she was curious and concerned. Wild herb foraging did not abuse the body to the extent of Marie's cuts, bruises, and general fatigue. Whatever she had been up to, it had taken a lot out of her, though her manner was as relaxed and calm as ever.

Leone didn't show up for supper. Instead, Amy and Marie opened a chilled Semillon to enjoy with the fish. Part of Amy was relieved not to have to face Leone so soon after their sexual friction. Another part wanted to know how it had affected her. Only now did Amy feel distanced enough to examine the afternoon's standoff. It all was immaterial anyway. Leone had sloped off, and Amy had come here tonight to ask an entirely different set of questions.

"Marie?" Amy broached the subject that had been bothering her since last night's editorial meeting. "I looked at some of Connie's previous work in the older almanacs. I found an illustration with similar marks to the ones you wanted me to add to the goldenseal paintings."

Marie glanced over, immediately engaged. "What illustration would that be, Amy? Can you tell me the year?"

"Umm." Amy had not expected the question. "The plant was angelica, and I think it was ninety-seven. Why do you need to know?"

Marie shrugged. "Just trying to recall if I can remember anything unusual about that year, but I'm afraid I can't think of anything offhand."

"So, what are these marks about? And don't tell me it's cataloguing or a form of Connie's signature, because I won't buy it."

Marie carefully pushed aside her plate. "I can't say I fully understand the system. It's a form of classification that will allow us to pull together an anniversary almanac at some point in the future. Hence asking you the year of the angelica marks. It's important to Leone that the goldenseal illustrations are treated in the same way. I'm sure there's nothing more to it than a special Garoul almanac edition."

Amy still looked skeptical.

"Come here." Marie stood and moved toward her office. "Let me show you what Leone's working on aside from this year's almanac."

Amy rose to follow her into the small back room. Marie's desktop computer was shut down but Leone's laptop sat blinking. Marie tapped the keyboard and Leone's screensaver flared. Bosch's Garden of Earthly Delights danced before them.

"What are we looking at here?" Amy asked.

Their heads met over the screen, Marie's hair cascading forward in a dark wave. She reached up and twisted it into a more manageable knot behind her head. Amy glanced over, eyes widening. Marie's neck flashed through the swirl of hair. Dark red scratches ran from her hairline to under the loose collar of her shirt. They disappeared in a flash of ebony and silver so quickly Amy thought her eyes had deceived her.

"God, Marie—" she blurted before she could stop herself. It was none of her business. She blushed wildly as Marie stared at her with guarded eyes. "What is it with the Garouls and that pig-ugly painting?" She waved a hand at the Bosch screensaver.

Her awkward save worked. She received a rueful smile and shrug from Marie before she clicked to pull out some document folders for Amy to see.

"This is a mock-up of the four hundredth anniversary edition to come out two years from now," Marie said.

"Wow, four hundred years. I never knew the Garoul Press went back that far."

"Further, if you count the French Garouls who arrived in New France in the late fifteen hundreds. In old Europe they were a publishing family, too. The Garouls have been around forever in one shape or form." Marie smiled proudly. "But this almanac is to celebrate our migration to the Americas and the eventual formation of a new Garoul Press."

For the next hour they discussed Leone's anniversary edition ideas, and the history of the Garoul Press on this side of the Atlantic. Yvette Garoul had arrived disguised as a man in the early sixteen hundreds. She had become a fur trapper and traveled across the continent, eventually arriving in the Pacific Northwest. There had been some interbreeding with the local tribes, and before long she had claimed the Silverthread valley for her growing family. It was an amazing story that Amy never tired of hearing. It had snared her imagination as a child and never let go. The original French family had faded into obscurity a long time ago, though Marie believed direct descendants were scattered all across Europe and beyond.

Amy checked her watch and stood. "I'd better go. It's much later than I intended. I had hoped to work in the studio for a few hours tonight, but I'm too tired now."

"Rest and get an early start in the morning." Marie accompanied her to the door.

"Get those scratches seen to. They look mean."

"I'm going to jump in a hot bath with some alder bark and vinegar. With a night's good sleep I'll be fine." Marie looked out across the compound, a faint frown creasing her brow. "I wish Leone had been here to explain everything. She'll be annoyed she's missed you."

"Oh, there'll be other times." Amy was diplomatic; perhaps it was best not to mention she'd seen Leone earlier that afternoon and as usual they'd sparked hard enough to be a fire hazard. All she wanted to do now was to relax with her library codebook and mull over what Marie had just told her about an anniversary almanac. It felt as if she had another part of the puzzle in her hands, but she was not sure how it all fit, at least not yet. With time it would. Amy was nothing if not tenacious. She stepped down from the porch toward the path home.

"Thanks for supper, Marie. I'll drop by tomorrow after I get caught up on my work. Good night."

"Good night, Amy. Sleep well."

❖

With a snifter of cognac Amy settled on her couch to read for an hour or two. Reading always calmed her down. It had been a strange evening, and she didn't know what to make of the deep scratches on Marie's hands and neck. There was a residual sadness about Marie these days. Amy could understand that. She must be missing Connie dreadfully, and worried sick. But she had to look after herself, too. Neither Amy nor Leone would want Marie falling sick as well.

Amy set her troubling thoughts aside and picked up her library book. She was soon absorbed in the rudiments of code making, cipher breaking, and all manner of locks and keys. It was a fascinating subject, and she was determined that this was what Connie's superfluous marks were all about. There was some sort of message hidden in certain illustrations. But why, and what did they mean? In what way did they relate to the anniversary edition?

Again she brought down a few random almanacs and carefully scrutinized the pages. She found nothing, but knew it was only a matter of time before she did. It was all to do with familiarity. She had recognized the first set of sigils through her knowledge of the angelica plant. Soon she would find other specimens she knew well that had the additional marks, too.

Once again she idly browsed through the Wiccan book of love spells, just in case there were any clues in Connie's other work. There were none. So it was all related to the Garoul Press projects.

At a chapter on incense spells something caught her eye. Scullcap. Wasn't that the stink Leone had burned to scare off the termites?

Scullcap. Burn this incense in the presence of your lover to strengthen commitment. Let it burn slowly into her heart.

What is that big lunatic doing burning it in Connie's cabin? If anything, it might attract the freakin' termites—Oh...oh!
Amy blinked. Oh?

She looked off into the middle distance with a glazed stare. She was being wooed? With witchcraft! Leone was casting love spells?

Exasperated, she put the book down and sat back to think. She didn't know what to make of it. Did Leone wanted to reconcile? But why? Why move backward? It was ridiculous. And using magic? What nonsense. A small smile crept across her lips. She couldn't contain it. She felt amused and curiously...what? Powerful?

Her smile was soon followed by a frown. Forewarned was forearmed. Amy would have to be careful around her would-be suitor. Leone knew all Amy's weak spots, and blindsides, too. She could easily run snapping at Amy's Achilles' heels. For Leone there was very little difference in love and war, there was only winning what you wanted. Amy knew that of old.

CHAPTER TEN

It was nearly midday and Amy and Elicia strolled along laughing and planning what to make for lunch, eventually deciding to eat at Jori and Elicia's place as it was closer. They'd had a lovely morning wandering along the riverside looking for a bitter cherry for Amy. Elicia had watched fascinated as, page after page, Amy filled an art block with skillful sketches and precise color swatches. In a few hours they were done and heading back.

Amy looked at the overcast sky. "Here comes the rain. I'm glad we got an early start on the day."

"Come on. Let's try and outrun it." Elicia lead them on at a quicker pace.

After about twenty minutes Amy stopped to look around. "Are we on the right track?"

Elicia hesitated. "I haven't been paying attention. I thought this was the trail we came by." But the Silverthread was no longer to their left. Somehow they had managed to go deeper into the forest.

"No, there are a few hunting trails leading off it. I think we're on one of them because I'm not seeing anything familiar," Amy said.

"Okay. Let's turn around and go back the way we came. Guess we won't beat the rain now."

It was a sensible plan until they came to a fork on the path.

"Crap. Where did that come from? We must have missed it on the way up," Amy muttered. She was becoming totally confused with a network of paths she'd have once sworn she knew well. She had no idea where Elicia had led them. "So, left or right, any ideas?"

"Mmm, I remember something about always turning right and you end up where you started?"

"Like back to the river? I don't think that's true. I can't even hear it now." Amy was very skeptical. "You weren't a Girl Scout, were you?"

"Yes, I was." Elicia defended herself. "Okay, so I never got my Orienteering badge. But I do have several Cookie Activity pins."

"Great, we can spell out SOS in gingerbread for the air rescue services."

"Hey, it's easy to criticize. What's your clever suggestion?"

"My clever suggestion is let's keep to the right, like you said." Amy looked at the forked path before them. "I mean, it's a fifty-fifty choice."

It was the wrong choice. That became apparent after another twenty minutes when the surrounding trees became denser, and the light gloomier. They came to a halt in a small circular clearing to work out their whereabouts with Amy's little handheld compass.

"Oh, I don't like this. It's creepy in here." Amy looked around, suppressing a shiver. "How the hell did we lose the river? I mean, it's friggin' enormous."

"I blame you. You're the one who agreed with me to turn right— What was that?" Elicia suddenly looked over her left shoulder, very ill at ease.

"Huh? What?" Amy found herself almost whispering, totally spooked.

"I thought I heard something."

"Like what?"

"Dunno. Just a noise."

"Shh. Let's stand still and listen." They did, and heard nothing alarming. In fact, they heard nothing at all.

"Crap, I hate it when the birds stop singing. It's all they ever do around here," Amy said. As she spoke she felt the hairs on her neck rise in what she now realized was a calling card. *Oh no, not that spooky bear thing again.*

"Amy." Elicia's voice grew as small as her eyes grew large. She was focusing on something over Amy's shoulder.

"What?" Amy was frozen by Elicia's wide-eyed stare. *Please don't let there be a bear coming up behind me. Please, please.*

"Look at the trees," Elicia whispered.

Slowly, Amy turned her head as if she were in a neck brace that might snap at any sudden movement. At first she didn't see anything, because in reality she was expecting a rabid grizzly to be standing right behind her. Her shoulders relaxed when there was nothing there. "What about them?"

"Look. Look at the bark."

And then Amy saw it. All around them in the small clearing, nearly every tree was lacerated. Torn apart by long, vicious clawing. On some the bark hung in shreds, the gouging going deep into the living wood. Others had huge patches of bark totally missing, the raw wood a madding crisscross of frenzied slashes. Amy swallowed hard as she absorbed the brutality. It was so unnatural, so destructive and sinister, the air in her lungs reduced to a sickly unbreathable syrup of pure horror.

"That is so not right." Elicia was in awe, totally dismayed.

"The poor trees."

"It's very high up." Elicia managed to croak. She looked shocked at the devastation. "Whatever did this was very tall."

"Like a moose?" Amy squeaked, not caring for her "bear thing" theory anymore.

Elicia shook her head. "No, those are claw marks. This is vicious, Amy. Totally insane and vicious."

"Oh." Amy found Elicia's words curious. No matter how nasty it looked, it was still just an animal, granted a humongous animal, sharpening its claws. What concerned her more was the stillness in the forest surrounding them. For her that meant something else, something much more sinister. "Let's just go. We need to get home," she said.

"Which way?"

"I don't care. Let's just go."

They started to move back the way they'd come. Amy still felt that claustrophobic tightness in her chest that screamed danger was nearby. She wanted to get away quickly but not alarm Elicia, who seemed oblivious to the sensations Amy was picking up on. *Maybe it's just me? Maybe I'm losing my marbles.*

A silken blur melting from tree to tree caught the edge of her vision. She squinted into the murk, but there was nothing solid, nothing she could define. Her breathing hitched. It was not a bear. Bears didn't move like that. Bears scratched trees, they didn't gut them. Not like back in the clearing. Elicia was right. That was insane. That was something else. And whatever was stalking them now was big. Big and clever. *And it wants me to see it. It wants me to know that it's out there.*

"Let's just get back as fast as we can, huh?" She kept a wary eye on where she'd last seen the flicker of movement.

"Left here." Elicia had moved on ahead, taking charge of their retreat.

"Are you sure?" Amy frowned, but followed anyway. The last thing she wanted was to freak out Elicia, especially if she was pregnant, but they needed to get the hell out of here right now. Hopefully they'd soon see the river sparkling through the trees.

After several minutes of quick paced tramping Amy blurted out, "Where the hell are we going?"

"Toward the river." Elicia kept the pace going strong, moving determinedly forward. She obviously had some sort of plan.

"I think we're lost again." Amy came to a halt, growing more confused with the path they were on. She didn't recognize anything.

"It's only a few more minutes along here." Elicia paused impatiently. "Come on, Amy. Follow me."

"Are you sure? The forest's getting denser, not thinning out. You're a teacher. Don't you teach the kids about geography and moss growing on the north side of trees and stuff?"

"I teach kindergarten. I'm a failed Girl Scout. My mind is so freaked by that tree mauling back there, the only thing I can think of right now is 'The Wheels on the Bus Go Round and Round.'" Elicia kept up her pace, looking determinedly forward. "You're the wildlife illustrator. You're the one meant to be in harmony with nature. You do something."

Amy looked at her in consternation. "Me?" Glancing around, she suddenly pointed. "Oh look, it's *Trillium ovatum*."

Elicia scanned the forest floor, trying to see what Amy was pointing at, then spotted the timid groundcover plant. "I see it! What does it do?"

"Maybe it can grow feet and run for help?"

"You're such a bitch, Fortune. I really thought you had a plan," Elicia huffed. But she dithered, no longer forging ahead. She slowed and seemed to hesitate.

"Hey!" a voice hailed them.

"Jori." Elicia broke into a run. Jori stood on the trail several yards up ahead so deep in shadow they hadn't seen him until he moved forward. He wrapped his arms around Elicia protectively.

"Where were you? I made lunch…but no you?"

"We took a wrong turn and got lost. Come and see this." Elicia turned back the way they'd come.

"See what?" he asked, following.

"Do we have to go back?" Amy said. Now that they had been more or less rescued, she was anxious to get the hell out of this creepy part of the valley.

"Yes. Wait 'til you see this, Jori. The trees back here are mangled." Elicia dragged him along by his shirtsleeve, braver now that he was with her.

"It was only a moose. Let's go home," Amy whined, still facing the way home.

"No way was that a moose and you know it," Elicia said. "Come on, Fortune. Or we'll leave you standing there like a jar of honey."

Amy quickly caught up.

All along the route back to the clearing she kept glancing from side to side, expecting her spectral stalker to reappear. Only Amy had been aware of it. Elicia hadn't been spooked. All Elicia had done was quicken their pace after seeing the claw marks. Fortunately, she'd managed to lead them straight toward Jori.

Now Amy stood again in the small clearing looking at the

wanton damage surrounding her. Her blood ran cold. It was unnatural and crazed to her eyes. What sort of animal did this?

Jori stood silent, taken aback.

"See, see. Look what's wandering around your valley." Elicia waved an expressive arm around her. "You have to sort this out, Jori."

Jori didn't respond at first. He stood tense and still, as if picking up a subtle vibration. His chin lifted slightly and his nostrils flared. Watching these tiny details with morbid fascination, Amy was reminded of a hunting dog picking up a scent. The moment passed and she shook herself out of her stupidity. She was here to cover Connie's project, not get distracted by all this "it's a bear, it's not a bear, what is it" nonsense. At least there were now witnesses to what she had experienced. That was good; on some level she needed the validation.

The Garouls managed these woods. They were more than capable of dealing with any marauding animal in their valley.

❖

Lunch with Jori and Elicia was a chatty, laughter-filled affair. They were obviously very much in love, and it warmed Amy to share in their glow.

When Elicia ducked inside to grab some napkins, Jori leaned in to whisper conspiratorially, "What ya think, Amy? I'm going to ask Elicia to marry me."

Amy gave him a big hug. "She's a lovely person. You're very lucky to have met her, Jori. I'm so happy for the both of you."

"It's kind of quick but I never met anyone who felt so right. We really understand each other—" He broke off as Elicia returned.

Amy decided it was time to go and leave them in peace. With a happy wave good-bye, she set off for home. She wondered about the pregnancy test kit she had seen in Elicia's shopping and immediately dispelled it from her mind. Jori and Elicia were in love and going to be married, which was the best news Amy had heard all year. There would be some party when Jori made his announcement.

Thinking about Jori and Elicia's happiness pulled her back into her own past, to a time when she too had been deliriously in love. She detoured past the creek and wandered along the riverbank until she came to a massive granite outcrop jutting over the water.

It was the first time she'd visited this place in over seven years. She didn't know why she was here, but it seemed like the right time to come and say hello.

It used to be her magic place. Her sarsen stone. Now she sat perched on it, her feet dangling six feet above the gurgling river. It was wide enough for two to lie side by side after a swim on a hot summer's day, and let the sun dry their naked bodies. She knew that for a fact. She smiled as she remembered a hundred lazy sunny afternoons spent just like that. And with that smile, the floodgates opened to her bottled-up memories of Leone and being in love with her.

On her first ever visit she had lost her sandal over the edge of this rock and cried big splashy tears as it swirled away. She could still recall the pink plastic shoe bobbing downstream and the fear that her mom would be mad and shout. Even at five years old, Amy was keenly attuned to her mother's mood swings and erratic stress levels. Then Leone, ever the little otter, jumped in fully clothed from all the way up here, and swam out and rescued the sandal. She brought it back triumphantly, soaked through, tall and proud. For the rest of that summer, and many summers after, Amy's awestruck eyes saw only her wonderful hero. Leone was older, taller, prettier, and much stronger than the boys, and so very protective of her, the little blond girl who came to stay for vacations and followed Leone everywhere.

On this magic rock Amy had chalked early masterpieces, cloud watched, stargazed, and years later finally kissed her hero. Her Leone. She had fallen in love here, lost her virginity—and her heart. They'd whispered plans for great adventures, for traveling the world over; silly teenage dreams of a wonderful future together.

The rock held bad memories, too. One summer, the body of a drowned man lazily swirled by, caught up in the current farther out. He wore a hunter's vest. Amy had been horrified as he drifted past face down, and full of dismay and fear, she ran for a grown-up. The Garoul children had simply stood in a line along the bank, dark eyed and silent, watching him sail away.

That last magical summer, she had sat here for hours waiting for Leone. They always met here on those balmy summer nights to watch the stars sparkle and the moon break over the valley lip. The stone was their secret rendezvous, where they would meet and talk, and make love until dawn.

Leone never showed. Eventually, tired of waiting, cold and worried, Amy had wandered down to Marie's cabin. It was empty.

Back home Connie gently broke it to her that Marie and Leone had left for the airport. Leone had a job at Garoul Print in Vancouver.

No time for good-byes, no farewells, no promises to wait forever. Leone had simply gone. In an angst-filled phone call the following night Leone had been cool and remote, explaining that her family came first, and that was why she had to take this opportunity in Vancouver. She and Amy had great fun that summer, but that's all it was. Fun. And she wished Amy well for the future.

A week later Amy was in London, making that future happen. All belief in love and magic lost. She took their dreams of travel and adventure and lived them alone.

Now, Amy stood gazing into the rushing water and allowed the old hurt and confusion to wash over her again. It was diluted by time and by her own emotional maturity. The pain had numbed, the lessons had been learned. She and Leone had been young and foolish. Real life had always been waiting in the wings, and it still was. She would complete her work, see that Connie was okay, and then move on as she had before. As she always did.

The weather had brightened and she decided to collect another sketchbook and head out again, grabbing every opportunity she could to tick plants off her specimen list.

Dicentra fromosa, bleeding heart. Amy knew of a shady ravine where she was bound to catch this plant in fall flower. Bleeding heart had always graced the valley with both a spring and fall show of its delicate pink blossoms.

It took a lot of nerve for her to go out alone after the morning's spookiness, but she had to do it. The work had to be done. Unless she wanted to beg Leone to escort her everywhere, she'd just have to steel herself and get on with it. She was not going to give in to Leone's wishes. Especially now that she knew Leone was pining for another "summer of love" with all that love potion rubbish. No way was Amy walking into that trap. Leone might think it would be a fun way to pass the next few weeks, but Amy knew it would take her back to her old heartaches, wants, and needs. And for her that was a journey more frightening than any walk in the woods.

She found her bleeding heart exactly where she expected to, and spent the rest of the afternoon recording the shy, dainty plant. Content with her day's work, she packed up and settled back against the trunk of a fir tree. Time for a snack bar and hot drink, she opened her thermos and—

"Phew." Her nose wrinkled. Something stank. She sniffed her thermos but it wasn't her coffee gone seriously off. Nope, not that.

She looked around her but saw nothing obvious. No skunks, no stinky flowers. A breeze blew up and the stench became stronger. It seemed to carry on the wind. She swung her head back and gazed up into the branches of the tree. Twenty feet directly above her dangled the head and shoulder of a large elk.

"Ew." She leapt to her feet and moved away. Aghast, she examined her find from a safe distance. It was disgusting. Only half the animal's carcass remained; the rest was torn away. Flies massed around its huge milky eyes; entrails dangled from the lower branches like Christmas streamers. From the look and smell of it, it was an old kill. Amy knew what she was looking at, a larder. She was just surprised to see one here. The last time she had witnessed this type behavior she was watching a leopard in the Serengeti.

She scooted around to the rear of the tree and examined the trunk. There were deep, ragged gouges where the predator had dug in its claws to drag its meal up into the branches. They reminded her of the savage scores she had seen earlier that day. Vicious, penetrating lacerations. It had probably suspended the heavy carcass in its jaws as it slowly climbed up to a safe spot to gorge on its kill.

Amy's appetite was gone. She recapped her thermos and put away her chocolate bar, deciding to make tracks for home. Bad weather was coming in over the valley ridge. It would bring an early dusk, and she didn't want to be caught out late. Especially not this close to the larder of something so big and menacing it could haul an adult elk up a tree.

❖

It took Amy a couple of hours to make her way back down to the central compound. It was late and most of the cabins were in darkness when she finally arrived at her halfway point home. As she cut across the clearing, she noted the lights were out in Marie's cabin. Was Leone asleep, too? It felt strange to have gone a full day and not have her pestering presence popping up somewhere. Maybe she was too embarrassed after losing her cool on the porch yesterday? Head down, Amy doggedly trudged homeward.

Halfway along the home trail, with a crescent moon peeking out between the racing storm clouds, she passed a part of the Silverthread where the river pooled into a creek. This was a safe swimming hole, and tonight she heard the rhythmic splashing of a night swimmer.

Curious, she pushed through the trees, ducking under overhanging branches until she reached the shore. The moon crazed across the rippling water, and a lone swimmer cut through the liquid silver with strong, powerful strokes. It was Leone. Even from here Amy recognized the curve of her shoulders, the graceful arc of her arm, and the dark mesh of her hair clinging to head and neck. She cleaved through the water, animalistic and erotic, affecting Amy at a very base level. *At least I'm honest enough to accept she is one hot mama. Even if I can't trust her not to burn holes in my heart.*

Amy sighed at the truth of it and turned to depart as silently as she'd arrived, until she saw Leone's clothes heaped on the bank where she had stepped right out of them.

Would you look at that? Practically lying in a mud puddle. Inwardly scolding, Amy wandered over, her obsessive-compulsive gene demanding she at least fold the clothes on a rock, off the muddy ground. She bent over and grabbed a sweatshirt by the collar. The fabric was already soaked through and badly stained. Her hand felt sticky. The dampness was not the consistency of mud, but thin and viscous, and it smelled coppery. She raised her hand to her face and looked closely. Blood! Her hand was covered in blood! It was all over Leone's shirt.

Anxiously she checked the jeans. They were also stained a dark red. All Leone's clothes were soiled with blood. Amy clawed through the pile, sick with alarm—

"My wallet's in my other pants." The deep voice came from directly behind her, causing her to jump.

"Shit. Do you want to give me a heart attack sneaking up like that?" She spun around to face a very naked Leone, her body gleaming in the moonlight. Rivulets of water ran down her long frame. Amy's eyes widened, momentarily overpowered with her gut-wrenching reflexes of alarm, attraction, and anger. She was worried at the blood on Leone's clothes—and annoyed at her standing before her gloriously nude, obviously unharmed, and as cocky as ever.

Leone gave a small grin, noting the reaction to her nakedness. She enjoyed the sensation of cool air and cold water on her skin. Now she reveled in Amy Fortune's gaze fixed on her body, despite Amy's obvious internal struggle to break away and look elsewhere. She felt every small shift in Amy's perception of her, and knew yesterday's fight on the porch had left Amy feeling off balance around her. Leone had catapulted Amy out of her staid little comfort zone. Had broken her out of her safe cocoon. But Amy had to understand, this valley was not a cocoon, and neither was it safe. Amy needed her, if only she knew it.

It was a bonus to meet up with her tonight while she was still so off-tilt. Leone knew she simply needed time and favorable circumstances to sway the odds back in her favor and win Amy back. Standing naked before her was so natural and right; watching Amy's befuddled reaction was a mischievous pleasure.

Finally, Amy managed to tear her eyes away and wildly scan the nearby skyline. *Has the woman no shame?*

GILL MCKNIGHT

"Your clothes? There's blood everywhere. What the hell happened? Are you hurt somewhere I can't possibly see?" she demanded, annoyed that her initial concern had been turned into something else by Leone's brazen, knowing look.

"I went into town with Claude for a brew. We hit a deer on the way back. It was messy. I didn't want to walk blood into Mom's cabin so I jumped in the creek." She shrugged as if it was an everyday occurrence, and mild inconvenience. "I'll throw the clothes in the laundry later."

"Here." Amy pulled off her jacket and handed it over. "Marie's gone to bed. She won't want you running the laundry at this time of night. Put this on and come back to my cabin." She nodded at the messy clothes in her hands. "I'll run these through a quick wash before they're ruined."

"Thank you."

"I'm doing it for Marie, not you." Amy turned abruptly and headed back up the trail.

Leone caught up with her in an instant, hugging the warm coat around her, enveloped in its owner's scent and delighted at this strange turn of events.

CHAPTER ELEVEN

Grab a quick shower to warm yourself up, and I'll make some tea."

No sooner had they entered the cabin than Amy was singing out orders, recovering her composure through brusque commands. She moved to the small kitchenette and dumped Leone's clothes in the washing machine with a large scoop of detergent.

Leone disappeared into the bathroom as she was told while Amy flicked on the kettle for making tea. With the water bubbling slowly to a boil she went to dig out some old shorts and a T-shirt of Connie's that might just make Leone's walk home a little more respectable. She pulled the clothing from the dresser and dumped it on her bed. It was obvious she was not going to get much studio work done tonight, so she changed out of her own mud spattered clothes and grabbed her pj's from under the pillow.

Amy almost didn't see the small cotton sachet tucked away underneath it. She examined it cautiously. It was gathered at the neck with a thin green cord, tied with what looked like an intricate series of knots. It smelled of herbs. She sniffed the fabric. It was a pleasant enough smell. She hadn't noticed it before so it must have been placed there after she made her bed that morning.

I bet if I were to look through the Wicca book I'd find this is one of Leone's hocus-pocus wooing concoctions. She's been in this valley too long. Has she never heard of dinner and dancing? She didn't know what to make of this bizarre side to Leone. It was endearing, yet also very annoying. She shook her head and replaced the sachet under the pillow. There was no harm in it and it did smell nice— Amy blinked.

Did the quilt just move? Another lurch from under the bedcover and her eyes widened. A horrible feeling crawled over her. Carefully she reached out and pulled the cover back with a swift jerk—and let out an unholy scream. A coiled, brightly colored snake was nestling in the dip of her mattress. It bunched up tightly, timid at the sudden exposure to light and the horrendous screech that accompanied it.

Amy spun on her heel and flew down the ladder, her feet barely touching the rungs. No sooner had she landed on the living room floor than she began to sprint for the door at top speed.

Leone burst out of the bathroom. The scream had sent her rushing from her shower in alarm. Amy was charging straight for her in an effort to reach the door, terrified out of her wits.

"Steady, steady." Leone grabbed Amy by the shoulders and just managing to stop her. They both nearly toppled to the floor. "What the hell's happening?"

"There's a snake in my bed. A snake. A big snake. It's big." Amy was seconds away from full-blown hysteria. Her eyes were wide and tear filled. She trembled all over, a victim of an inborn terror of snakes that common sense and woodland holidays had never quiet eradicated. Leone was well aware of this phobia and tried to calm her.

"Okay, okay. Keep calm. Let me take a look." Leone wound her towel tighter around her waist, uncaring that her chest was bare. "What color was it? Can you remember?" The color would give her an indication as to what might be awaiting her at the top of the ladder.

"Yellow—with black blotches—no, brown. Black. Oh, I don't know. Get rid of it, Leone. Please…please." Amy was a little calmer now that she had a champion. Leone reckoned if Amy had been on her own she'd be in Massachusetts by now, her feet a blur.

"Sounds like a bull snake. Big, you said."

"Enormous."

"Well, a male can be over six feet—"

"It was bigger than that…"

Leone snorted and headed up the ladder. "I've heard your fishing stories, remember."

Amy stood wringing her hands, anxiously watching her bare-breasted Amazon climb to the sleeping gallery. She had never been so grateful she'd brought Leone back to the cabin.

"Do you want a stick? Don't let it bite you. Please be careful." She tried to be helpful from a distance.

"It's a bull snake all right," the call floated down to her. "A young female. At least I think it's a female; they're usually a little bit chunkier, but this one's—"

"Who cares! Get it out."

Leone balanced carefully coming back down the ladder, both hands occupied with her hefty cargo.Approximately three to four feet of colorful coils wrapped around one wrist and forearm. Amy paled at the sight. The other hand grasped the snake just behind its head. It lay docile in her hands. As Leone passed her, Amy backed off until her shoulders hit the wall.

"Open the door for me, will you. My hands are kind of full." Leone nodded at the obstacle.

Amy pounced on the door handle in her enthusiasm to expel her unwelcome visitor. The night air reactivated the snake's senses and it gave a loud hiss as it passed her, making her scurry to the far end of the room. Leone moved off the porch and set the snake gently on the ground close to the tree line.

"There you go, gal. Go catch a big fat gopher for supper. Ain't nothing but chickens in there." She nodded back to the cabin.

"I heard that, and you're not funny."

Before returning to the cabin Leone stood and sampled the night air. The forest was lively, activity carrying on as usual. She could sense nothing strange or out of place. Far from content, she moved back to the porch. Hesitating on the top step, she sniffed the air again, accepting there was nothing out there waiting. At least not anymore.

By the time she entered the living room Amy was in the loft stripping the bed down with great gusto.

"How the hell did it get in here?" she cried as sheets, pillowcases, and a quilt cover parachuted to the room below. Leone gathered the various items together and took them into the kitchen, dumping them on the floor by the busy washing machine.

"Dunno," she called back. "They hunt in trees for birds. Maybe she fell onto the roof and found a way through the shingles into your rafters. I suppose she dropped on your bed and burrowed in for safety. In the wild they live in burrows and—"

"In the rafters?" Amy looked up horrified at the cross beams above her bed. "Oh my God. You've got to go up there and find the hole. This whole cabin's falling apart. Connie used to look after it like a newborn baby. Doesn't anybody mend things anymore? Who maintains the cabins around—"

"Hey. Hey," Leone called up to her. "Calm yourself. It was just a guess about the rafters. I'll check the roof in the morning, first thing, okay? And there's nothing wrong with the cabin. Stop getting in a tizzy. The snake's gone and…umph." A T-shirt and shorts landed on her head.

"Cover yourself up and make some tea while I finish this bed. There's bread and some cheese in the cupboard. Let's have supper."

Leone made a light supper and banked up the fire. Soon they were sitting snug on the couch before a warm blaze.

Amy sat and watched the fire, finally calming down after her encounter with the valley's reptiles. Absently she nursed her empty cup, its porcelain heating her hands. As usual Leone was sitting too close, but the heat from her body was relaxing and secure, and Amy was too frazzled to care about the close contact. Together they sat, watching patterns form and melt in the flames, the only sound the ticking of Connie's old mantel clock.

Amy sighed. *This feels so right. Like it's always been a part of my life, but I've been absent from it. Like it's always been here, waiting for me…and I was always somewhere else?*

"What feels so right?"

Amy jerked and turned to look in Leone's questioning eyes. *Shit. Did I just speak out loud?* "Huh?"

"You were mumbling something about things being right? You

are happy here, aren't you? I mean, everything is going okay with your work?" Leone didn't want to discuss their personal problems tonight. Now that there was peace between them. This was not the time to fall back into their circling dance, where Amy resisted the inevitable and Leone tried to lure her in deeper.

"Yes, yes. I've always liked it here. Love it, in fact. Once I get to speak with Connie I'll be a hundred times happier, of course. But the work is going well. I see no problems with it," Amy said. "I'm glad to be back in Little Dip."

Leone nodded in response. Her shoulders relaxed, she was happy with the answer. She reached over and squeezed Amy's hand.

"We're all glad you're back," she said, pleased when Amy didn't immediately pull free. She cleared her throat. "After you left I thought about you a lot. Where you were, what you were doing. Connie told me your news. How good things were going for you. Places you'd been to. It all sounded so much better than here…" Her voice trailed off, thick, faltering. Her question was—would Little Dip be enough for a hardened globetrotter like Amy? But she was unsure how to ask it.

Amy slid her hand out of the warm grasp. It had not been better than here. Nothing had been. This was home. Everywhere else was…not home.

She'd limped around Europe from job to job between her university studies, burying herself in work, carving out a growing reputation based on skill and a hell of a lot of luck. In the beginning she had been a timid student, shocked and hurt that a love supposedly so safe, so solid, could falter and fail. That such essential things could be wrenched away, leaving her with absolutely nothing. It was a hard life lesson. But Connie had nursed her through a heartache not even five thousand miles could dissipate.

Now she was a mature woman, a professional artist. She moved around the cities of Europe with ease. She spoke several languages, earned good money. She'd had more love affairs than she cared to remember. She had survived and she had changed, but she had never really been happy. Home was always missing.

It seemed they had come full circle. Well, almost full circle. Here she was, once again in Little Dip, sitting much too close to Leone, her creature of smoke and mirrors. A creature in whom she had invested every ounce of her young, inexperienced heart. Amy knew Leone was only trying to help her, to protect her. She also knew Leone still held feelings for her, even after all these years. Leone had not moved on with time. Amy could see that. She was engrained into this valley, entrenched within her family. She had kith and kin, hearth and home. All the things Amy had not. Leone might as well have been a tree, she was rooted so deep in this place.

"What did you do after you left, Leone?" She suddenly needed to know.

"Me?"

"Yes. After you left." Amy cautiously circled closer to that painful time. Leone seemed to instinctively know what Amy was asking.

"I went to Vancouver to learn about Garoul Print for the rest of the year. But you know that." Leone shifted in discomfort. "Then I came back to the Portland head office and started working at Garoul Press." Her answer was awkward, the words sticking, so she cleared her throat often as she spoke. There was no joy in the telling. It was obvious she had not been happy with her allotted tasks. But it had always been that way for the eldest of the Garoul children. They took over the family business, simple as that. Marie had given up medicine to take over from her mother, Leone had not even entered college when her call came. She looked over at Amy and asked, "Didn't Connie tell you?"

"I never asked."

They fell back into silence, the air around them still and melancholy.

"I better make tracks." Leone stood and stretched, exposing her flat brown belly with its small, deep navel. Amy's eyes locked on it, remembering out of nowhere, kissing the dark brown freckle that nestled on its rim.

A surge of panic, and distress, and something else a lot subtler, rose to swamp her. She didn't want Leone to leave. She didn't want to be alone in a cabin where snakes dropped from the rafters. She didn't want to lose the company, the relaxed honesty before the open fire. The melancholy had pulled her into a stupor, and she was afraid of the void when Leone left. She had a hundred reasons. But the real one was that tonight they had been close. Not in words, but in understanding. Tonight they had begun to repair something a long time damaged.

"Don't go," she blurted. Her face flamed as soon as the words left her mouth.

Leone's stretch stilled, and she slowly drew her arms back down to her sides. She said nothing, but looked expectantly at Amy.

"I mean…what if it comes back? I won't sleep. I know I won't. And I need to. I really, really need to if I'm to begin in the studio tomorrow," Amy explained anxiously, suddenly aware her invitation could be interpreted differently.

Leone nodded, understanding. "I guess I can sleep on the couch. At least my clothes will be bone dry in the morning."

She tried to sound matter-of-fact, but inside she thrilled at being asked to stay, to serve and protect. She was needed after all. And that meant somewhere deep down inside Amy Fortune, there was a small sliver of space for her. A little nook she could creep into and curl up in contentedly, like a kernel waiting to seed.

The hours of anxious waiting by Big Jack and the fight on the porch all melted away. She knew it was a long journey back to Amy's heart. She knew she deserved to crawl every inch of it on her hands and knees and be thankful for the privilege. There were also extraneous circumstances that could make her fail at any moment. But she wasn't even going to consider the possibility. She was wanted, needed, necessary, and had been invited to stay.

All the magic Connie had taught her was slowly coming true.

CHAPTER TWELVE

It was nearly three in the morning, and Amy had not slept a wink. Her anxious gaze swiveled from rafter to rafter above her head, looking for any signs of furtive slithering. The wind had lifted, and rain blew in from the west, tapping on the windows and pattering on the roof.

Below she could hear the fire popping and crackling, the couch creaking and blankets rustling as Leone rose to add another log. Amy squeezed the little herbal sachet she had found under her pillow. Squeeze and relax, squeeze and relax. Until it was twisted so out of shape it looked like it would burst at the seams. When she remade the bed it had fallen at her feet and some strange compulsion made her leave it at her bedside. Now she gripped it like a stress ball.

This is awful. I'll never sleep tonight. If Leone doesn't get the roof fixed tomorrow, I may never sleep again. My timetable will be a shambles! She worried her lower lip as she pondered her options. The wet weather meant she'd be better off working in the studio. She frowned as she realized something odd. Surely if there was a hole in the roof big enough for a twenty-foot snake to sneak in, then the rain should pour through, too?

The sachet squeezing became frantic. What if the snake had been planted there, under the bedclothes? But would Leone do that? She knew about Amy's snake phobia. But would she be that cruel? Her instincts told her Leone would never do that to her. On a deeper, intuitive level she knew Leone cared for her, wanted only to help and protect her. Her nose twitched. *Scullcap. She's burning that damned stink again.*

Amy remembered the spell book. It said scullcap was used in love spells; no mention of termite control. Was Leone burning it now for her?

A violent gust of wind made the rafters above creak. This was no time to ponder witchy wooing. With a terrified glance at the beams Amy's resolve broke into smithereens, she couldn't stay up here with all these snakes…

Leone lay watching the lazy swirl of incense smoke trail away overhead. She knew Amy was wide awake. She could tell by her breathing, light, a little fast, sometimes hitched and irregular when a bad thought surfaced.

The snake incident angered Leone, though she disguised it well. She dreaded to think what might have happened if she hadn't been here. Amy would have vacated her place of safety in seconds flat, and plowed straight into the forest and definite danger in a blind panic.

The rustling of bed linen and the soft pad of bare feet alerted her that Amy was on her way down from her loft. Leone closed her eyes and tried to relax her face muscles in a semblance of sleep.

"Leone," a small voice whispered from the foot of the couch.

"Yeah," she answered immediately. Propping herself up on an elbow, she saw Amy's troubled eyes and tremulous chin, and felt her heart break in two.

"Leone. The snake…it wasn't planted there, was it? It really did fall from the rafters? Nobody would play a joke like that on me here, would they?"

"Oh, Amy." Leone sat up and drew Amy down into her arms in a tender, reassuring embrace. "No one in this valley would ever do that to you. Never, ever. It was just a freak thing," she lied through her teeth.

They sat together swathed in Leone's blankets. "I promise I'll check the roof first thing in the morning."

"Thanks." Amy snuggled further into the warm blankets, and in doing so wormed deeper into Leone's arms. Encouraged, Leone held her tighter, surprised and pleased at this unexpected outcome.

She decided to try to reassure Amy even more if it made her snuggle in more.

"I mean, it could have been in here all along and you just never noticed."

"What?"

"Yeah, maybe it just sneaked in for some warmth? Or it could've been chasing a rat—"

"A rat!"

"Or maybe it was looking for somewhere to lay its eggs—"

"Eggs."

Amy drew her feet up under her, fingers fretfully plucking fluff off the blanket.

"Of course, some snakes don't lay eggs," Leone mused aloud. "Some give birth to hundreds of live—Hey."

Amy was nearly up and off the sofa before Leone could grab her and calm her down.

"Okay, okay." Leone tried to soothe her, realizing she had made a slight tactical error. Laughter bubbled in her voice. "Forget that one. No baby snakes, or even eggs. It's the wrong time of year. I'm sorry."

Amy glared at her until Leone apologized again. "Look, whatever it was, it was a one-off. It will never happen again. I promise you."

"Maybe that crap you're burning attracts them." Amy came right back at her with an agenda of her own. Two could play torture games.

"Huh?"

"That termite stuff."

"Mmm, no. It's okay to burn that." Leone shifted uncomfortably.

"I think you should put it out."

"No. It's fine—"

"Extinguish it. Just in case?"

"Connie said to burn it. I promised…termites…" Desperation crept into Leone's voice. Amy noted it with wicked glee.

Oh, so we can't snuff out the stink spell, in case all the love in the room goes poof?

Smugly she watched Leone squirm for excuses to keep the incense lit. There was no doubt in Amy's mind this was the spell from Connie's Wicca book. *Termites, my ass.*

"I think I'm allergic to it." She kept up the pressure, secretly gloating at Leone's discomfort.

"No. No, you're not. Are you?" Leone looked anxiously at her.

Inwardly Amy giggled at the ferocious snake-charming Leone, now reduced to casting stupid spells to catch Amy's attention. *I'll give her my attention, all right.*

"It itches my eyes. See?" She leaned in with widened eyes until they were almost nose to nose. Leone's breath hitched in response and her inky irises expanded at a million miles a second. It gave Amy a thrilling surge of...what, power, mischief? She enjoyed teasing big bad Leone Garoul like this.

Leone seemed to pulse toward her. She filled every inch of space. Every hair on Amy's skin rose. She tingled from head to toe.

Suddenly, it was no longer a silly game. In an instant it had become exciting and dangerous. She could feel the heat rolling off Leone's body, smell the warm spice of her skin, and practically count those long dark eyelashes. She used to do that...a million years ago. Try to count them, as they lay entwined in meadows, on the riverbank, and once...only once in Leone's bed. Now their gazes locked, and they bewitched each other all over again.

Hesitant, then suddenly sure, Amy leaned in and simply rubbed noses. She used to do that a million years ago, too. Time collapsed around them, and a million years compressed into this single moment, erasing all the time between here and yesterday.

Leone was still and careful. She didn't so much as twitch. She swallowed everything, every detail. Amy was playful with her, warm with remembering, softened by the happy times, and offering—offering what?

A low growl rolled in Leone's throat; she was heated, unsure, wanting. And then Amy moved toward her once more, and her lips poured over hers with the sweetness and satiny heat of melting chocolate.

In that moment, without question, doubt, or reservation, Leone Garoul believed in magic.

Her mate had been returned to her. She had burned a thousand candles. Offered up enough incense and herbs to woo the whole world. Leone had woven her spells and cast them around her chosen one. Amy had been conjured by her, and for her, and was never going to leave her again.

With a throaty growl she spilled Amy over onto her back, covering her. Fingers whispered through silken curls, traced the nape of neck and throat. Stroking her from shoulder to wrist and back again, enjoying the contours, the texture of Amy's skin, so pale against her own. Leone nuzzled the sensitive spot below Amy's ear, the hollow of her throat, her eyebrow, her hairline. She dropped kisses down to the small dent just below the full lower lip. Leone breathed her in and lapped her up, scent, and texture, and heat, covering every inch of Amy's face in an act of worship.

She swept the flat of her tongue across Amy's rosy cheek, dragged her teeth slowly down Amy's throat, to lay in thrall over the trembling pulse point, waiting until the hum of Amy's life blood harmonized with the pounding of her own heart—

"Ow, stop nipping."

Leone rose from the scented throat, eyes unfocused. She was suffused with everything that smelled, tasted, felt, like Amy Fortune. She tried to concentrate on the flushed face scowling at her through a mass of snarled curls.

"Don't you dare mark me. I see you're still a biter," Amy said.

Leone looked at the scarlet bruises already forming on Amy's neck, and decided not to mention them. She burned with excitement and energy. Slowly she lowered her mouth and claimed Amy's with a deep kiss that shut out the rest of the world.

Amy moaned and buried her fingers in hair as heavy and dark as a midnight sky, twisting and knotting it into hungry fistfuls. She wrapped herself around Leone and held on tight. Legs and arms entwined, they rocked against each other, the air thick with moans and murmurs, growls and whimpers. They were not gentle with each other. They never really had been. And they were hungry now.

It had been a long time. Their kisses were urgent, hands greedy. They tussled and tugged at each other's clothing like the teenagers they once were, until the ripping of material startled Amy. Leone had shredded her pajamas in her haste.

"Damn it, Leone. These cost over fifty dollars. Go easy. And no biting."

Unheeding, Leone's mouth devoured her breasts, gorging on the soft tissue, torturing the sensitive tips with urgent tugs and nips. She sank her teeth into creamy flesh that rippled under her tongue— Amy grabbed her by the ears.

"Hey, Ruff-Stuff. No teeth. I like things different now."

Leone's eyes glittered, her white teeth flashed through blood red lips. Flushed and breathless, she was reckless in her immediate need. She trembled with primal energy. Amy had never seen her so beautiful, desire spiked through her like quicksilver. Every instinct, nerve, sense her body had was urging her to bond with this woman. It screamed at her to do so, but Amy was adamant this was going to be her way.

Things had changed. She was no longer the inexperienced teenager who allowed Leone to run amok over her body as they eagerly discovered sex for the first time. To this day she still bore a mark, a small pink rosette on the back of her left thigh, a bite mark that had never faded.

Tonight, Amy was determined they would not fall back into that heady chaos. There would be passion, but her way, how she wanted it. And tonight she wanted to make love, and it was damn well going to be on her terms. Tonight they would finally close the door on a painful past and move on, freed from it. So she hung on to Leone's ears, until those flashing eyes focused on her face.

"I don't like having my breasts mauled. I like them to be kissed—slowly—all over." She watched Leone intently to ensure the words were seeping into her lust-puddled brain. Amy took the big, black blink to be an affirmative.

"Then I like my nipples licked with long, swirling strokes until they are rock hard." This was greeted with a second slow blink. She had all of Leone's attention now.

"That's when I love to have them sucked. Not hard, but not too soft either. Suck them just right, and I'll come for you. All over this couch." There was no blink this time. It seemed Leone had lost the power to her eyelids; she just stared at Amy, and swallowed hard.

Finally, as if she felt responsible for the thick silence that had wrapped around them, Leone blurted in a choked voice, "They're bigger than before—your breasts."

Now it was Amy's turn to blink.

She responded carefully, with deliberation, "Yes. It's been a while. I became a woman."

With Amy's words the years apart opened up like a chasm for Leone. So much had changed for Amy. So much worldly travel and new experiences. She had gone out and lived, while Leone had sat and brooded. Fear coiled in her guts, freezing her with uncertainty. She felt alone, teetering on the edge of an abyss. For Leone understood the balance, had mastered the tilt of it. She stood on the brink of a life worth living, or an existence alone.

If Amy rejected her there was none other, and it was done with. She would have selected her mate and been refused. A long time ago she'd lost Amy through her own inexperience and lack of courage. What would be her excuse now?

Amy raised her head and gently claimed Leone's hesitant mouth, remembering another time when she thought of these lips as all her own. The day the teenage Amy lost Leone Garoul, she lost Little Dip, and her home, and a little bit of herself, too. It had taken many years of traveling and living her own adventures to put her wholly and firmly back on the map of her life. And what had she done? Where had she gone? She'd run right back to Little Dip. Straight back to the Garoul valley, to Connie's cabin, Leone's arms, this madness, with all the ingenuity of a lemming.

Here was home, here was shelter, here she felt whole and satisfied. And a big part of that, an agonizing part of it, was the woman lying beside her on this skinny little couch, taking up far too much room as usual.

The kiss deepened. Leone tried to be tender, tried to remember. But firm breasts pushed against her own with only her borrowed

T-shirt separating their flesh but not their heat. Leone wanted more. She wanted taste, and deep scent, and essence. She wanted all of Amy. Slowly, she began the act of claiming.

Amy squirmed against her, arching into Leone's belly, rocking on her thigh. They molded to each other, sinuously rolling, caught in an ancient rhythm that at the same time was solely their own. Amy's nails trailed patterns across Leone's long, lean back. Leone's rumbling growl resonated against Amy's throat, making her skin tingle; she arched her back into the strong body covering hers. Her breasts were lavished with wet, sucking kisses until they flushed pink, their tips hard.

Leone sucked with a delicate passion, sensitive to Amy's murmurs and the frantic movements beneath her. She was quickly learning Amy's secrets, a mixture of old and new, marveling at the pleasure the act of loving Amy brought both of them.

When she finally abandoned the breasts they were swollen and firm, glistening with her saliva, the areolas puckering in the cool air. Amy murmured in disappointment and Leone grinned into the soft skin of her stomach. Her hair trailed across Amy's belly as she dropped kisses all the way down to her navel. Leone crooned happily to herself as she circled Amy's belly button with wet kisses and dipped her tongue into the salty indent. She teased and played until Amy's hands caught fistfuls of her hair and guided her on to their joint goal. Amy quickly raised her hips, spreading herself open, offering herself to Leone. Without hesitation Leone plunged onto her sex.

Leone had been patient; she had been careful; she had paced herself to the wishes and rhythm of Amy's body. Now Amy's scent was too strong and Leone's needs too great.

With a deep growl Leone nuzzled the tender folds. She drew the plump clitoris into her mouth and drove Amy relentlessly toward the precipice. Leone's hair was pulled, her shoulders scratched as Amy cried out to her for that one, elusive, torturous touch that would shatter her into stardust.

Amy knew this was going to be big. She knew Leone would take her there. Every molecule of her body centered on her lover—

and then she came, a tidal wave of pure heat that melted every bone in her body and blew off a dozen pyrotechnics in her skull. Above her shuddering cries she faintly heard a deep panting growl. Amy's eyes fluttered open and she briefly glimpsed a dark devilish stare shining up at her. Leone's eyes danced with pride and love. Her tan cheeks and chin glistened in the firelight, damp and pungent with Amy's essence. The air around them was thick with sweat, and sex, and scullcap.

Leone crawled up her body and kissed her with sweet, salty lips, sharing the joy she had tasted. And as they kissed Amy cradled her in her arms, tightening her thighs around Leone's waist, and held on to her as if she were drowning.

CHAPTER THIRTEEN

Amy poked her nose out from under a heap of blankets and knew immediately that she was alone. Leone must have sneaked out early in the morning, leaving her to sleep on peacefully. The fire smoked and crackled, spreading warmth into the room. Leone had relit it without waking her. She was grateful for the heat but would have preferred waking up snug and warm in Leone's arms. In the kitchen she found a small bunch of wildflowers nestled by the coffeepot, anchoring a note.

> *Sorry. Something very urgent has come up and I have to go. I wish I could have stayed and watched you wake. Can I see you later tonight? I really am sorry.*
> *L.*
> *PS. You look beautiful when you're sleeping.*

It was an awkward, shy note, emotionally clumsy and a little unsure. The star-pointed flowers were a perfect accompaniment for the sentiment. They were shy and delicate blossoms. Amy knew Leone had hunted these down in some far-off stony area. They did not grow in the rich loam by the river. It was a sweet gesture, a poignant throwback to their teenage years. Again, Amy felt a pang of regret that Leone had gone. She wanted to be with her. She needed Leone's reassuring presence after their night of lovemaking. From the timbre of the note she knew Leone needed hers, too. Whatever had taken her away had to have been important.

With a sigh, Amy put the flowers in a tumbler of water and started making breakfast. She relaxed on the couch with her coffee and idly flicked through the pages of the Wicca spell book. She wondered who the publishers were. She'd never heard of the Wiccan Wheel before. *I must ask Marie. This is her area of expertise.* She scanned a few of the love potions and recipes. It was sort of laid out like a cookbook... Amy frowned. She was looking at a potion that included angelica. The gram amounts used were very reasonable, but something jarred her.

She sat back and gazed off into the middle distance, collecting her thoughts. Where had she seen angelica recipes recently? In the almanac. Right beside Connie's illustration with the weird marks.

Amy went to Connie's desk, opened the almanac, and found the angelica illustration. The recipe with it was one of Marie's. An herbal infusion for colic...and curing the bite of wild dogs. Wild dogs? *Bloody hell, Marie.*

Unlike in the Wicca book, the ingredient measurements in Marie's recipe were all wrong. *This would choke you. Even I know that.* The recipe went on to mention another botanical ingredient, lady's bedstraw, again in bizarrely inaccurate amounts.

Amy flipped to the page with the illustration for lady's bedstraw. The illustration had extraneous markings just like angelica. Amy didn't have to be overly familiar with the plant to see them. Once she suspected they were there, they practically leapt off the page.

What the hell was going on? The weird measurements she guessed were linked back to the plant illustrations, but in what way? By looking at the recipe amounts she could guess which plant illustrations would have hidden sigils—the ones with the crazy gram measurements had the marks.

Amy checked out other almanacs at random. Her theory worked. Each had a weird recipe among the real ones, and for every strange herb dosage she found the related plant illustration had discreet markings hidden in it.

It was all part of the code she had suspected from the moment she had seen the marks in Connie's work. But the marks meant nothing on their own. She still needed the missing link. All codes and ciphers had a key. She'd read about it in the library book.

Okay, so she could link the confusing recipes doses to certain illustrations, but that wasn't enough. A key, she had to figure out the key.

Amy knew this had nothing to do with the anniversary almanac idea Marie tried to sell her last night. Connie would have talked to her about that. They shared their ideas and swapped opinions. They had always worked like that. Pooling knowledge, sharing research. Connie would not have kept information about an anniversary almanac from her. But would she have withheld a code?

Amy chewed her lip. Maybe this was something Connie didn't know she was involved in? She wished Connie was available, even on the end of a telephone. Amy wanted to reassure herself that all this strange, mysterious stuff had nothing to do with Connie being ill. She desperately wanted Connie to let her in on the secret. If Connie was part of it, that was.

Amy doubted either Leone or Marie would tell her the truth. The code was there for a reason. This was secret knowledge, and only the almanac's exclusive readership would know it was embedded in the books at all. Amy would have to solve the mystery by herself.

A tapping on the roof shook her out of her reverie. Was Leone up there fixing it, as promised? What about the urgent business that took her away so early?

Amy stepped outside. The wind had risen and snatched her hair, whipping it around her shoulders. She looked up at the shingles, concerned Leone was looking for snake holes in such blustery weather.

"Leone? Are you up there? Be careful. It's too windy."

Leone was nowhere in sight. The overhanging tree branches dipped and swayed, knocking on the cabin roof. That had been the tapping noise.

She wandered around to the rear of the cabin, hoping Leone might be back there doing some other repairs. Amy missed her already, and wished— She jarred to a halt, looking in horror at the back wall of Connie's cabin. It was completely lacerated. The surface wood hung in gouged-out tatters. The surround and sills of the small bathroom window were splintered apart. No wonder she could barely open it. It was ruined, and it wasn't recent damage either; it was sustained.

Amy slowly backed away to the front of the cabin where she felt safer.

"Okay." She took a dry swallow. "I've got to tell Claude and Marie there's something in the valley damaging property as well as trees."

She went back indoors and dragged on her coat. She wasn't exactly sure what the Garouls could do, but it wasn't acceptable for whatever it was to get this close to the cabin. Especially Connie's cabin, which was farther out than the compound ones. Was that why she kept a gun?

❖

The wind had died away by the time Amy arrived at the compound. She rounded the corner of Claude's cabin and came to an abrupt halt. Before her on a huge A-frame an adult deer hung by its hind legs. Its body cavity was opened and gutted. The carcass was headless and the stump of a neck was totally mangled, as if the head had literally been ripped off. A fly-infested bucket sat to the side. She assumed it held the entrails.

"Hi, Amy."

The soft voice came from behind her. Spinning around she saw Paulie approach, an impressively wicked knife dangled from his hand. He smiled at her before blushing fiercely. Amy wondered if he had perhaps developed a little crush on her. He seemed very awkward around her.

"Hi, Paulie. Is this the deer Claude and Leone hit with the truck last night?"

Paulie blinked before burning an even brighter shade of red. "Um, they brought it in last night. Claude dressed it, but left the rest for me to practice skinning on. Do you want to watch?" he asked eagerly.

"Mmm. Sure."

Amy wasn't at all sure if she wanted to watch, but she didn't want to dilute his obvious enthusiasm for the chore left to him. He moved to the carcass, and with great concentration drew the blade around the tethered hooves before slitting the inside of each leg down toward the pelvis. Slowly, he began to peel back the hide from the fetlocks, scrubbing at stubborn patches with the blade. Amy winced.

"You've got to make sure the hide doesn't touch the meat," he said. "No one wants a hairy steak, do they?"

His casual words broke Amy out of her horrified trance.

"Yeah, that would be yuck," she said, vowing herself back to vegetarianism. "Paulie, why's the head missing and the neck so mashed up? Is that where the truck hit it?"

"Maybe," he said, concentrating on the job in hand. But even with his back to her she could see his ears glow. He was finding her questions difficult, and she wasn't sure why. "The head's in Claude's freezer. He's taking it to a friend who's a taxidermist. He wants to get it mounted as a gift for Leone's birthday. Don't tell her. It's a surprise," he added hastily.

"Nope. The secret's safe with me. Hey, thanks for the demo, but I need to go find Marie. I'll catch you later."

"Okay, I'll save you a couple of loin steaks." Again he blushed furiously, and again Amy was uncertain what it was that made him so awkward around her.

"Amy," he called after her. "There's no one over at Aunt Marie's. They've all headed out."

It had occurred to Amy that the compound was very quiet for the time of day.

"Who's they? And where have they gone?"

"Most everyone. Claude told me to stay here and finish skinning the buck. I'm not sure where they went. They took off very sudden. Elicia just left a minute or two ago. She looked upset. I called but she just kept walking. Didn't hear me." He shrugged in a typical teenage fashion.

"Do you know which way Elicia went?"

He waved his knife toward one of the exit routes. "Maybe the parking lot?"

Amy turned to follow his directions. "Thanks, Paulie."

He turned back to his deer. Amy ran curious eyes over the headless carcass one last time. If the head was intact enough for mounting, and the body was intact enough to butcher for meat, then the only real damage to the animal was to its throat. How the hell did a Toyota truck manage to hit an adult deer bang on the neck? And apparently hard enough to rip its throat clean out?

Nothing was adding up this morning. Amy's frown deepened.

She jogged down the to the parking lot hoping she could catch Elicia. Maybe she knew where all the Garoul adults had gone? This had to be the urgent business Leone had been called away on. Had the Garouls cornered the tree ripper?

A flash of red caught her eye; it was set back in the woods. She squinted. Someone was out walking in the forest. Was it Elicia? Elicia had a red coat.

"Elicia," she called.

The figure didn't stop and was soon swallowed up by the trees. Was it Elicia? Amy was indecisive; should she follow or head down to the parking lot? Maybe Elicia wasn't going to the car. Maybe she was looking for Jori.

It had to be Elicia; Paulie said she'd come this way, and she had a bright red coat. Yes, it was probably Elicia. Another splash of red moved between the firs, and Amy made up her mind.

"Elicia. Wait up." Amy plunged into the forest after her.

❖

No matter how well I think I know this valley, I always find a track I've never seen before. She was angry with herself for acting impulsively and following the elusive red coat. Amy had no real idea if it was Elicia or not. It could be Santa for all she knew. Glimpses of red had popped up here and there, flashing at her through the trees. Always a little too far ahead for her calls to be heard. Amy was well and truly pissed off.

She decided to keep pushing on in the hopes of finding a path home. In fact, any path would do at this point. In her haste that morning, she had forgotten to bring her backpack with her water flask, hand compass, trail mix, and all the other things that made getting lost in the woods semi-tolerable.

Finally her bad luck broke and she crested a small rise to find she had doubled back on the Silverthread river. It wasn't a section she recognized, but she knew all she had to do was follow it northeast and she'd pick up a trail soon enough. She skirted around fireweed and goat's beard, noting a licorice fern, which was on her to-do list and not the easiest plant to find either. *Better remember the way back here. Damn, I wish I had my backpack. I could have sketched this one.*

Amy was so busy berating herself she almost missed the squat cabin sitting amongst the trees on the opposite bank. She clambered down to the riverbank and stared across at it. It seemed uninhabited. The windows were barred, like a prison, or a secured store. That was all she could make out from this distance. Curiosity got the better of her. She might as well explore while she was this close.

With boots and socks in hand, and pants rolled up well past her knees, she waded across a relatively shallow part of the river.

"Goddamnit." *It's bleedin' freezing!* Safely on the other side, she hastily laced up her boots before approaching the little shack.

The closer she got, the less abandoned it looked. Wood was neatly stockpiled by a side wall. It was a seasonal collection, not a damp, mossy heap leftover from previous years. This was good firewood. Yet the chimney wasn't smoking. The windows had iron bars on the outside, but the glass was smashed and shards lay all over the ground. Pretty gingham curtains fluttered in the breeze, incongruous with the damage surrounding them.

Even more intrigued, Amy crunched up a well-worn path and around to the front porch. There she hesitated. The door was hanging by its hinges, its wooden panels snapped clean in two. Broken porch furniture was scattered out over the dirt path. All was silent, eerily so considering this was a scene of recent and incredible violence.

"Hello?" Amy's voice wobbled. It was too late to beat a retreat; if someone was inside they knew she was here by now. "Anyone... home?"

Silence. Amy was more than a little relieved. She cocked her head and listened. Nothing. There was definitely no one in the cabin.

Slowly she mounted the porch and carefully stepped over the remains of the door. It was a one-room shack, in a shambles. Every stick of furniture—which consisted of a bed, table, and chair—was in pieces. Newspapers, bed linens, torn-up books, and spilled foodstuffs littered the floor. Even the wood burner lay on its side, its cast iron door torn off, the chimney pipe bent.

Amy entered, and broken glass and crockery cracked under her boots. On the window sill, tucked beside the gingham curtains, lay a roll of cherry-flavored candy. A bizarre nod to normality in amongst such chaos.

"You shouldn't be here."

Amy yelped in fright as the voice rang out directly behind her. She spun around to find herself nose to chest with Claude. "Jesus, Claude. I could've dropped down dead."

"Sorry, hon. Didn't mean to scare you. What are you doing out here?" His kindly eyes smiled down at her as he stepped out onto the porch. She followed him out the door and down onto the packed earth path.

"Walking. Looking for plants. What is this shack? Why are there bars on the window? Why's it all broken up?"

"It's an old storage hut."

"With bars? It looks more like a jail."

"They used to keep dynamite there in the forties." He drew her further along the path, leading her away from the cabin and onto a nearby track.

"What did they want dynamite for?"

Claude chuckled at the relentless questions. "It was to blow open a new logging road up near Leapers Bluff, but the war came along and work stopped. Least that was what I remember being told as a kid."

"So why are there furniture and books and stuff in there? Is someone living there?"

"Told you. Storage. Marie keeps stuff there for furnishing the other cabins."

Amy frowned. She wasn't buying it. "Claude, someone was staying there. It had been lived in. And now it's all smashed up," she said.

He shrugged indifferently. They were a hundred yards or more from the cabin and he was leading her along a trail parallel to the river. "Dunno. I suppose it could be used to rest up if someone was out this far on a night hunt. I'll let Marie know it's been vandalized. She'll know what to do."

"But who would come all the way out here to smash up a storage room?"

"Vandals. Losers from town."

"All the way out here?"

"Young idiots. No doubt poaching. They enjoy destroying Garoul stuff. Probably kicked the door in and wrecked the cabin for the sheer hell of it—"

"But, Claude, the door was broken from the inside." She looked anxiously at him. He frowned darkly at her logic. "Somebody kicked their way out."

"Look, Amy. I don't know. I'll tell Marie about it later. Right now all I want to do is get you back to the compound."

"Where is everybody? What's happening? Have you seen Leone?"

"We're out hunting."

"I haven't heard any gunshots for it being such a big hunt. Is it bear or cougar you're after? Or wolves? Is it whatever's shredding the—"

"We're hunting, that's all there is to it. That's where everyone is, and that's why you're getting out of here quick. Okay?"

"Why can't I stay with you? After all—"

"No arguments, Amy. I'm taking you to your cabin."

"But why—"

"Nope."

"But when—"

"Nope."

"I didn't—"

"Nope."

"Rhymes with rope?"

"Nop—Ha ha. Very funny."

"Do a deal with you, Claude. Take me to the parking lot and lend me your truck. I need to pop into town for a quick message. I was trying to catch up with Elicia to grab a lift with her, but she went into the forest instead."

"What? Elicia's in the forest?" Claude's head whipped around.

"Well, I think so. I saw a red coat. And it looked like her from the back."

"Are you sure it was Elicia?"

"I don't know. She never answered when I called. Hey, I recognize this path." They had taken a few back routes that had eventually opened up to one of the main trails into the compound. "I can make it from here on my own."

"Are you sure?" Claude dithered. Amy knew he was torn between taking her all the way to his truck or returning to the hunt now that she was so close to safety. She pushed him a little bit more.

"Of course I'm sure. Give me your keys. It's only five minutes down the path. I'll be fine."

He handed her his truck keys. "Okay. Leave them under the visor when you're done. And be good." With a wave he headed back the way they had come.

Amy trudged on to the parking lot, mulling over the wrecked cabin. Okay, so Claude had no answers. *But he had no questions either, and to me that's strange. And for a man out hunting, why didn't he have a gun?*

Claude drove a beat-up Toyota truck. Amy hesitated by the hood. The fender was dirty and thick with mud, and looked like it had been that way for weeks. No way had it hit a deer last night. This truck had not impacted with anything recently, other than muck. Leone had lied about the accident, the deer…and her bloody clothing.

CHAPTER FOURTEEN

Virgil Bloomsy looked delighted as Amy entered the library. "Back so soon? You must be a quick reader."

"Actually, I didn't bring the book." she said apologetically. "I'm afraid I forgot it. I can bring it back tomorrow, if that's okay?"

"My dear, there is absolutely no hurry. Bring it in when you're ready. In fact, feel free to borrow anything else that catches your eye. Remember you're a library member now."

"Thank you. I don't suppose my friend Elicia dropped in earlier?"

"I think I saw her across the street. She didn't come in here, but she could be at the store. You are my first, and probably only, customer today. It's always quiet coming up to a holiday weekend."

"Okay. I'll go find her. But first I'll have a quick peek at your shelves, seeing as I'm here." Amy moved to the back of the library, keen to find more volumes on code breaking. Now that she had the link between the illustrations and the numbers in the recipes, she needed more information as to how the keys worked. She stood and read the spines for inspiration, at a loss at what direction to go in next.

So, I have some weird numbers hidden in recipe amounts, and some weird book page sizes, and some weird marks on Connie's artwork. What would Captain Midnight do? He'd wave his decoder ring at it, and it would all make sense, that's what he'd do. She sighed, wishing it really were as easy as that.

"You seem to like those code games. Does Connie still play

word puzzles? I could give you a few magazines to pass on to her."
Virgil passed, his arms stacked with books.

"What? Oh, no. I'm not sure if she still does." Again, Amy
was reluctant to tell the townsfolk anything about Connie's current
health. Not even Virgil, who claimed to be a friend. In fact, Amy had
never heard Connie mention him, and her natural reserve made her
hesitate to tell him any personal business.

She was still scowling at the spines when he passed by again.

"Can I help you with anything? You seem a little bemused."

"No. Not really."

He fluttered around her for a second longer, and suddenly she
found herself grasping at straws. "It's more like a number puzzle
anyway. Not words. I've got numbers, and on another page lots of
squiggles." She shrugged, scanning the shelves before her. "And
I'm not sure how the two match up."

"Oh, numbers and graphics. That's different. Sounds like
cipher-text. You need the key."

"I need the whole goddamn door."

"Maybe it's a pigpen."

"Huh?" He had her attention now.

Virgil gave a sharp little smile. "Yes, the pigpen, one of the
most basic ciphers. Also known as the Freemason's cipher, as it was
used by the Knights Templar in medieval France." He launched
into a mini lecture. "If there are multiple keys, then you have
layering, cipher over cipher. That would be difficult to break, but
not impossible. Once you have one of the keys, of course."

"There's that key again."

"Well, you are more than welcome to bring your numbers and
squiggles in and we can try together." He waved a hand around the
empty library. "As you can see I'm hardly run off my feet. A good
puzzle would certainly help while away the time."

Amy saw it as an offer made more out of loneliness and
boredom, than a burning need to help. Even so, she was reluctant to
share, especially as there was a connection to Connie's work and the
Garoul Press. If it did turn out to be some promotional code game
embedded in the anniversary almanac, it was not her place to make

it public through her own nosiness. Her gut instinct was to keep her research to herself.

"…and that's why it's called the Caesar cipher, because it's attributed to Julius Caesar. Today, of course, any Boy Scout could decrypt it in five minutes…" Virgil was in the middle of another narration, unaware he'd lost Amy ages ago. She tried to concentrate but felt annoyed that he was eating into her time with useless information. What she needed to do was pick the right book and go and find Elicia. Not stand here listening to Virgil rattle on. "…but frequency analysis can help break the plaintext into recognizable word patterns." *Now he's just showing off.*

"Oh, but you don't have any text, just numbers and sigils, isn't that right?" His question brought her back to the conversation with a snap.

"Mmm, yes…sigils. Well, weird marks really…" *Did I say sigils? There are marks, but I never implied they were mystical.*

"I'd really love to see them…"

"Oh, they're in a heavy old book, and it's not my place to remove it from the cabin—"

"Ah, it's one of Connie's books, is it? She has such a wonderful collection. You know I'd be happy to drop by on my day off?"

"To be honest, Mr. Bloomsy, it's not my book to play around with. I may be interfering with—"

"Please, call me Virgil. Well, the offer is there if curiosity gets the better of you. I can suggest a few other books that might help?" He started reaching for his selection when she interrupted.

"To be honest…Virgil, I should be working in the studio, not clowning about with puzzles. Maybe I'll let the runes rest, while I do what I'm being paid to—"

"You think they're runes?" He jumped on her words.

Amy blinked at the overt enthusiasm. "I really have no idea."

"But they might be runes?"

"I don't know. I wouldn't know a rune from a road sign." She was beginning to feel cornered. He pulled back, as if realizing he was being too pushy, and shoved his hands in his pockets, nodding, but he looked tense. His lips pursed and his cheeks flushed brightly.

"Well, I'd better go and find Elicia," Amy said. She was glad of the excuse to leave. Virgil was just a little bit too bored for her liking. It was a pet hate of hers, people who expected others to alleviate their boredom, rather than make their own entertainment. He had a whole library, apparently to himself. You'd think he could find something fun to do.

She thanked him again and left, heading over to the pharmacy and Johnston's store to see if Elicia was there, though she seriously doubted it. There was no sign of Jori's Jeep, and Amy could think of no other way for Elicia to get into town.

A quick glance through the window told her Elicia wasn't at the pharmacy. Next, she dropped into the general store. Norman Johnston glared at her from behind his counter.

"Good afternoon, Mr. Johnston. Can I have a bottle of water, please?"

"Still or sparkling?" he asked huffily.

"Sparkling, please." *Just like you*. She managed a bright smile despite his lack of courtesy.

"Seems quiet around town today," she said as he checked her change. She noticed the way he had grabbed at her five-dollar bill and fondled the coins he took from the till. He was having a love affair with money; she bet the whole town knew it.

"People startin' to head off for the Labor Day weekend." He gave Amy her change, his face vexed.

"I'd have thought with school out there'd be a ton of teenagers just hanging around here drinking Cokes and coffees?" She casually twisted the cap off her bottle, deciding to linger and chat. Maybe she could clear up something that was troubling her. Something Claude had said.

Norman Johnston eyed her suspiciously. Amy suspected most of his customers paid begrudgingly for his overpriced goods and left as glumly as they'd arrived. Her hanging around and chatting had him flummoxed.

"They're all over at Covington." He bitterly spat out the name of the largest town in the area. "It's got a mall." He might as well have said *gonorrhea* from the look of distaste that crossed his face.

"Oh, that'll do it." Amy chuckled as if he'd said something

clever. Norman rearranged his chewing gum display and eyed her carefully. Slowly, he relaxed.

"Better to have them out from under your feet," she said, noticing his thawing attitude. "I was out walking in Little Dip earlier and found what looked like an abandoned hut some kids had trashed."

Norman frowned at this, and for a moment Amy worried she'd misread him completely. Luckily, now that he trusted her with his considerable opinion, he was eager to enlighten her.

"Damn kids would never go into Little Dip. Nobody likes it there…too much strange stuff. And the Garouls are all over everything. You can't have nothing around here without the Garouls taking it off ya!"

Even with the abrasive history between the townsfolk and the Garouls, Amy was still surprised at his vehemence.

"Oh. Well, maybe I was mistaken. What strange stuff?"

"Humph." Norman sniffed dismissively, but continued. "I remember you from when you were a brat, hangin' out with all them other Garoul brats. You know fine rightly what I mean. There's a creature in that valley, and you all know it! Even the animals know it. And that bitch Marie Garoul and her mother before her were witches if ever I seen one. That's why they don't want anyone near. That's why you won't help the town."

Amy was aghast. *All that crap coming out the wrong hole.*

"Hey. Just a minute, Mr. Johnston. I spent every summer in Little Dip, year in, year out, and the Garouls are lovely people, and there's nothing going on in—"

"Hah. Believe what you want," he rudely interrupted. "I got no time to argue. I'm running a business here. Now, if that's all?"

"Not only is it all, I believe it will be everything," Amy replied haughtily, and primly stomped out, leaving her half-drunk water on the counter.

Her mind was in a whirl. Unpleasant as it was getting it, at least she had confirmation that the storage cabin probably wasn't vandalized by local kids. *I knew it. Claude was talking trash through his 'stache.*

Amy had done all she could. The mysteries were piling up

around her until she felt buried alive. She could give no more time to strange codes and spooky cabins. What she needed to do was an honest day's work in the studio. Even Nancy Drew had to pay her bills. Sighing, Amy returned to Claude's truck and sat a few moments thinking over her morning.

Leone's weird story about the deer still didn't sit right with her. Her fingers played with the key fob and she half smiled at the silly little picture on it of a pig wearing a nun's wimple. Claude had such a childish sense of humor. The picture reminded her of an image she'd seen somewhere before. Perhaps in a childhood storybook?

With a shrug she started the engine and pulled out of the graveled parking lot, heading back to Little Dip and the sanity of her studio.

❖

Amy made a light lunch and sank thankfully on the couch, resting her tired feet on the hearth, toasting her toes. A small metallic glint winked at her from beneath the dresser. It caught her curiosity, and with a little burst of energy she went down on her knees and reached for the glittering object. It turned out to be one of the bullets she'd dropped when she was searching for the scarf and found Connie's Bearcat revolver instead. She held it up to the light, twisting and turning it until it twinkled in the firelight. She decided she liked it, so shiny, and new, and silvery. It was dangerous and pretty all at the same time.

The clock chimed, reminding her it was time to move to the studio. Without a further thought she dropped the bullet in her jeans pocket, like a lucky charm, and headed off to work.

It felt so strange and nostalgic to sit at Connie's workbench. As a child she had spent so many hours sharing Connie's special space with her, watching every movement Connie made, hanging on her every word. The young Amy had thrived at Connie's side, soaking up her knowledge like a germinating seed.

Some kids stood on a kitchen stool and eagerly watched their moms bake, waiting to lick the spoon as reward for helping to mix and fold, weigh and measure. Others held the flashlight for their dad as he rummaged under the car hood, passing him tools as he changed a filter or checked for loose wiring. Through such simple acts children learn, and develop skills and interests. Bonds are built, and memories made.

Amy's mother did not bake; she drank. Her father had no car; he took taxis to airports and disappeared for months at a time. But Connie always had a stool for her to stand on, always needed brushes or palette knives passed to her. Patiently passing down her own recipes. Not for cheesecake and shortbreads, but for sketching, watercolor, and detailed illustration. Slowly, Connie shaped the raw talent of the child at her elbow into as gifted a craftswoman as she was herself.

Amy bit back her longing for those early days, and her longing to see Connie right here and now. Instead she busied herself around the studio, setting up the paper she'd stretched the night before now that it had dried and was tight as a drum. She reviewed the devil's club sketches she and Leone had singled out for the insets.

Just thinking of Leone made Amy's heart bloom, vibrant, happy, and certain in its choice. She was content with the choices she made last night, for both of them. It surprised her, this clarity to her emotions. She could see right into herself, to what she was feeling, as crystal clear as cool, reflective water.

Her intellect was more hesitant. It cautioned her to tread carefully. Reminding her she had crossed the minefield of loving Leone Garoul once before and had been blown to bits.

Amy deliberately turned her mind back to the job in hand—scaling down. Her field book was the European A4 standard she preferred working with. However, the insets were an irregular size. They had to be one eighth of the overall page to fit with the text. She would have to make a grid to reduce the scale and keep the perspective. It was the only way to make the transition between her sketch and the actual artwork correct.

The grid calculation to get the aspect ratio was a basic math formula. As Amy concentrated on the measurements, the figures began to loop in her head. She looked at her roughly penciled calculations. Déjà vu oozed up from the scrap paper she'd scribbled on. Amy frowned and studied the numbers again. They resonated somewhere in the back of her mind. She had seen these figures recently. She knew she had. Lists of numbers—Figures of?... Figures for?—The potions! The recipes! The weird measurements on her scrap paper matched the grams in Marie's brews.

Amy leapt to her feet and hurried to the almanacs. It was true. The crazy dosages in the recipes related exactly in to the grid measurements for the strange page sizes. Amy stared at the ash-filled hearth. For several long minutes she sat and thought it through over and over, casting sums around her head until her logic finally concurred with her guts.

"Oh, my God, I think I found the key."

❖

The page grid is the key? Amy sat perplexed. She had made several grids on acetate plastic using Marie's strange recipe amounts as scaling measurements. Much to her excitement she found each grid fit exactly over the marks in the illustrations. A grid made to the recipe measurements for sweet cicely had every strange little squiggle in the painting falling perfectly into the center of a grid square. It was the same for every weird plant illustration and recipe Amy could find. She knew there were untold ciphers she would never find. The almanacs went back over the years, almost forever. Lord knew how many were archived away.

Now what? She had all these squiggles sitting inside her grids... So what the hell did it mean?

Well, this is just rubbish! I thought the grid would show me words or something? She sat back and frowned. There had to be another key—one that made sense of the grid, one that told her how to use it. Typical of the sneaky Garouls not to make their code nice and easy. She knew how to get the marks off the page and onto the grid, but not how to make the grid tell her something.

Amy set the books aside in disappointment, and stood and stretched. One door opened, and another slammed shut in her face.

Enough! She needed to work. Codes and witchcraft—between the two, the Garouls were eating up too much of her time. But something was nagging her.

Leone and Marie had lied about the marks in Connie's work. Leone had lied about her bloody clothes. And Claude was very evasive about the vandalized cabin.

Amy didn't feel she could trust the Garouls anymore. Tiredness and disillusion drained every ounce of vitality from her. She had never felt so isolated in her life. Was she wrong to doubt these people? After all, they were like a second family to her. Her only real family after Connie.

That worried her, too. Connie was in their care at some mysterious retreat up north. What had really happened to her? The Garouls were definitely keeping all sorts of secrets from her. Had they a right to? Why?

The weight of the world lay heavy on her shoulders. Amy wondered if she had been too hasty in sleeping with Leone. Her common sense berated her for her emotional weakness. Had she been too carried away by cozy couches and soppy memories of teenage love? Not to mention the sharp sexual frizzante that still sparkled between them. A vintage that unfortunately only seemed to improve with age.

CHAPTER FIFTEEN

L ate into the afternoon Amy concentrated hard on finishing the final details on her insets, though for once she was not totally immersed in her art. Her mind was caught up with her latest discovery, and constantly swirled away like the colors off her brush in the water jar. It was probably this sliver of inattentiveness, of not being wholly inside her other world that made her aware something was wrong. A sustained rustling outside the studio made her sit up sharply.

She sat motionless, alert. There it was again—more than a rustling of leaves, more than the rattle of rain on the skylight, or the tapping of twigs on the shingles, more…of what?

When the prolonged screech came Amy jerked in shock, jarring the table. Water spilled over the workbench and brushes clattered onto the floor. The noise of slowly splintering wood was excruciating. It dragged on, inch by inch, like chalk on blackboard, like locomotive breaks, like agony. All along the outside of the studio.

Amy slid off her stool onto trembling legs, wide-eyed in horror. She could trace it, feel it, the length of the western wall of the studio. From one end to the other it was subjected to a slow, savage ripping. The small of her back was rammed tight against the workbench. She could follow the malicious trajectory right into the far corner—then it ceased as suddenly as it started.

Thick silence filled the air around her. Thicker and heavier than the lump in her throat. For a long time she stood frozen, waiting for whatever came next. Whatever horror could possibly come on the heels of that noise? That insane tearing? Finally, she shook herself into action, and slowly backed toward the living room door, her eyes never leaving the corner of the studio where she was certain something stood, waiting to see her reaction. Carefully, one step after another, she backed— A hard rattle came from the skylight directly above her. Amy gave a startled cry. Her head whipped up, her gaze darting across the ceiling. It was on the roof! It was trying to get in.

Amy lunged for the door. A quick fearful glance over her shoulder slowed her retreat. A branch tapped on the glass, not a creature. The wind had risen and tree branches were lashing the wooden cabin. Amy had always felt secure in this sturdy cabin, now it felt as fragile as a matchbox. Her protection was being slowly and systematically ripped to ribbons.

This had happened when Connie was here. Amy knew it beyond all doubt. It all fit together. She knew what Connie had gone through, the stalking, the attacks on her home. The terror. No wonder she had guns, no wonder she'd collapsed.

Amy turned and fled for the small dresser by the door. She pulled the drawer right out of its runners, spilling scarves and gloves out onto the floor. The Ruger shook in her hands. It felt heavy, and evil, not at all comforting.

Is it loaded? Can I shoot a bear? Or a wolf? Can I even shoot a gun? Like Connie, Amy considered herself a fisherman, not a hunter. She had never wanted to learn to shoot. In Britain there was a totally different attitude to gun ownership and it had solidified her ambivalence toward them. Weapons were not necessary in her life. But then she seldom had rabid animals trying to claw their way into her home in southwest London. Amy fumbled with the box of bullets and scattered them all over the floor.

"Shit! Shit, shit, shit…shit!" She scrabbled on her knees trying to scoop them up. "Shit."

In the rising wind, every creak and groan of the wooden cabin freaked her out. Whatever was out there could claw through the walls at any moment. Could explode through them for all she knew.

"Yoo hoo. Anyone home?"

Her hands stilled. She hadn't expected that.

Amy peeked out the window and did a double take. Virgil Bloomsy stood before the porch steps carrying a plastic shopping bag. The wind whipped his waterproof slicker around his skinny body. He seemed unconcerned that there was a marauding man-eater out there with him.

Quickly stuffing pistol, bullets, and her hysteria back into the drawer, Amy took a deep breath and opened the door.

"Mr. Bloomsy? Virgil. What on earth are you doing all the way out here?" She knew damn well what the snoopy old duffer was up to. But it didn't matter; he was there and the thing was gone. Maybe his approach scared it away. It seemed only Amy and Connie had shared the luxury of its presence.

"I really hope you don't mind. After I lock up I like to go bird-watching. I know it's private land, but so far no one has grabbed me for trespassing. And this valley is full of the most wonderful birds. Did you know there's a taiga merlin's nest up by the logging road?" He flushed with excitement at his disclosure.

"Wow, a merlin?" A quick scan over his shoulder and Amy knew the coast was clear. All her senses told her the creature, whatever it was, had gone.

"Yes. A pair of them. How rare is that? These two didn't migrate," Virgil said. "Of course, it was Connie who told me about them. Otherwise I'd never have known. Oh, that's why I'm here." He reached out the carrier bag. "The book she ordered came in late yesterday afternoon. I forgot to give it to you earlier. I hope you don't mind a private delivery, but as I was in the neighborhood, so to speak…"

Amy took the parcel and indicated he should follow her indoors. "No, not at all. Would you care for a coffee? Or there's juice, if you'd prefer."

"You know, I'd rather have a glass of cold water if that's all right with you."

Amy led him into the cabin, momentarily amused at the way his hungry stare ate up the erudite coziness of Connie's home. He fixed on the bookshelves, a ravenous glint in his eye. This was obviously his first visit here, despite his protestations at being Connie's good friend.

"My, look at this collection. It's a nature lover's paradise. So much knowledge, and so beautifully presented."

Amy smiled indulgently as she filled a glass with ice water from the fridge.

"It's a lesson to us all. Collect every book you can about the subjects you love, and care for them as if they were your babies." She brought his drink over. "And before you know it you'll have a literary summation of who and what you are."

He hadn't moved, still standing transfixed before the shelves. "If I lived here I'd never go outside again."

"Maybe that's why Connie has a reputation as a recluse. And who can blame her? She's got that beautiful valley just outside her door, and this wonderful world lining her living room. I'd never want to leave either."

"How is she?" He turned to face her now.

"Mmm, fine. She's not here. Recuperating elsewhere."

He nodded. "I suspected as much. I'm sorry. It's not my business to pry. Just…just give her my regards, please."

"I will."

He set the empty glass down on the side table beside the almanacs. The plastic grids lay askew across their covers.

"Oh. I see you're still plowing on with the ciphers?"

"Not so much now that I've begun to paint. Like I said, it's just a puzzle to while away the evenings." Amy moved toward the door to try to lure him away from her study material. He took the hint and reluctantly followed.

"I think the weather turned in your favor," she said. The wind had died down allowing a little heat for the last few hours of the day.

"Yes. I better make the most of it. Thanks for the drink."

"Thank you for delivering the book." She waved good-bye as he trudged off.

Back in the cabin Amy unwrapped the parcel he had delivered. She frowned at the book cover. It was the autobiography of a contemporary of Connie's, a man she discreetly disliked. It looked familiar. Amy wandered over to the shelves, and after a minute found Connie's copy. It was a signed gift from the artist. Why the hell would she order a book she already had, about a man she didn't even like? It was obviously a prefabricated excuse for Virgil to call in person. Which meant he knew already that Connie wasn't here.

Amy's initial annoyance at Virgil's nosiness now became alarm. *What the hell is he up to, and why is he so fascinated with Connie and that goddamned code? Just what I need, another freakin' joker in the pack.*

CHAPTER SIXTEEN

Y ou've got to let her go." Her mother's voice was hard, her eyes cold.

Leone glared back, hot and overloaded with emotion. "We're going to be okay. We're older, wiser."

"You'll hurt her."

"I'd never hurt her. I'll be careful—"

"You were meant to protect her, and you slept with her instead. How's that being careful?" Her mother's harsh question cut deep.

"She's still safe. I'll keep her safe."

"She's not safe. You've tainted her. She's like Connie."

Each was coiled tight with tension in this standoff in Marie's kitchen. On the stove one of her potions bubbled in noisy readiness.

"Here." Her mother turned and distilled the simmering brew into a flask. Leone could smell the disappointment oozing from her every pore. Her mother was tired and upset, and didn't need any more worries. A part of Leone felt guilty about bringing more stress onto her. Another, bigger part, knew Marie was wrong. This was the right time. Maybe the only time Leone would ever have.

"Take this down to the cabin." She handed Leone the flask.

Leone took it and turned to go.

"Leone," she called after her, pulling her up short at the door.

"You've got to let her go. Or they'll kill her."

❖

Back in the studio Amy mopped the water from the floor and tidied the mess on her workbench. Luckily, her work had escaped unharmed. She needed the mindless cleaning chore to steady her nerves and focus her mind.

Finally, she faced up to the inevitable and ventured outside to see what damage had been done to the studio wall. She had barely gone two steps outside the door when she saw Paulie farther up the trail. He was scanning the ground and then raising his face to the air. He didn't even notice her, he was so engrossed in whatever he was doing. She stood and quietly watched his curious behavior until he moved away, taking the same path Virgil had followed earlier.

The sight of a friendly face rallied Amy's morbid thoughts. There was always a Garoul nearby if she ran into trouble this close to home. Fortified with that thought, she trudged around to the rear of the cabin to investigate.

The wall was deeply gouged in four parallel lines. Undoubtedly claws, but whatever they belonged to had Amy flummoxed. These were not any marks she knew of. Not that she was overly experienced. There was something weird out there. Something had shadowed her in the woods, too wily to be seen, but bold enough to allow her to notice its presence. It played games with her—the fish, the stalking, and now vandalizing the studio. It was big. Far too large to be wolves or wild cats. And it was not a bear, either. Definitely not a bear. So what the hell was it?

The trees deep in the forest had been shredded. And the Garouls knew about it. Something had been locked in that cabin. Something had torn it apart trying to get out. And the Garouls knew about that, too.

Amy examined the older scars on the walls, remembering with a shudder her horror at that terrible screeching. Now she was appalled at the flimsiness of the structure between her and whatever did this. The cabin had withstood a lot of damage. How much more could it take?

Norman Johnston's bitter words rang in her ears. "There's a creature in that valley, and you all know it." Was what he said true?

Connie had endured this…this creature, time after time. The

cabin walls were testimony to that. The Garouls knew this. The Garouls knew far too much. She was sure they did. *And they told me she had a breakdown over her work? Bastards!*

❖

"Tell me the truth." Amy stood in Marie's kitchen; her hands shook where they rested on the countertop.

"About what?" Marie shook her head, confused. Her eyes were worried, but guarded.

"Connie. Is she really all right? I know it wasn't a work-related breakdown. I know she was victimized, by some sort of beast."

"Amy, I'm not sure what you're talking about." Marie began making a pot of herbal tea. "Please calm down and tell me exactly what you mean—"

"I mean her studio being practically flayed open. I was in there this afternoon and something came and used it for a scratching post. It was terrifying."

"Oh my God. Did you see what did it?"

"No. Virgil Bloomsy came along and it slid off. Good thing, too. I had Connie's gun and if I'd have seen it, it would have lead fillings in its teeth."

"What? Hold on. You had a gun? And do you mean Virgil Bloomsy the librarian? Amy, here, sip this. Let's sit down and you can start from the beginning, okay?"

Amy settled onto the couch, determined to get to the bottom of it all. Marie sat beside her, seemingly mystified at Amy's whirlwind of information. Amy sipped her tea. The fragrant warmth was calming, and she drank a little more.

"First off, is Mr. Bloomsy as big a friend of Connie's as he claims? I mean, much as I appreciated his unscheduled visit this afternoon, he sort of creeps me out." Amy needed to know more about the man.

"I've never actually met him. Connie's the one with the library card. He's not a friend as far as I know." Marie shrugged. "Connie is an acclaimed, well-respected artist. Lots of people try to worm in close, or try to violate her privacy. One arts magazine even called her a recluse because she wouldn't be interviewed."

"She is a recluse. She loves the valley and seldom leaves it. Not even for her own openings if she can avoid it." Amy frowned. Marie had to know Virgil. Elicia had been returning her library books when they went into Lost Creek together.

"And he was here in Little Dip this afternoon, hoping to visit her?" Marie asked.

"He knows she's ill. And I know he knows she's not around. He made out he was real chummy with Connie, was some sort of puzzle pal, and he delivered a book he said she'd ordered. Only it's a book she already has."

"What?"

"A book she already—"

"No. The puzzle pal bit. What do you mean?"

"Well, a puzzle pal, I suppose. I don't really know what to call it." Amy was reluctant to reveal she knew there was a code hidden in the almanacs. She was pretty goddamn certain Virgil knew it, too. But whatever secret was in there, neither Marie nor Leone was going to share it with her. Until she found out what had really happened to Connie, Amy was going to be very select in what she told the Garouls, too. She looked Marie straight in the eye.

"So what's out there, Marie? What's in the woods?"

"The forest is always dangerous, Amy. Occasionally bears come over the ridge or cougars down from the bluff. What can I say? I haven't seen anything."

"Jori has. He's seen the trees all torn up. And now Connie's cabin looks the same. It has some really old marks on it, too." Amy was upset at recalling the damage. "It must have been really scary for her." Her eyes grew moist at the thought of Connie going through the same experience she had these past few days.

"Amy, I'm going to get Claude to check out Connie's cabin. I didn't know it was being damaged. Honestly, I didn't. She didn't say a thing about it. Please believe me." Marie reached for Amy's hand. Her concern shone clearly through her words. "Tell me about Bloomsy. Why was he visiting if he knew Connie wasn't there?"

"I don't know. Just a snoopy fan, I guess. Maybe he wanted to see her cabin while she was away, and it was safe to drop by with a made-up reason. He said he bird-watches in the valley and took the opportunity to pry."

"We'll be on the lookout for him from now on, and send him on his way. We don't want strangers wandering around." Marie looked very displeased.

Amy stood and wandered over to the bookcase idly scanning the book titles. The tea had de-stressed her. She suspected that had been Marie's intention all along. It helped because it hadn't clouded her judgment. She'd been able to ask what she wanted to know. It was just that the answers hadn't been what she wanted to hear. Nothing was any clearer than it had been before.

A pig in a wimple looked out at her from the spine of a book on Hieronymus Bosch. It was the same picture as on Claude's key fob. Always with the ugly art, she mused, turning back to Marie.

"I need to head back. Tell Claude to check the back of the cabin, especially around the studio. That's where the latest mess is." She gathered her jacket and bag. "I'll have to see Connie soon, Marie. I need to, if only to reassure myself. Can't I even phone her?" She rubbed her eyes. They hurt and her head felt thick. It had been a rough day.

"I'll try and organize something, Amy. I miss her, too."

The words were spoken quietly, but brimful of emotion. Amy knew Marie and Connie's relationship was a truly loving one. She believed Marie when she said she knew nothing about the clawed-up cabin. Her distress at this news was apparent on her face. That much was true. But if Marie was using the town library, then she sure as hell knew Virgil Bloomsy.

❖

It took Amy more than a little while. The trail was not very clear, and she had to be careful not to get lost again. This was an area of the valley she was not familiar with, and nightfall was only a few hours away.

Amy had left Marie's cabin dissatisfied but determined to investigate further. There were too many things that did not ring true for her. Fortunately she had a good idea where to start—at the broken-down shack with barred windows.

She managed to emerge a couple of hundred yards upstream from the little storage cabin. Even from a distance she could see that repairs had already been made. The smashed door and the broken porch railings had been replaced. The debris that had littered the way up to the steps had been tidied away. Amy faltered. She hadn't expected this.

Carefully she approached, tallying the repairs and changes since her last visit, especially the sturdy new door with the heavy padlock. The clearing the cabin stood in was very silent, as if even the trees were holding their breath. Nothing moved, no breeze stirred the branches, no birds sang, no small creatures rustled in the undergrowth. It was deathly still, except for the crunch of her boots and the quiet gurgle of the river.

Rather than mount the steps, she wandered around to the side. The window curtains were pulled tight. She could still see the candy sitting on the sill, same as last time. The woodpile had been added to as well. It was now twice its size. She supposed if hunters used the cabin, they would use the wood for cooking and heat. Still, it was a hell of a lot of wood for a few overnight visits.

She cocked her head. Was that a noise from inside? She could have sworn she heard shuffling. Standing still, she concentrated. There it was again, a little tap, the creak of a floorboard. Someone was inside.

"Hello?" Amy said in a wobbly voice. She cleared her throat and tried again. "Anybody there?"

She was answered with a soft moan, so gentle she almost didn't believe her ears. The whimper was almost mournful.

"Who's there?" she gasped, only to be greeted with silence.

"Hello?" She moved around to the front door. It was heavy and locked and wasn't going to budge an inch. Again, there was nothing but silence on the other side of it. After several seconds Amy began to wonder if she'd imagined it all.

"Come away."

A furious Leone strode across the clearing toward her.

"Where the hell have you been all day—and I'm not coming away. There's something in there." Amy stood her ground, relieved to see Leone, then immediately uptight. Leone was striding toward her at top speed, shaking her head in exasperation. It was obvious she had no time for this.

"It's a locked-up storage cabin."

"I heard something move. It moaned."

"It's an old cabin. The wind pours through and it creaks a lot."

"Do you have a key for the lock?" Amy already knew the answer but had to ask.

"No. Come on. Claude told you this area was being hunted. You're not allowed here."

"Why is it you're all out hunting, yet none of you have rifles?"

"People have guns." Leone looked more and more determined to move her away. "Come on. I'll walk you home."

Still Amy wouldn't budge. There was nothing but silence from the cabin and she was beginning to feel a little foolish. But her stubborn streak had set in, and she was not going to go anywhere soon without a fight, or a damn good reason.

Leone's shoulders tensed. Then she sighed. "Please, Amy."

Amy considered this, and decided an apology would do, too. It was better than a fight, but not as useful as a damn good reason. There was nothing to be gained here. However, a walk and talk with Leone might reveal other things. Besides, she had missed Leone, and could see in the soft glow of Leone's eyes she had been missed, too.

"Okay. But only because you said please so nicely."

CHAPTER SEVENTEEN

When they reached Connie's cabin, Amy walked straight to the back to show Leone the mauled studio walls. Leone stood dumbfounded. Her face paled at the ferocity of the damage. Amy watched her carefully. Like Jori, she seemed to absorb something else from the scene; she looked genuinely shocked.

"We need to move you into Marie's," she said. Amy shook her head.

"No. I need to be near the studio so I can work night and day as necessary."

"You've got to—"

"I've got to get my work done to help Connie. That's all I've got to do."

"For God's sake, Amy. Look at it. You've got to move."

"No. You look at it. You sort it out. I'm staying here to work." Amy had more than enough Garoul intervention today. "From the start you told me it was nothing. You even ridiculed me. Well, I think we both know it's not 'nothing' anymore. You want to help me, Leone? To be my big, bad protector? Well, you better do a better job than you did with Connie."

Anger and accusation poured off her. She was sick and tired of it all. Tired of the evasions, the secrets, of always being on the outside of this family. She wasn't really part of them at all. It was just a silly notion she still held of home. Amy felt tears well up and almost panicked that Leone would see just how weak and scared she was. How close she was to giving up. She had very little resolve left.

Quickly, she turned and walked around to the cabin's door, leaving Leone behind.

She nearly missed the book sitting on the porch chair. She lifted it. It was heavy and very old. With growing curiosity, she admired the beautifully tooled black leather cover. It was decorated in a repeat pattern with a series of moon phases. All along the outer edge the eternal moon cycle of wax and wane was beautifully rendered in gilt, from new, to crescent, to full, and back to waning. The center panel was very strange. It portrayed an old passkey, with the body of a naked man bent double, hanging halfway through the round of the key's bow. Amy leafed through the thick, yellowing pages. It was a dictionary for a language she was unfamiliar with. It looked like an older version of modern French, but she couldn't be sure. The Garouls still used French, but an old langue d'oc dialect. This must be one of Connie's books being returned. But why leave it out here when the door was always open?

The crunch of Leone's returning footsteps coming up behind her made Amy hurry inside. Without another thought she set the book aside.

Leone followed her in.

"If you won't go to Marie's, then I'll stay here," she said.

Amy snorted. Leone was annexing her life, just like before. When would she ever learn that this Amy Fortune was not the one Leone remembered?

"Like you protected me from the snake? What are you going to do, Leone? Fuck me safe?"

Leone jolted as if slapped. Amy left her and locked herself in the bathroom to prepare for bed. As far as she was concerned, the matter was closed.

❖

Leone was gone when she returned. It didn't surprise her. There was a thin line inside Amy, garrote thin, and the moment she got anywhere near crossing it to the side of her that allowed Leone into her heart, Amy felt as if she were slowly cutting her own throat. Just one night she had spent with Leone, and less than twenty-four hours later she was at a loss with her life.

She had uncovered secrets and lies, and now Leone was trying to herd her out of her studio and bury her deeper in the mystery. Once she moved to Marie's, Amy knew Connie's place would be locked up tighter than that storage cabin, and she'd never be allowed back in. She'd never be able to access Connie or her home again. Amy would rather wait here alone with the Ruger than lose that.

The pillow was cool against her fevered thoughts. In the dark of night they spun and swirled and clamored in her head until she thought her brain would burst. Slowly, Amy tried to map them all out. Looking for links. Looking for something that made sense.

She was certain neither Leone nor Marie knew of the attacks on Connie's cabin. They had not abandoned her to this torture, and for that Amy was grateful. But for some reason Connie had kept the damage from them. Why? Like Amy, had she not trusted the Garouls? Amy sighed. There were too many locked doors in this valley.

A quiet click came from the room below. Amy's eyes flew open.

Instantly alert, she raised her head cautiously from the pillow. She had heard the door latch open. Footsteps padded quietly across the living room to the foot of her bedroom ladder.

Slowly, Amy rose to a kneeling position, scrabbling with a free hand for her makeshift snake thumper—a hockey stick, kept by her bed. The ladder creaked under the weight of her night visitor. Quietly, a rung at a time, one, two, three…coming closer. She counted each tread with rising fear. Her grip tightened. She raised the stick as a dark head slid into view. Coal black eyes looked directly up at her.

"For God's sake, Leone. I nearly decapitated you. Don't ever sneak up on me like that again."

Trembling with anger and relief, she dropped her weapon and sank onto the bed. Leone mounted the final rung and stood before her totally nude.

"Where have you been? Have you been outside naked?" Amy was astounded.

Leone shrugged.

"I've been looking around. I left my clothes downstairs." With that she lifted the blankets and slid in beside Amy.

"What the hell are you doing?"

"I'm staying here tonight."

"No, you're not."

"Yes, I am." Leone's eyes glittered fiercely. Amy puffed and spluttered and threw back the covers.

"Fine. Do what you damn well want. I'm sleeping on the couch." She swung her legs out of the bed, but before she could rise Leone's arm coiled around her waist and easily hauled her back. She was spooned against Leone. Hot breath blew past her ear.

"Don't you ever leave our bed in anger." Leone growled, then roughly tongued the rim of Amy's ear, pulling the lobe into her mouth, nipping it gently.

"Ow. How dare—" Amy's words were drowned by the rip of fabric as her T-shirt was hoisted over off her body and flung away like wrapping paper. Leone dragged Amy closer, pushing her curls aside to nuzzle a sensitive spot right behind her ear. Her hands came around to cradle Amy's breasts and begin a sensuous, squeezing massage. Amy tried to twist away, but she was pinned tight.

"Let me go."

The heat pouring from Leone's body was overwhelming. Her mouth teased and sucked at just the right places on Amy's neck. Amy couldn't stop herself; she was instantly turned on, as if programmed to respond. Leone knew her far too well. She'd loved to be cradled like this when they were first together. To be spooned from behind while Leone played with her body until she became a puddle.

Young and inexperienced, they had fumbled along until they found a way that felt all their own. Leone had been the initiator then as well as now, her stronger sex drive carrying them through hot afternoons and sweaty nights of breathless exploration. Those strong arms again curved around Amy, cupping her breasts, pressing them into the heart of Leone's palms, against the mounts of Venus and Luna, the lines of life and fate.

The slow massage flamed down to her groin. Amy moaned and pushed her buttocks back into crisp, scratchy curls. She gripped her pillow, her other hand digging into Leone's hip, pinning her closer. Leone's rumbling growls deepened in response to her touch. Amy knew the power of her own hands on Leone's flesh, too.

Leone's teeth clamped on her nape in a sucking kiss she found incredibly erotic. Her hand strayed over the curve of Amy's belly. Amy moaned as their hips undulated in a luxurious rhythm. Leone carefully circled her clitoris, stroking with tender pressure. It was a knowing touch. Amy pushed into the hand. Their hips danced in sweaty harmony, the air thick with whispered breaths and sighs and that deep rolling hum that reverberated in Leone's throat when she was totally blissed.

Leone carefully increased the pressure, gliding through the silky wetness, cresting the tiny, super-sensitized organ, and matched Amy's excited hip sway. Thoroughly in control, she reveled in texture, scent, and sound. Amy's body sang for her with deep moans of pleasure. Amy pulsed against her, rolling along the length of her body.

Time fell away for Leone, as if all the long years of waiting no longer mattered, had never even existed. This was where Amy was meant to be. This was natural and right. Leone held her with hands and thighs and teeth, biting her shoulder, arm, the nape of her neck. Tasting, owning, marking. Letting the world know Amy was hers.

Amy rolled against the lean body spooning her. Leone had always been the perfect lover for her. Even as nervous teenagers their rhythm fit, their chemistry so complementary, so complete. She felt her clitoris swell under Leone's touch, her breasts full and heavy, tingling at the warm and addictive pleasure pouring through her.

"Mmmm, so good," she moaned, trying to twist onto her back. She needed to touch Leone, too. Needed to see her, to connect with her. Leone growled and held her in place.

"I want to see you. I want to watch your face," Amy whispered and tried to turn again.

Instead Leone rolled her onto her belly. The dry warmth of Leone's skin flowed across Amy's back like desert sand; her long hair trailed silken shivers across her heated flesh.

Leone dropped delicious licks and nips down her spine, slowly kissing toward the flare of her hips. There she stopped, resting a cool face on the curve of Amy's buttocks. Her arm snaked in under Amy's waist, holding her tight. Amy raised her head to try to face her. The grip on her waist tightened pinning her in place. She lay totally still, her entire body goosefleshed as hot breath caressed her bottom, and listened to the deep breaths of Leone inhaling the intimate curve of her flesh. *This is different...this is very, very different. I'm not sure about this...*

Amy was experienced. She'd had many lovers. After all, she was a healthy, young woman. But she was shy about this. Uncertain. There had only ever been the one time, with one lover. An act of sensual discovery. That lover was lying with her again tonight.

A low, hungry growl reverberated against her cheek as if to confirm the memory. Leone had always led the way, could never get enough. When she was younger Amy used to think Leone's passion would swallow her whole. Now it pinned her to the bed in turmoil.

Gingerly, she tried to move but found herself trapped by Leone's strength and weight.

"Leone?" she said quietly, then expelled a sharp gasp as her ass was roughly snuffled and nipped.

"Leone." Amy tried to jerk away, squirming. Several more nipping kisses covered both her butt cheeks, and a deeper growl commanded her to keep still. All uncertainty at Leone's intentions was stripped away as her crease was parted and a thick tongue run along its entire length. Amy's head kicked back, and she gave an involuntary whimper. The tongue laved her again and again, and suddenly she was back there, in the past, drowning in the dizziness of Leone's power and sexual energy, her body enslaved with every lusty act of worship carried out upon it.

Amy tried to clench but immediately Leone pushed deeper, this time concentrating solely on her anus, worrying it and rimming it firmly. Amy's skin prickled, her nerves leapt and quivered. Her mind screamed disapproval of this animalistic act, but her body was more than eager to embrace the sensations dancing along every nerve ending. Wriggling under the attention only increased the grip on her waist and the ferocity of the investigating tongue. Her weak attempts to pull away seemed to excite Leone into delivering more punishing nips and bites across her buttocks. All were designed to make Amy twitch and squirm deliciously.

Amy's face burned at the hot breath on her intimate flesh. Her heart hammered, fueled by her moral dismay, and a volcanic heat burned in her groin.

Leone's free hand wormed between her thighs and unerringly found her clitoris, which much to Amy's disbelief was incredibly plump and erect, totally connected to this new sexual high.

"Leone," she managed to blurt before the practiced fingers began to thrum. "Oh, God."

She was being cleverly played by a knowing lover. These hands knew her body, remembered it well. The sly tongue knew even more. It knew secrets even Amy was unaware of. Her thighs splayed, offering more of herself to the questing fingers, pushing her ass higher into the hungry mouth. She was panting now, her burning face buried in the pillow, clutching the sheet, her entire body rolling on Leone's tongue and fingertips. Her mind was spinning like a tossed coin. Orgasm tore her apart without warning, and she screamed into the pillow—another thing she had only ever done with Leone. No one else could make her cry out like a lost and wounded animal.

Finally, she lay belly down, stunned and gasping, trying to recover her breath. Leone rose and straddled her. Large hands squeezed her buttocks together firmly as Leone ground her own wet, aching need into her. She came quickly and quietly, after just a few short strokes, grunting Amy's name softly into the dark.

Leone lay sated and relaxed, looking over contentedly at her panting, prostrate partner. Amy managed to roll onto her back with great effort, and Leone reached over to brush the damp curls from her forehead.

"Never leave our bed again. Don't you know you're mine?" she said.

"Yours?"

"Mine. All mine. I love you. I always have. I've never stopped." Leone played with another stray curl. Amy reached up and stilled her hand.

"That's our past, Leone, not our future. I don't want to be owned. I want us to be lovers. Real people, who share, and talk openly and honestly, not ghosts from some unresolved past."

"You're my mate. You always have been." Leone's face tightened.

"We're lovers, Leone. There's no rejection here. We've been down this road before, and we both know where it can end. I'm here for a few weeks' contract, and to see how Connie is. Then I'll go back to London and my life. Let's just see where this takes us over time."

"Why are you denying this? You can't leave. Have you been talking to Marie or Connie? How can you take their side? Can't you see we're meant to be together?" Leone sat up, agitated.

Amy scooted upright, too. She leaned back against the headboard, drawing the sheet up over her chest.

"Leone, I need to go slow. I was hurt all those years ago. I lost so goddamn much. Confidence, self-esteem, trust in my own emotional decisions—and it wasn't as if I had that much to start out with. I lost you as my best friend. I lost you as my first love. In a way I even lost this valley, a place where I felt safe, and loved, and protected. I felt as if I'd lost my home. I was young, and losing you exploded my whole world in so many ways back then. But I can't afford for that to happen again. The sex between us is fantastic, it always was, but it's not going to be all there is."

"My world exploded, too. They sent me away. They said we were too young. That I was bad for you." Leone floundered, the explanation drying up in her mouth. Guilt poured out of her. She ached for this to be right. To be able to make it right, but years of waiting had not prepared her for this conversation. It had popped up in the wrong place at the wrong time. Leone couldn't explain—not yet.

"They?"

"Marie and Connie. I went to Vancouver and you went to college in London. They wanted us apart. You know the rest."

"Marie and Connie sent us away. To stop us being together? But why? We were young, but we weren't that stupid. We were doing no one any harm. Why did they do that?" Amy was genuinely hurt at this revelation. There had to be some reason behind it. Marie and Connie were not hurtful, domineering people. Amy knew as a child she had been cared for, in fact, practically raised, by both of them. Their disapproval made no sense.

Leone looked away. Amy could see her intense unhappiness. She placed a hand on the tanned shoulder.

"Leone, why did you ask if I'd been speaking to Connie? How could I? She's in the retreat." The shoulder stiffened under her touch.

"I...I meant earlier. Years ago. I wondered if you'd ever discussed it. That's what I meant." She looked defeated, miserable, and angry. Amy wanted to hold her in her arms and make all the hurt go away, but they had to have this talk. This was their new foundation. She was determined if they had any chance at all they had to talk now. She also knew if she reached out to comfort Leone they would be thrashing all over the bed again, avoiding the main issue. It was Leone's way of old, to hide in lust and hope all those unspoken emotions would simply sort themselves out.

"Tell me the truth about last night," Amy said. Leone whipped around to face her, eyes guarded.

"The truth?"

"About you and Claude hitting the deer. About why you were covered in blood? I was driving his truck today, and it's fine."

"I never said it was Claude's truck. We were in Robért's. He's taken it to the shop to get hammered out." The answer was too quick, too glib. Amy tried to remember the exact words of last night's conversation and gave up. She knew she was being lied to. Her heart shrank. She tried again.

"Then tell me about the anniversary almanac you're planning with Connie. Why does it need those strange marks all over the illustrations?"

Leone's face became a hard, defensive mask. "You want to be told a lot about other people's business. Why don't you tell me about your work? How much have you done, if any? I see you everywhere you shouldn't be. Ignoring my advice and my orders. Have you done any work between your childish acts of autonomy?"

Amy bristled. "You're attacking me and my work? My work? You shit—"

"Very professional, Amy." Leone flew out of the bed and headed for the ladder.

"What? You started an argument and now you're leaving? What happened to not leaving our bed in anger?"

Leone kept moving, ignoring her.

"Typical of you—make a run for it when talking has to be done." Amy was furious. "Is this our future? Is this us communicating? Is this your friggin' protection? Fuck and run."

Amy was up on her knees shouting at Leone's back before she dipped down the ladder and out of sight. Leone spun around and in a flash was crouched on the bed beside her, nose to nose. Her eyes glittered with anger. Her lips pulled back into a snarl, her breath heavy with Amy's sex scent.

"Yes, Amy. We fuck. Fucking is what we do because you won't call it love."

Before Amy could blink she had turned and practically leapt down the ladder. She flung open the door and walked naked into the night with a bitter parting shot. "And if fucking is all you want, I can do that for you, too."

Amy watched her go, dismayed at the morass they had descended into after such intense intimacy. She blushed at the memory of what they had just done. It would be so easy to see the sexual tsunami they were surfing as an indicator of their emotional state. Leone certainly saw it that way. But it was not so for Amy. Leone was too forceful in bed. Too quick to grab at the pleasure and try to avoid the painful self-examination they both had to make. Leone was erotic and animalistic. She saw love as heart-numbing, mind-bending sex, not the complicated mix of trust and compromise it actually was.

Amy had the audacity to want more, to demand more. She wanted truth and honesty, not just a climactic high that for one brief, existential moment wiped away all the worries of the world. She wanted a real, hard-won, forever love—but only if Leone was going to fight for it alongside her.

If Amy was going to buy into a happy-ever-after story, she was damn well going to write the ending herself.

CHAPTER EIGHTEEN

Amy slept in the following morning. Heavy overnight rain and the satisfied hum of her body lulled her into a deep and desperately needed sleep. It was too miserable outside for fieldwork; today she was studio bound.

Taking time for domestic chores, she threw some clothes into the washer. In the pocket of her jeans she found her lucky bullet. *Maybe it's a bad idea to have live ammunition in your pocket.* The wash cycle hummed along as she examined her tiny lucky charm. Was it tipped with silver? How bizarre. A silver bullet. In the movies the whole casing had to be silver to kill the werewolf. Was this another of Connie's charms from the Wicca book? At least it explained the smelter in the studio. Amy giggled; if she dug deep enough she was bound to find a spell that said you needed a dozen of these, and the blood of a mermaid.

Was it even a real bullet? Could you mess around artistically with live ammunition, adding decorative embellishments? Why not engrave them: "With Love," or "Surprise."

Amy snorted and fetched the Ruger Bearcat. The bullet slid home happily. *Well, there you go*. She emptied the chamber and left the gun on the mantel, dropping the bullet in her jacket pocket where it hung by the door. It was still significant to her. Maybe even charmed? She would keep it for luck. Though she scoffed, she was uneasy with her discovery. Amy didn't like it that Connie was into witchcraft and playing with silver bullets. It seemed so unlike her stoic aunt. Was all this related to the code, too?

The code now firmly back in her thoughts, Amy pulled the mysterious book from last night down from the shelf. Something about its cover played on her mind. She stood turning the heavy handmade tome in her hands. The cover art was beautiful, if not a little macabre. What was pulling her? She examined the entire book. Whatever it was it was not registering on her consciousness.

With a dissatisfied sigh she began to slide the book back into its new home. Again, she paused. The spines on the bookshelf all blended into one another in a colorful mass. Amy stood and waited for her thoughts to clear. This often happened to her when her head was elsewhere, buried in the details of an illustration, or in this case the mechanisms of a cipher. She knew from past experience all she had to do was stand still, and whatever was tugging at her mind would slowly materialize. Sometimes it was something as silly as the laundry dial needed setting. Other times she had maybe forgotten to make a call to the bank, or had a dental appointment. A few times she had nearly missed a lunch date with friends. If she relaxed and cleared her head the answer would come to her. Something was bugging her, but what?

A little pig in a wimple sat on the spine of a Bosch art book, the twin of Marie's copy. Hieronymus Bosch? Amy frowned. The pig was from the Hell section of his Garden of Earthly Delights triptych. A painting that was everywhere in Little Dip. She'd seen it on Claude's key fob, Marie's wall, and Leone's screensaver. She'd even noticed it emblazoned on a T-shirt across Paulie's skinny chest.

Amy stilled with the new book not quite slotted into place. The naked man hanging through the passkey on its cover. That was Bosch symbolism if ever she saw it. It was certainly his style.

She pulled out the Bosch art book. Its dustcover was a detailed rendition of part of his famous Garden triptych. Spreading the cover out on the table, she was better able to look at the painting in detail. There he was, the man halfway through the key, in Hell, poor bastard—The key! Halfway through the key! She was halfway through the code. The book was the halfway point. It was so obvious. Now that she saw it, she felt incredibly stupid.

With trembling hands she fetched the acetate grid she had used to scale down her artwork and that also matched Marie's bizarre recipe amounts. The same grid, that when placed over Connie's illustrations had each mysterious mark falling dead center of a square. But that was all she had found—something had been missing, a second key to make sense of it all. Now it was here in her hands. A book in an ancient language. It had been secretly gifted to her last night. She had an ally. Someone wanted her to break the code and find the Garoul secret.

The Garden of Earthly Delights was the third element of her cipher. Somehow it was the link between the almanacs and the langue d'oc dictionary. Amy frowned at the dust jacket on the table before her. Her artist's eye sized up the book cover with the grid. It wasn't a good fit. This was the wrong rendition of the painting. The scale was incorrect and parts were cut away to fit in with the book design.

Amy needed a full copy set in the original dimensions. Only that would match up properly. And she knew just where to find one.

In Marie's office.

❖

The rain did not let up for her walk down to the compound.

"Yo, Amy. Don't tell me you're out working in this?" Jori met her halfway across the central clearing.

"Hi, Jori. No, I'm working indoors today with all the sensible people. Is Marie around?"

"Leone drove her into Covington. Time to stock up the larder."

This was good news; a larder run to the largest nearby town's food markets was practically an all-day chore. Hopefully, she'd have more than enough time to try out her theory on the print over Marie's desk.

"Okay. I'm going to do some work over at her place. I'll catch up with you and Elicia later."

The first thing on the agenda was to make sure her guess was right and the Bosch triptych was part of the overall code. With the painting laid out on Marie's big cedar table, Amy pulled the acetate grid from her backpack. She carefully aligned it with the edges of the actual print, not the frame.

It fit.

Amy held her breath; several painted figures now fell neatly into some of the squares, just as the marks had done. She peered closely at them. They were the weird hybrid animals, half-man, half-fish, fowl, dog, boar, wolf, whatever misfit Bosch had imagined. Amy was unsure what they were meant to represent, they were all so fantastical. She did know that every depiction of a human hybrid, half-man half-beast, fell into the center of a grid square as if prearranged to do so.

"I know what I'm looking for. I know how to break the code," she whispered in awe to the empty room.

Borrowing an almanac from Marie's library, Amy opened it to an illustration with embedded sigils. Laid over Connie's illustration, each mark fell within a square. Gently, she traced each mark onto the acetate grid with a soft lead pencil.

Next she placed the marked grid over the print of Bosch's painting. As it was a triptych, she had three choices. She set it on the first panel, The Garden of Eden, Bosch's representation of creation. Nothing matched up. The traced sigils marked on the plastic grid did not align with any figure or structure in this panel of the triptych.

She tried again with the central panel, The Garden of Earthly Delights, depicting mankind's activities on earth. This time a few of the marked squares fell over particular painted figures—the man-beasts. These sigils she transferred to a blank sheet of paper, positioning each as accurately as it was on the grid.

Finally, she moved onto the last panel, Hell, a grim and gory chaos. Several more fantastical human hybrids filled the remaining marked squares. They too were transferred to the writing paper in the positions they were found in.

Now she had a sheet of paper dotted with sporadic squiggles. It still made no sense, but there were probably hundreds of other marks hidden throughout all the almanacs. At best she would only ever find a few to decode.

"So basically, a mark in the illustration is only used if it lines up with something in the Bosch painting. That's the key. That's all there is to it?" Amy was skeptical. It seemed far too easy now that she had all the elements before her. But then, she supposed that's how codes worked. They were easy to use once you had the keys.

The other plant illustrations Amy knew about gave her marks that related to different hybrid figures in the painting. Now they too drifted across her paper pad. Some floated in space; others snuggled up close to each other, forming rough alphabetical letters.

Amy foraged through Marie's almanacs and found a few more marks in the illustrations of Solomon's seal, mandrake, Belladonna, cowslip—all from different years, and all in Connie's work. How long had the Garouls been doing this? She had no idea how far back it went, but believed probably since the beginning of the Press. Maybe even since the time of Hieronymus Bosch?

Her head ached. Her eyes were tired and dry. She had barely half a page with a few words and half-formed sentences sprinkled here and there, and all in a nonsense language.

It was late in the day and she didn't want to be here when Leone and Marie returned. She was not prepared to confront them with this until she knew exactly what she was decoding. It could be a recipe for steamed fish for all she knew.

She was thirsty and went to fetch a glass of water from the kitchen. Marie had been partway through a recipe before she'd left. Idly, Amy examined the dried and fresh herbs sitting out on the bench. Henbane, juniper berries, and white wine. In the right quantities, and in the hands of an expert, this infusion would be a strong and very effective painkiller. A quick glance at the recipe notes amazed Amy. This was a whopper dose. Even a layman like her could see that a spoonful would flatten a horse. She stood and glared at the pan and its contents. What was the point of making such strong potions? Who were they for, and what good could they do?

Baffled, she headed back to the office to tidy up. She could do no more here. She had used all the secret marks she knew of in Connie's work and had not even a paragraph to show for it. Once she'd straightened up, she decided to head back to Connie's cabin. She needed to stop and think. She was so close…she could feel it. But close to what?

❖

The heavy overcast weather had not lightened any. In fact, it looked like a storm was approaching fast. At least the rain had ceased, making the walk back a little easier.

Halfway home, and deep in the forest, a mournful howl rang out, rooting her to the spot. Its echo ricocheted through the trees, giving her no idea where it originated from, except that it was close by.

The hackles on the back of her neck rose and the blood drained from her face down to her toes, rooting her to the spot. Was the prowler back? She looked around anxiously, but all was quiet. Eerily quiet. Amy quickened her pace, wishing home were closer. A second stricken howl curdled her stomach. This one was filled with pain. With no hesitation, Amy broke into a steady jog.

The last curve in the track opened up onto the small clearing before Connie's cabin. There she skidded to a halt. Blood was splashed over the porch steps. Her door lying wide open. A trail of wet crimson led into the cabin.

"Oh, crap." Cautiously, she approached; the only other option was to run away into a forest filled with howling wolves. It was best to get indoors and quickly, providing indoors was safe. And there was only one way to find out.

She slowly mounted the porch and peered with trepidation into the gloomy interior. There was a lot of blood. This was not a small creature. She thought of the elk hanging gutted in the tree, and the snake burrowed in her bed. Had something decided this was now its pantry and left a tasty morsel for her to find?

A moan from inside made her jump back a few feet. Then she surged forward; it was a human cry. It was Paulie!

"Paulie! Oh God, Paulie. What's happened?" She fell on her knees beside the naked youth. He was semiconscious and his body was shaking, she assumed from shock and blood loss. He was covered in blood. She dragged a blanket off the couch to cover him, to keep him warm, and scrabbled to remember her first aid lessons.

She had to get help. A series of howls sang out the length and breadth of the valley. More cries than she could ever recall hearing. How many wolves were out there? It creeped her out. Amy didn't want to leave Paulie here like this, but how was she going to get help? She needed to draw attention to the cabin.

She grabbed the revolver from the mantel and checked that the chamber was loaded. She ran out to her front porch. Aiming in the air, she pulled the trigger. Shots rang out sharply into the darkening sky, making their own echo down the valley. That had to get the attention of any Garoul in the vicinity. The howling immediately ceased. That unnerved her, too.

Back in the room she knelt beside Paulie. He had passed out. With a handful of soaked dish towels, she washed the blood off his face and body, trying to see what damage was underneath. His face was unhurt. Most of the blood must be from his other wounds. She cleaned his shoulder. It had a nasty series of slashes. His hands were unharmed, just very bloody. She wiped them clean. In fact, apart from the wounds on his shoulder, he was relatively unharmed. So where had all the blood come from?

A shadow filled the open doorway. She looked up to see Claude. She was relieved he had arrived so soon.

He knelt beside her, examining Paulie with deft efficiency.

"It's his shoulder. It looks bad, but I don't think it's all his blood. His wound is just seeping now," Amy said. Claude nodded and wrapped the blanket tighter around Paulie, easily lifting him into his arms. Paulie moaned, starting to come around.

"It's okay, son. You did good," Claude murmured. Turning to Amy, he said, "Yeah, you're right. It is superficial. I'm taking him to Marie. She has all the stuff I need to fix him up."

Amy stood, ready to go with them. "Aren't you going to get a doctor?"

"Marie and I can see to this."

"But he's been attacked. We need to get him to a hospital."

"Marie's a doctor, remember? She may not practice anymore, but she can look after Paulie." Claude was adamant.

Amy was confused. This was important. Paulie was hurt. Marie had given up medicine years ago to take over the Garoul Press from her own mother, just as Leone had taken over from her. Surely Marie would want Paulie to go to the hospital?

"But—"

"Amy. Let it be." Claude was turning away with Paulie in his arms. "I know what I'm doing. It's just shock. His body is in overload and has shut down. I have to go now, okay?"

Amy silently held the door open for him to pass through. Now was not the time to ask more questions about overloads and shutdowns, but she was hurt at being excluded.

She watched him disappear down the track. The Garouls always closed ranks on her: first over Connie, then the code, and now Paulie. But then Amy had always been the outsider; even as a child she had been aware of it. She used to put it down to the fact she came and went every vacation. Or that she wasn't really blood kin. But most of the younger Garouls came and went for the summer months, too. And Marie was Connie's partner, and had been like an adopted aunt to Amy.

Amy knew her excuses were threadbare. On some deep, unfathomable level she had been kept on the outer edges of this family and its secrets. The real question was how could she feel so connected lying in Leone's arms, yet so isolated in the real world of this valley?

Amy filled a pail with soapsuds and sluiced down her floor and porch steps. She was incredibly upset. She liked Paulie and was distressed he had been hurt. The wounds in his shoulder had been jagged and vicious. Deep, lacerating claw marks that reminded her of the marks on the trees, and on the studio wall. And that made her shudder.

❖

It was late afternoon when she finally curled up on her couch with her piece of paper and its curious drift of letters and half-formed foreign words. The day had taken its toll and she was listless and defeated. The dancing flames in the fireplace mesmerized her, so much so that she had to physically shake herself to get up and actually do something before the day slid away.

Instead of heading for the studio as she half expected to, she found herself pulling the passkey book from the shelf. She returned to the couch and began a painstaking search for her partially completed words in the langue d'oc dictionary. Slowly, she translated her marks and squiggles, guessing at some of the words and crude lettering. She worked for hours until finally she could do no more.

Then she sat back in the mellow glow of her reading lamp, and with disbelieving eyes read, over and over, her half-formed sentences.

> *You are Garoul. Honored are you in the sacred groves of Gaul. Feared by Rome, the voices of Celtica sing your name...*
>
> *O Keeper of the Beast within...*
> *...the moon is in thine eye and all shall...*
> *Long may you hunt...and...the mountain. Long may you walk among man.*

CHAPTER NINETEEN

Keeper of the Beast? She read the words over and over until her eyes swam. A beast? Of course there was a beast. She knew that. She'd known all along, but was just too stupid to actually accept it.

The Garouls locked it away in the old storage shack—except for the times it broke free and ran amok in the valley, ripping up trees, and elk, and Paulie? Her eyes widened as she thought about the claw marks on Paulie's shoulder.

At the storage cabin she had been aghast at the destruction. The door hanging off its hinges, furniture broken and strewn across the floor. But the curious cutesy curtains? Was that an attempt to give a prison some comfort?

Amy jolted. The cherry candy on the windowsill? Connie had been in that cabin. Connie had known!

What had she known? She must have been trying to break the code, too. Had she stumbled across it during her work for the Garouls and investigated the beast for herself? Was that why they had taken her away? Or had it attacked her like it had attacked Paulie?

Amy leapt to her feet in panic. Connie had realized her work was part of an elaborate code. And being Connie, she had set out to break it. Amy recalled Virgil; the prim librarian had sidled up to her every time she looked at the code books on his shelves. His interest bordered on downright nosiness. Had he really been a puzzle buddy to Connie all along? A secret ally she had kept from the Garouls?

Was he helping her with the code? It all made sense. Someone had left the langue d'oc book as a clue for her. And it appeared after Virgil's visit.

Connie had disappeared, and Virgil didn't know who he could trust anymore. He had to find out if Amy was friend or foe. That's why he was always snooping around. Could Virgil tell her what had really happened to Connie? He must have some idea what was going on.

Certain in her course of action, Amy grabbed her jacket and headed out the door. It was late, but if she gunned it she might get to Lost Creek before the library closed. She jogged down to the parking lot and made straight for Claude's truck. Thankfully, his keys were tucked under the visor where she'd left them,

Amy took the turn for Lost Creek and sped along the dirt track as fast as she was able, throwing up plumes of dust and grit. It was a single-track road with frequent cut-outs for a vehicle to pull over and let another pass, and coming toward her was Leone's truck. She could clearly see Leone and Marie in the front seat, returning from their larder run, looking back at her in surprise. Amy kept up her speed. She knew if she capitulated first and pulled up into a passing bay Leone would stop alongside her to snoop, and then doubtless interfere and try to boss her around.

Determined, Amy hogged the road ahead in a bizarre game of chicken, not slowing down at all. With confused faces Leone and Marie pulled over and Amy blew by without so much as a glance, eyes fixed firmly ahead. She could feel Leone's glare burning into her, but she drove past, relieved the little confrontation had so easily gone her way. By the time Leone had driven Marie to the compound and found out about Paulie, Amy would be in Lost Creek getting her answers at last.

❖

There was a light on in the office window when Amy skidded to a halt outside the library. Frantically, she rapped on the door. A dim light lit the hallway, and a bolt slid with a loud metallic snap. A few more rattles and clicks followed before Virgil Bloomsy opened the door a crack and squinted out.

"Amy?" he said in sharp surprise.

"I'm sorry to disturb you, but can I come in?" Her request was so urgent he didn't hesitate to open and let her enter. Deftly he locked it behind her in a reverse series of clunks and clicks. He seemed very nervous.

"Are you okay, Virgil?" Amy picked up on his twitchiness.

"Yes, thank you. A little stiff with all this rain." He indicated the barred door. "I'm just security conscious. I like everything locked up nice and tight." He smiled weakly.

I bet you do. She thought he looked tired and pale, but decided not to comment on his discomfort. After all, he had no idea who or what she represented as far as the Garouls were concerned. He was probably taking a real risk letting her in at all.

"I'm sorry to call so late. I know you're heading home for the night, but I needed to talk to someone." She moved to the reception desk. Virgil followed. He moved stiffly and was watching her warily. "Actually, I needed to talk to you."

"What's the matter, Amy? You sound very upset."

"I broke the code. I know what it means—well, some of it. Just a few lines, to be exact."

He stood in stunned silence.

"I'm guessing you and Connie were working on it together when suddenly she just disappeared. Am I right?" she said.

"You broke the code?" Virgil was still digesting this news. He gave a small, mystified shake of his head.

"It wasn't that difficult once I figured out the keys. There were three of them, so it was a little more complex. It's like a combination, each key points to the next, and all three unlock the code."

"Three keys."

"Yes, the almanac illustrations that Connie already knew about. The langue d'oc book that you had. I guessed it was you who left it for me. I knew I had outside help. And I figured out the third by myself—the Bosch painting."

"Bosch?"

"The Garden of Earthly Delights." Amy nodded, impatient to get to her point. "I need to know what happened to Connie. I know they have a beast hidden away in the valley. Some sort of monster." She hoped he would trust her. "Virgil, tell me everything you now about Connie, right up to her disappearance."

She could see the shadows flit over his face. He was still hiding something, holding back. Unsure. They stood in silence for a second while he thought things through and Amy silently pleaded with him to trust her. To tell her the truth.

Then sighing so deeply his shoulders sank, he said, "I killed her."

Amy watched his lips curl into a thin, cold smile. His words sounded as if they came from underwater, spoken to her in slow motion. Her body went numb. She floated out the top of her head and watched herself…and him, from a distant point somewhere in the library rafters. Connie was dead. Connie was dead. Connie was dead.

"…and after the wolf eats grandma, silly Little Red Riding Hood arrives. Talk about life echoing fiction." He was still talking. Always talking, always sounding so smug.

Her Connie was dead. He'd killed her. And now he was standing before her talking about nursery stories?

"Beware false prophets who come amongst you in sheep's clothing, for inwardly they are ravening wolves." Virgil had moved on to sermons now. Amy pulled back her fist and with all her anger punched him square on the nose.

It popped under her knuckles with a satisfying crunch. Blood spurted over his chin and shirt. He screamed in pain and surprise. Amy took another wild roundhouse swing for his head. He ducked, but she managed to cuff his ear. Then she faltered. His sharp cry had mutated into something else, something feral that froze her. He snarled—a nasty, sly snarl.

His eyes gleamed eerily up at her from his defensive crouch. His hands holding his bleeding nose looked hooked and horrible.

"Bitch!" he spat through a mouthful of blood. "I'm going to mail you to Leone Garoul, piece by piece. Starting with your cunt."

Amy stumbled back, startled at the poison pouring from his mouth. He was clawing at his clothes, wrestling them off as if they were on fire. She could see bloodstained, badly wrapped bandages across his scrawny chest. He'd been hurt. His chest was wet from the nosebleed she had given him, and he was slobbering copiously in thick, oily cords. And rank—he smelled rank. Werewolf. The Beast was a werewolf. And it was Virgil Bloomsy. Connie had found him out! Her mind screamed at her to run, but her feet were glued to the floor.

Amy recoiled at his slow, ugly mutation. His face distorted and twisted. His jaw thickened and elongated in wretched crunches and creaks. Teeth tore at his lips, much too sharp, all wrong for the shape of his human mouth. Except it wasn't quite a human mouth anymore, it was pulling and twisting all out of shape. Cheek skin stretched like rubber, close to tearing. His head shook and shook, as if full of bees; his spittle and bloody mucus flew like water off a dog's pelt, spattering her face—and waking her out of her horrified trance.

She ran for the door, but it was barred with bolts and chains, and slides and locks. She had little time. Whatever it was he was turning into he was nearly all of it. This was his only moment of weakness. These were perhaps her last moments on earth and she wanted to make them count. Amy threw all her body weight on the nearest section of shelves and pushed them over onto Virgil's crouched, convulsing body with an enormous clattering crash.

Lightweight as they were, they still hurt when they hit him. His bellowing roar was little satisfaction. She changed course and ran to the rear of the library where she knew the fire exit was probably her only chance. Behind her came loud bangs and thuds. She glanced back to see the bookshelf cast aside like broken twigs. He was free of it. On the wall opposite, his shadow rose from crouch to full standing. He was vile in silhouette, with a stooped, shivering back and a stubby, twisted muzzle. His sloping forehead ran up into low pointed ears. His whole body pulsed with excited savagery, quivering with bloodlust, like a dog on the scent of an easy kill. Amy knew in her gut all his kills were easy. His whole posture screamed to her of a craven coward wrapped in the body of a malicious bully. She would not let him win; she would never let him win. Not after Connie. She would fight him to her dying breath. She would hurt him before she died.

"I can smell you. I can smell Garoul all over you. Whore. Like Connie—a Garoul whore." His voice was dry and raspy. He moved slowly, limping. Amy realized he had not fully changed. Perhaps he was too weak from his earlier fight. She had no doubt he was responsible for Paulie's injuries, and that Paulie had landed some telling blows of his own. She also realized this was another advantage. Virgil was prowling, threatening and taunting her because he couldn't chase after her and tear her to shreds.

He would try to corner her, to terrify and intimidate her, but he had overlooked one thing. Her hatred for him. He had killed Connie and she hated him more than she cared to live.

"Do you go down all fours? Does she mount you from behind—"

Her answer was to elbow the fire alarm glass, the smash setting off a shrill bell. Low emergency lighting flickered, casting an eerie green glow over the darkened aisles. It was a risk. There were two alarm buttons in the library—which one would he turn to? And could she slink away in time if he chose hers? It was worth it, though, because now he knew a bright blue light was flashing on the front of the building and the county fire department had been alerted.

As if to underscore her gamble, the telephone began to ring. Probably an automated response from the emergency switchboard over in Covington, but it would pile pressure on him. Remind him the real world was just outside the door, and soon it would be knocking, wanting in.

Luckily, he chose the far corner and the wrong alarm. She darted to an adjoining aisle and hurled herself against another shelf, tipping it over onto him. Adrenaline buzzed in her veins, giving her that extra edge, that extra meanness she needed to attack back. But he was quick and caught this one. Books cascaded off the shelves, but he held on to the framework and simply flipped it back at her with easy strength. Except that she had already slipped away, disappearing into the maze of bookshelves.

"Thank you for the code, Amy. After you share it with me— and you will—I will know all the Garoul secrets, and I can take everything away from them. You are so much more cooperative than your aunt. She wouldn't share at all."

He was getting desperate; she could hear it in his voice. Time was running out for him and he knew it. Soon the place would be crawling with people. All she had to do was avoid him, but the library was cramped, and shrinking by the minute. She wasn't allowing him to outmaneuver her, but eventually she would run out of places to hide. Guilt washed over her that she'd been so stupid to trust him. How could he be the beast the Garouls served to protect? It made no sense.

Amy hadn't time to wonder. She had to keep moving.

"No. Connie wouldn't share at all. Not even when I bit her." He continued to bait her, hoping she'd give away her position. But Amy was literally one step ahead.

"She screamed, Amy. She was so scared...and in so much pain."

He was slithering closer. She could smell him, that funk that oozed through the patchy, greasy fur on his chest, back, and genitalia. He wasn't aware of it. He probably lived with the stench every chance he could, sliding through the Garoul valley like an evil little skunk. She quietly and carefully unhooked a fire extinguisher and slid farther way from him and his callous taunting. How he didn't hear her heart thumping she never knew. To her ears it sounded like a turbine engine roaring, fueled on hate and anger.

"She was in terrible pain. And, Amy? It wasn't quick."

Rescue was taking too long. She hated him. A deliberate rap with her toe drew his attention to where she was hiding. Positioning herself carefully at the end of an aisle, she raised the canister like a baseball bat, ready to deliver the biggest Dry Powder surprise of this bastard's life. She waited, alert, sure he had been tricked by her tapping. Anxiously, she kept an eye on first the right-hand aisle, then the left. Quiet, it was too quiet. So, he'd decided to finally shut up? That's how she knew he was creeping up on her.

The tiniest scratch, a little creak—and she knew. He was coming for her over the top of the shelves. Sliding along the row above where she stood, hoping to surprise her by dropping on her from up high.

Well, Amy Fortune had a few surprises, too. With shaking hands she loosened the nozzle and waited. The stink increased as he drew closer. She waited. Stern, composed, and terrified, but patient, she waited. Finally, with one last tiny scrape, the top of his matted head peeked over the shelf above her. She raised her canister and blasted the suffocating dry powder straight into his eyes. The harsh rasp of the extinguisher couldn't quite drown out Virgil's outraged squeal. He clawed at his burning eyes.

Adrenaline pumping, Amy threw her full weight into this shelf and toppled it with Virgil scrabbling blindly on top. He hit the floor in an ugly heap. Amy fled for the rear fire door, running for her life. Time was up, no more hiding; she had a few precious moments to get out of the building. Hopefully, there would be a fire engine in the middle of Main Street, along with all of Lost Creek's nosy residents. That was the only safety net she had—witnesses.

She cannoned along the far aisle to the fire door. She could see it. See the exit sign illuminated with promise. He was right behind her. Limp or no limp, he was tearing up the aisle after her, vicious, murderous, grunting, growling. She wasn't going to make it. An agonizing five feet to go, and she wasn't going to make it. She had run out of time, luck, life. Her body tensed for his pounce.

With a splintering explosion of wood, fiberboard, and fragmented metal, the fire door disintegrated before her eyes. The outside alarm flashed blue streaks across the sleek fur of another enormous monster. It stood nearly eight feet high, densely muscled and sleek. Its coat shone and rippled in the emergency lighting. Long, strong limbs ended in large clawed hands and feet. Its flat muzzle was pulled back in a rabid snarl. This one was bigger, stronger, faster and much more dangerous than Virgil. This was a true predator. She couldn't believe it, two of them, two beasts. She was a goner. Then from behind her she sensed Virgil's dismay, and heard the quick skitter of his hasty retreat.

With shaking hands she raised her fire extinguisher. It was her only weapon. Face-to-face with this brute, it seemed so paltry. With a stifled, exasperated growl the creature threw out a long arm and swept the extinguisher from her hands. It sailed through the air to the far side of the room crashing into a wall, leaving her defenseless. Amy closed her eyes and waited for it to come for her.

Except it didn't want her. Instead, it pushed past into the library, its deep, menacing growl rattling the rafters. It was after Virgil.

Amy spared no time to wonder. She flew out the door and raced for Claude's truck. Sirens sounded over the mountain roads. The sheriff's car was heading this way. She was not going to wait around. She drove out of the parking lot as fast as possible, swerving onto the road. Let the sheriff's office deal with a library full of werewolves.

She was nearly a mile out of town when her truck shuddered at a tremendous crash from the rear. It creaked and dipped awkwardly, as if it had slammed into a pothole and broken an axle. Amy looked in the rear mirror in terror. Something had landed in the bed of her truck. She could see nothing in the darkness.

Suddenly she was showered in glass. She ducked her head, and with a grinding snap the sunroof was ripped clean off its hinges, opening the cab to the stars. With a graceful movement, the black-furred monster from the library dropped through into the passenger seat beside her.

Amy jerked the steering wheel in abject horror. The truck swerved fiercely one way, then the other. Terror rolled through her in clammy, gut-slamming waves. This nightmare had no end. The creature grunted and hung on to the dash until the truck had straightened itself. Amy screeched to a sliding stop, throwing them both sharply forward, then back into their seats.

They both sat for a stunned second. Then the beast leapt onto its haunches beside her, surprisingly agile for such a hulking brute in such a small space. It leaned in close. Amy was as frozen in fear, waiting for her head to be ripped from her shoulders. The stubby muzzle with its row of cruel teeth drew closer. Above it, amber eyes blazed with cunning intelligence. Its wet snout tenderly sniffed at her ear for a moment. Then the side of her neck was clamped in bone-crushing jaws. *So, this is how I die. Headless in Oregon.* A soft nip and a big, rolling tongue washed over her skin. And she was released.

Shocked, Amy swung her head around, the beastly face mere inches from her own. Its breath was meaty, it panted, the tongue lolled, the teeth glinted with saliva, white and diamond hard. She was fixated, fascinated, like a mouse before a cobra. Her neck was wet from the lick, yet her skin had not been broken, and that amazed her. Those razor-sharp teeth made the blood chill in her veins.

A sharp tap with a long claw on the plastic dash broke her stare. It tapped the truck's dashboard again, pointedly. She was to look there, pay attention. Dazedly, she managed to turn her head and gaze stupidly at Claude's litter. This was too surreal. Her brain felt starved of oxygen.

The monster leaned into her ear and damply snuffled her again. Inhaling her, delivering another little nip. She tingled all over. She could smell its fur, hot, spicy, musky; lots of scents she couldn't quite place, but which felt immediate and intimate to her. Her belly clenched and she trembled all over. In fear, she thought, and then realized it was excitement. Her body was responding as if programmed, completely disassociating from her mind, which was currently screaming that there was a werewolf in the cab with her and maybe she should get out?

She closed her eyes.

Leone. Her eyes flew open. She knew this feeling. It existed for only one person.

"Leone?" she whispered to the empty space beside her. She was alone. The passenger door was gone, lying bent and broken on the dirt road.

The creature had gone, faded into the woods, like an old dream melting away to nothing. She stared after it; she stared at the

GOLDENSEAL

dashboard and all Claude's junk—then she looked after the beast again.

"Leone." Her shocked whisper swirled away on the night breeze.

❖

He was in the air, foul and polluted. He poisoned both worlds, both states of being, with his greed and brutality. An ugly creature, neither human nor wolven.

She was easily closing in on him, stronger, faster, smarter; a lifetime of training and honing her genetic characteristics had made her a consummate predator. Rogues normally avoided natural born wolven. They had no place in the order of being. Fearful loners, they could cope with neither the city nor the wilds. This world had no place for them. Their days were numbered and they knew it. For him to come so close to a settled wolven den was an indication of his ambition and madness.

He was wily, cunning, but also a coward. He attacked the weak. Humans and adolescent wolven like Paulie. But Paulie had gotten a few good bites back and chased him off. Virgil still hurt from that miscalculation. She could see it in his tracks. He moved stiffly; he didn't heal well. Polluted and unnatural, his suppurating wounds were probably what slowed him and saved Amy.

Her mate was unhurt. She had attended to her, worried that his filthy bite had caught her. But Amy was safe, and Leone's rage eased from red-hot, belly-burning fear into a cold, calculated determination to hunt him down and kill him.

As she followed him through the backwoods straight to Little Dip, it was clear he had a well-worn route. She was closing in. He had harmed her clan, intimidated her loved one. She would kill him…for Paulie, and for Connie. But most of all for trying to harm Amy, her mate, her very own.

❖

Amy jolted forward, jamming the gears, toward Little Dip. Her eyes again focused on the dash. What had she missed? What was she to see? It was strewn with crumpled paper, chewed pens, candy, and empty coffee cups. All Claude's trash. Candy. There were several packs of unopened cherry candy. Connie's favorite brand. This wasn't litter; this was candy Claude had bought for Connie. Connie!

Banging rapidly into high gear, she increased her speed. Connie was safe. She realized that in her guts she had never really believed Virgil's claim that Connie was dead. It had never felt true—but the thought of it had made her so very, very angry.

And her rescuer, her protector—that was Leone. Every molecule of her mind, body, and soul knew this.

Barreling down the back roads, she was determined to see this through. She would follow the cherry-flavored clue and find Connie. And she would find out who, or what, in hell's name Leone Garoul really was.

CHAPTER TWENTY

It seemed like good manners to put Claude's keys back under the visor. Despite his truck having a passenger door missing, no sunroof, and being littered with broken glass. When she checked the bed, it was so bent it looked like a dairy heifer had parachuted into it. Well, Claude could just suck it up. He'd lied to her.

On rubbery legs she pounded up the trail to the compound to find it mysteriously empty of Garouls. Early evening was when they usually congregated around the barbeque or fire pit for beer and supper. Undeterred, she burst into Marie's cabin.

"Hello? Who's there…Amy? Is that you?" Paulie's croaky call came from Leone's bedroom.

"Paulie?" Amy found him struggling to sit up in bed. "Oh, hon. I'm sorry I woke you. Here, let me help." She eased him into a sitting position. His wound still caused him pain, though it had been treated and bandaged.

"I see Marie has been working her magic," she said.

"Yeah." He wriggled into the pillows she had plumped up for him. "Thanks, Amy."

"Did he hurt you much?"

"Nah. Marie says she's more worried about dirt and infection—" He pulled up short when he realized what he was saying. His face flamed at falling for her trick.

"I know Virgil attacked you," Amy said. He looked at her in amazement.

"The librarian? Wow. You know more than me. I just thought it was a rogue."

"Rogue?"

"Yeah. No clan. Dangerous guys with no proper Alpha to control them. They often snoop around other dens, drawn in by scent."

Amy sat back and digested all this. Virgil, she knew was a werewolf. But a rogue werewolf? They had names for him, for his kind? Dens and clans? What the hell did Paulie mean by clan?

"Paulie, can I ask some stupid questions? And please be honest with me, because I met with Virgil earlier today and only just escaped by the skin of my teeth." *Thanks to the skin of Leone's teeth.*

He tensed. "I'll try, Amy. But I'm making no promises." She admired his open honesty and plain common sense, something sorely lacking in his elders, as far as she was concerned.

"Okay. I know the Garouls have a werewolf." She came straight out with it. Out loud it sounded so stupid she immediately tried to qualify it. "Look, I broke the almanac code and found out some information. I know you guys have a beast to look after. Generation after generation." She took a deep breath. "And I know it's Leone."

"She told you that she was the only one." This was more a statement than a question. He almost sounded offended.

Unsure what she was really answering, Amy nodded. "Sort of," she said. Ambiguity seemed the best way forward.

"Typical."

"Huh?"

Paulie sighed. "We each have a werewolf to look after, Amy." There was a twinkle in those black eyes that reminded her so much of Leone.

"That's ridiculous."

"Why?"

"Because the place would be crawling with…" Her sentence trailed away as the truth dawned on her.

"The Garouls are a werewolf clan, Amy."

"Jesus." Amy sagged onto the bed.

"I don't think you read that code right," Paulie said sympathetically.

"I don't think I did either." She raised her head to look at him. "All of you?"

"The minute we hit puberty the change begins and we come here for Claude to train us. Little Dip is our family home. We learn to hone our wolven skills here on hunting breaks like this. We need to get by as hybrids in the modern world, but still be able to survive in the natural environment. So yes, I guess there is a beast. Many of them."

"Fuck. Excuse my language."

Paulie shrugged. "You should be with Claude when he gets stuck in a thorn bush."

Amy sat up. "Do you know what happened to Connie?"

He shook his head. "I only arrived last week to learn to hunt. Connie was…ill, before I arrived. But she's safe." He shifted uncomfortably and Amy sensed there was something he wanted to keep from her. And guessed she knew what it was.

"If a rogue wolf attacked a human, would they become a werewolf, too? Like in the movies?"

"That's a really harsh thing to happen. Even if someone survives an attack from a rogue werewolf, the shock to their system when the change begins can kill them. Few get past that stage, and if they do manage, then there's the addiction. The wolven side brings such a high, and if you run with the change too long, or too often, it sort of psychos you out. It's one of the first things we learn." Paulie paused, and looked hard at her. Amy knew he desperately wanted her to understand. "The real struggle is to control your humanity, not your beast. The wolfskin is more real, more in harmony with the natural world than the human side. It's harder to be human."

"So it's easy to become addicted to the raw power of the beast side, and harder to revert back to human?" Amy mulled this over. All the movies she'd seen had it the other way around. The full moon had always been the struggle for Lon Chaney, not the twenty-eight days in between. She'd imagined the fight was to deny the beast inside, not the day-to-day struggle to survive in the human world.

"Paulie, Virgil bragged that he'd bit Connie. Could it be like that for her now? Shock and addiction?" She was scared at the possibilities of Connie's situation. Virgil had hurt her, but had he changed her?

"Connie's lucky. She has all of us, and Marie's specialized knowledge to help her through. But it'll be tough on her." He held her gaze. "Marie's been nursing her, but she had to be moved away. Sometimes the change can get a little…violent. And Marie had to subdue her. Everyone has been caring for her, Amy. Please don't worry."

Again, Amy found some reassurance in his words. "I want to see her."

"Not tonight. It's the full moon; it's going to be hard on her. Connie's not trained to cope with its pull. Look at the damage she did to her own cabin walls last time she went on a rampage. But now that you know, you can talk to Marie about it. There's nothing to hide anymore. No reason why you can't be with Connie."

"Why hide it from me at all?" She was angry now. Connie had damaged her own cabin? Amy was shocked, she'd thought it was Virgil torturing Connie just as he'd tortured her that day in the studio. Just how out of control was Connie, how bestial had she become? Paulie shrugged in a typical teenage fashion.

"Probably the work you're doing. I imagine Connie was attacked for what she knew. Bloomsy probably reckoned she was the weakest link, being the only human in the whole valley."

"An easy target. Why did he go for you?"

"The same reason. Easy hit. I picked up his trail from your cabin. I didn't realize what I was following." He smiled ruefully. "Inexperience. I was lucky I hurt him harder. After he ran I found I couldn't hold my shape. I began to change back to human form too quickly. Not a good thing."

Amy nodded. "Claude said you were suffering from an overload. I wasn't sure what he meant."

"You would have been next, Amy. Virgil would have come for you. We were all guarding you. It's just a pity no one knew who the rogue werewolf really was."

"Bastard. I hope Leone got him."

"Leone?"

"When he was after me, a second wolf appeared and chased him away. He nearly had me. It was so close." She shook her head in wonder at her marginal escape. "It was Leone," she whispered softly. The mystery was no more. Leone's secret was out in the open. All that was left was what they had now.

"Well, she is your mate."

❖

Amy left Paulie tucked up and recuperating and started out for the most logical place she could think of, the storage cabin. Connie must still be there, being administered to by Marie and her horse-felling potions. Amy had to see her to set her heart at rest.

It was terrifying running alone along the forest trails. Amy failed to understand how her body was still operating and not curled in a fetal ball under a bush. The only thing that kept her going was adrenaline and her anxiety to see Connie.

Nevertheless, the nighttime valley had never looked so frightening. The full moon hung heavy, its bright light illuminating and shadowing simultaneously, giving her guidance on one hand but playing on imagined fears with the other. Every rut and stone along the track was visible, and her feet flew over them. At the same time, every darkened branch, hollow tree, or shady undergrowth hid another imaginary monster. Amy ran on, as if the hounds of hell were after her. For all she knew, they were.

Her mind was in turmoil, seething with questions, conclusions, and frustrations. The Garouls were werewolves. Had been so since time immemorial. Had Connie known this? Marie was her partner, so she must have known. It seemed only Amy was in the dark all these years. Why? Was she untrustworthy? Had her teenage romance with Leone tainted her into being the perpetual outsider?

It hurt an incredible amount, so much that her chest cramped at the implication that these people were not the second family she had always thought. That Connie, her only real family, colluded with the Garouls, and in doing so had been wounded and…and possibly mutated into a monster herself.

I should run away. Leave them all and go to Europe, like before. This secret could become a cage if I don't run now. But she remembered the massive furred beast in the cab of Claude's truck, leaning in to caress her neck with a maw that could rip a deer apart. And its clumsy attempts to get her to notice the cherry flavored candy, to bring her back to Connie. Amy knew there was nowhere else on earth she wanted to run but here, along this spooky moonlight path, straight into danger for the people she loved most.

The moon was clearly her ally, for she found the storage cabin easily. Cautiously approaching from the front, she could see the door lying open, swinging gently in the night breeze. There was no damage, but the air of abandonment didn't bode well.

The crawling sensation she now associated with Virgil slid over her skin again, like a cold, oily rag. So, he had escaped the library and the attention of the emergency services. She knew he was somewhere nearby, spying on her. Amy hesitated, fretful and uncertain. Where was the threat coming from? If she ran to the cabin, would he be in there waiting? Maybe staying in the woods gave her more options for escape.

A flutter of movement from the shadowy doorway nearly had her bolting for the river. He was in there! She caught a flash of red—a red jacket. Squinting, she took a hesitant step forward. Elicia appeared, quietly but frantically signaling her inside. Amy made a run for it and leapt onto the porch and through the door, slamming it behind them.

Elicia retreated into a corner, hovering anxiously beside the neatly made bed.

"Did you see it?" she whispered fearfully.

"Since I arrived in the valley, I knew there was something in the woods following me around. I thought it was a bear at first."

Elicia nodded. "I wasn't sure if you could sense it. Some people can't. They walk around blissfully unaware." She moved closer to Amy, whispering fervently, "But they're everywhere. Beside you in the supermarket aisles. Behind you on the subway. Teaching your kids, pumping your gas, cutting your hair—"

"Checking your books out at the library."

Elicia's dark eyes widened. "You know?"

"I know he's hurt Connie. I'm guessing he's outside waiting to try to hurt her again." Amy looked around the tidy interior. "I'm glad she got away."

Elicia shook her head slowly. "He's here for me."

"You?"

"He wants to rip out my cubs. They're Garoul cubs. He wants to eat them."

"Cubs…" Amy's mind was spinning. "Jori's? Elicia, you're pregnant by Jori, right?"

"Yes. We didn't plan…" Elicia began to cry; her shaking hands covered her face. "I love him so much, and now he'll hate me."

"Why did you say cubs?" Amy asked quietly. "Elicia, do you know about the Garouls?" Her answer was a sad nod.

"Well, you knew more than me." Amy sighed and moved to comfort her. "I've known Jori all my life, Elicia. And I know he won't hate you. He loves you. He'll be so happy about the…cubs."

Elicia sank onto edge of the bed, sobbing in deep cracked gulps. Amy crouched and put her arms around her.

"He loves you. We all know it. That's why you're here, in the valley. No one comes here unless they're practically a Garoul." She tried her best to reassure Elicia, all the time keeping an ear open for any prowling outside. "Elicia. You'll be all right. Everything will be fine. I promise. Look, I have to go check that all the windows and doors are locked. Are you okay for a minute?"

"It's no use." Elicia wiped her wet cheeks with her palms and sniffed. Regaining a little control, she kicked off her shoes.

"Believe me, this is a stout cabin. I've seen the damage it took to get out of the damn thing, never mind in." Amy was rattling the shutters. Combined with the bars on the outside, she felt certain the windows were secure.

"It's no use." Elicia sighed dejectedly. She shrugged off her jacket and loosened her belt.

"It buys us time. The Garouls know who he is, and he's been

stupid enough to come into their valley." Amy barred the door with a hefty plank used for that purpose. It should hold; she was sure it would.

"It's no use…"

"Elicia. Trust me, we're safe."

"It's no use…because I'm in here with you." Elicia's voice had dropped an octave and rasped harshly in the quiet.

Amy stilled. Slowly, she turned to look at Elicia. Or what used to be Elicia.

"You've got to be kidding me."

Amy stared at the convulsing woman before her. Elicia was doubled over on the bed in pain. Amy recognized her facial twitching and twisting as the same process she had witnessed with Virgil's change.

"Elicia. Please don't be a werewolf. Please."

"I'm trying so hard not to be tonight," Elicia answered with a sickly smile, her face bathed in sweat. "It's the moon. It's hard—" She broke off with a deep moan.

"Can I do anything to help? Will the cubs be okay?" They were incredibly stupid questions, but Amy felt compelled to ask. Elicia's reply was to curl up tighter in a cramped ball.

"Okay. Okay. Elicia? If you can't control this…will I be safe in here with you?" Another stupid question, but it was clear to her Elicia was not managing to subdue her mutation. Her fingers had truncated to painful hooks, the nails had coarsened to thick, yellow flakes. Nasty and needlelike. The veins on the back of her hands bulged out like a corded roadmap. Her face was turned to the wall and Amy knew this was deliberate. Elicia was ashamed of what her body was doing. She guessed Elicia probably had no clan but was another one of the rogues Paulie had talked about.

Amy had no idea how this might go. Virgil was malicious; he'd hated her and wanted to attack. Elicia did not have the same malevolence, but did that mean Amy was safe? Would Elicia strike through fear and instinct alone? Did it work like that? How did any of it work?

"Go, Amy. Go." Elicia's whisper was hoarse and filled with

pain. Amy stood for a moment considering this. But it was not really an option.

"I can't. If I leave, he'll come in here after you and the cubs. I can't lock you in safely, the outside padlock is missing."

Anyway, where could she run? Out the door and straight into—what? She couldn't leave Elicia behind, alone and defenseless. Not with Virgil prowling in the trees.

"Please, Amy. Go. I don't know what I'll do. I've only been like this for less than a year. I don't know how to…" Elicia's words trailed away in another grunt of pain. She gulped for air. Then she slowly relaxed, her body uncoiling from its tight muscular contraction. It reminded Amy of a woman in labor, the little bouts of relief between the shuddering, cramping pain.

Uncertain, Amy reached over and smoothed Elicia's forearm. Maybe she could help just by talking calmly. Leone had sat beside her in a small truck and hadn't been a ravening beast. Perhaps a werewolf didn't need to be dangerous, unless it wanted to. Maybe if she simply talked to Elicia she could ease her through the pain, and help her retain control.

"Less than a year?" she said, deciding to try her theory out.

"I parked too close to the Dumpsters one night. I was lucky to survive," Elicia explained bitterly. "The papers called it a 'savage dog attack on local woman.' A month later I knew what it was." Her voice was a little stronger now. More like her natural voice. More confident she was helping, Amy perched on the edge of the small cot and continued asking questions.

"You're doing fine. Stay with me. Tell me more, Elicia. What did you do when you found out what was happening to you? It must have been terrifying."

Elicia laughed dryly. She rolled onto her back so Amy could see her fully. She had the same flattened muzzle with sharp, vicious teeth under a curled black lip that Amy had seen on Leone. Her dark skin had become leathery, covered with a soft black fur, thin around her face but thickening over her head and down her throat. That was the extent of her change as far as Amy could see. Elicia plucked ineffectually at her blouse, her hands misshapen and knotted.

"Do you want me to help you undress?" Amy asked softly. The clothes looked tight and restricting. Elicia nodded a little shyly. Quickly Amy helped her disrobe; the skin on her body was dark and burnt looking, and very coarse. The musculature was far more pronounced. Elicia's breast tissue had all but disappeared, flattened onto an expanded rib cage. Distress and anxiety streamed from her, and Amy's heart went out to this woman who had to cope with this terrifying ordeal all on her own.

A deep moan ripped from her throat and she doubled up, cradling her stomach as if protecting her cubs.

"Breathe, Elicia. Breathe through the pain." Amy tried to remember every hammy medical television show with a birth coaching scene. It worked. Minutes elapsed with no sound other than the breeze in the trees outside, and Elicia's deep panting. Her body did not mutate any further.

"There are others like me." She finally relaxed, her trust in Amy established. "Virgil collects us. He's set himself up as an Alpha with his own rogue pack. He wants what the Garouls have."

Amy's jaw dropped at this. Elicia was aligned with Virgil? Well, initially. It seemed she had changed sides somewhere along the line. Clans, and packs, and rogues, and loners. There was an entire society of these beings out there. Amy's precise, logical world shattered even further. The supernatural didn't feel so super anymore. Not when it was incredibly real and sitting on her doorstep.

"Is that why you started seeing Jori? To infiltrate the Garouls and the valley?"

Elicia grunted. She was more comfortable now, but still hurting. Small convulsions ran forcefully through her body, caught in its half stasis. Amy watched it all carefully, praying she had made the right choice not to run away and abandon her.

"But we fell in love, and now I'm pregnant, and I've betrayed Jori." Elicia's upset quivered across her face, and her eyes slowly caramelized into a lighter, golden color.

"Hold on there, Elicia. Good thoughts only." Amy placed a calming hand on her shoulder. "Remember, I told you no one comes here unless they're already accepted. Jori and you have to talk. But he'll be delighted you're carrying his babies. Trust me."

"I don't deserve your kindness, Amy. I tricked you to go to the library so he could meet you. Marie didn't have any books to return. I did as he asked and never questioned it."

Marie had denied knowing Virgil Bloomsy; now Amy knew it was true. Virgil had flushed her out of the woods that day straight into the path of Elicia. Not that it mattered anymore. "Hush, Elicia. It's okay. It was all Virgil's doing."

She was answered with a sad little whimper and continued to stroke the furred shoulder, conscious it had been flesh only moments before. In the end, if Elicia couldn't hold back the tide, Amy needed a plan B. It was obvious Elicia couldn't control this. Her face was almost fully wolven now and Amy could see it distressed her. Elicia had not come to terms with her survival as a werewolf. She wore it with shame. Amy hadn't thought of it that way. Leone was so statuesque and majestic; Paulie spoke with such pride in his heritage. Even Virgil was drunk with the vicious power of it. Elicia was frightened and unschooled. She feared it.

"You know, you're sort of pretty…for a werewolf." Amy felt terribly for her. Elicia's eyes flitted suspiciously at her. "Okay, *handsome* is the better word. Like Leone."

"You've seen Leone? As wolven?"

Amy nodded. "She kicked Virgil's ass and saved me."

"I'd loved to have seen that."

"You don't like him, do you?"

Elicia shook her head. "Never. But what did I know then? He made me feel even dirtier. Then as I got closer to Jori and his family, I saw a different way. They were so close-knit and warm. They were a real family, and I began to understand the pack mentality was not about power and hierarchy, but togetherness and bonding. They have such control over their wolven side," she said in awe, before another wave of pain rolled over her. They sat quietly until it freed her.

"You were the one who helped me, weren't you? You left the langue d'oc book on the porch. And you tried to lead me here, to

Connie, when I first found this cabin. Why?" Amy said, realizing it had been Elicia all along, and not Virgil as she had assumed.

"I stole his book. I wanted you to know. I hated the way you were kept in the dark, opened to the same threat as Connie. I liked Connie so much. She was always kind to me when she came to the city to see Jori. Please, can I have some water?"

Amy helped her sip from the bottle sitting by the bed. Elicia licked her dry lips. "I knew Leone was trying to protect you, but Virgil always managed to get close—" She gasped, more pain. The spasms were coming closer together, and though Amy could see no more outer signs, she was unsure what happened to the human physiology on the inside. Would Elicia being pregnant complicate her change?

With a powerful gulp Elicia continued. "I took you to the trees because I wanted you to realize you were in danger and make the Garouls tell you the truth. You and Connie are more important than the stupid code. But when I saw them, what he had done to those trees, I knew he was out of control."

"Thank you," Amy said simply. Elicia had given her a lot and placed herself at risk in her rejection of Virgil and his plans. Amy was glad she had decided to stay in the cabin and comfort her.

"Amy?" Elicia whispered into the dark.

"Yes?" She leaned in closer to the quiet voice.

"You smell like food."

"Oh." She pulled back.

"You need to go. Tell Jori I'm sorry, and I love him."

"No." Amy stood and spoke forcefully at the creature curled up on the narrow cot. "You can do your own goddamn dirty work. When you're ready I'm going to open that door and we both run for it. Once we get out, we go our own ways. Don't you dare come after me! Find some other food. Just go and hide until morning."

Elicia blinked at her, eyes shining likes twin moons in a dark, muzzled face. Her teeth glinted, her mouth swimming with saliva. Amy knew she smelled like supper, but this was their only chance.

"Elicia. Listen to me, concentrate. You have to do this for your cubs. You have to protect Jori's cubs. These are Garoul babies, and you are in the Garoul valley. This is home. This is your home, and your cubs' home."

The cot creaked as Elicia rose. She towered over Amy, but was not as tall as either Virgil or Leone had been. It struck Amy that a lot of the pain must be in bone, muscle, and ligament mutation. Amy moved to the door and lifted the wooden bar. She held on to it; this was her only weapon. It might well prove useless as a weapon, but she felt marginally safer armed.

"On the count of three, we run." With a nod at Elicia, she lifted the latch and pushed at the door. Her body tensed ready to spring out and run like hell.

"One." The door swung slowly open.

"Two—" On the porch before her, side by side, were two massive wolven. Silent and sentinel. Amy realized with a sickening lurch that all this time they had simply stood and waited for the stupid human to open the door.

CHAPTER TWENTY-ONE

Both beasts looked in surprise at Amy's wolven companion. Behind her Elicia whimpered and pulled back into the depths of the cabin. Amy raised her plank; she'd be lucky if she landed one blow.

With an irritated growl one of the beasts reached over and, taking the tip of her weapon in its claws, simply shook it loose from her grasp and casually tossed it aside. Amy frowned. It was all so reminiscent of her fire extinguisher incident with—

"Leone?"

The other wolven brushed past her, intent on reaching a cowering Elicia. Amy turned protectively toward Elicia, confused at this new wolf's intentions. But it merely greeted Elicia with muted growls, and was answered by her sad whimpers. It had to be Jori. A massive brute, taller, with more densely packed muscle than his sleeker sister.

Leone retreated, and Amy followed her out to the porch and into the moonlight. She was relieved to be out of the stifling confines of the cabin, leaving Jori and Elicia to deal with their own lives. She had a life of her own to deal with, and it was in shreds at the moment.

Exhausted, she partially collapsed to sit on the porch steps. Her hulking companion stood nearby, watching her intently with those eerie amber eyes.

"I could sleep for a thousand years and still wake up to this friggin' nightmare," Amy told no one in particular.

It was too much for her system. Her brain was beginning to shut down.

"You wouldn't believe the day I've had," she told the werewolf she now knew was Leone. "Is he still out there?"

It raised its nose to the air, nostrils quivering as it inhaled. The lip curled and a low growl rumbled deep in a broad furred chest. Amy had no idea what that meant, but assumed there was no danger present. From afar a distant howl echoed into the night.

"Which cousin is that?" Amy said bitterly. The beast squinted at her, quiet and curious. Then it moved away, down to the river, and waited, looking back at her. Amy guessed she was to follow. Slowly, she pushed herself to her feet. Her body felt leaden and her head groggy. She had reached her limit a long time ago and had been running on empty ever since.

When she reached the bank she stooped to unlace her boots. She'd have to wade across, and despite the fact she'd spent the night being attacked by werewolves, holing up with werewolves, and finding out her entire adoptive family were werewolves, it seemed important to not get her feet wet and catch a chill.

With a snort the beast reached for her and scooped her up. She found herself carefully cradled in its arms, feeling like a small child. It was ridiculous. She clung on as it waded into the water, uncaring of the cold. Amy was stunned. She couldn't remember ever being held like this by her parents.

I never get my families right. I never fit. Her head sank onto a dense, matted shoulder and she found herself crying. A furry cheek briefly rubbed across the crown of her head, and the creature kept on walking.

It didn't cross to the other bank; instead it waded upstream, thigh deep, using the river as another trail through this part of the forest. When the current got too fast or too deep it plowed out of the water and along the bank. It carried Amy back to their rock. Their teenage rock, their lover's rock.

The beast carefully laid her down, then spooned around her, pillowing her head on its arm. The heat from its body could have driven a steam engine. It felt warm and secure, and in her exhausted state she allowed herself to be cuddled into the safest place she knew in the whole goddamned valley.

A wet nose snuffled her ear, hair, and neck. She was settled in closer still. She smelled its earthiness, its musky fur, and found it comforting. Falling asleep was her body's natural defense now that she was safe. Deep fatigue crawled over her. She could not have stopped it even if she tried. She was done.

The creature cradled her and gave comfort. She knew it was Leone, but it was also still a beast to her. Unnatural and unknown. It cared for her, but she wasn't sure what she felt for it. Her Leone. Her mind was too tired to think about it now, to process this discovery's effect on her heart. Her last thought before sleep overtook her was that after all these years she had never really known Leone Garoul. Not at all.

❖

Her mate slept. Dull, exhausted, and wounded on a level licks would not heal. Salves and potions wouldn't help either. The bleeding was too deep within her. Heart blood, rich and ripe, all full of love, and it was seeping away and Leone didn't know how to stop it.

She had followed Virgil until his trail crossed Jori's mate and began to circle her. This concerned Leone greatly. Jori's scent was all over Elicia; it should have protected her from a rogue.

Soon she'd found Jori. He was aware Elicia was in trouble. He could see Virgil was actively hunting her down. Together they tracked their quarry to the cabin by the river. They knew Elicia was hiding inside, so they lay in wait for Virgil to make his move. Once he was sure it was safe to do so, he would attack the human woman. It was his way. But in the distraction of Amy's arrival Virgil had become uneasy. Sensing a trap, he had slunk away.

Jori had a lot of soul-searching to do tonight. Leone felt for him and this new revelation about Elicia. She curled more protectively around her own mate. A brave fighter. Leone was proud of her. She was never going to let her go.

Dawn was still a few hours away. She would stay with her mate, on the special rock. She would mutate back to human form with the sun, in her sleep, the traditional and less stressful way to revert. And in the morning her human self would be there to protect and comfort Amy, too.

Leone was in Connie's cabin again. The fire blazed out warmth, and Amy was by her side. They were happy and in love. She could feel the love energy coursing through her. It made her heart beat stronger. Her blood pounded steady and sure. She felt younger than she was. Amy looked younger, too. She looked like she did the day Leone realized she was her life mate, forever and ever.

Laughing and smiling, they were so close, so together, it felt perfect. The air was scented with pine, and the logs on the fire crackled. So good together—and then she began to change. She couldn't control it, couldn't stop it.

First, her hands. The nails blackening and thickening. Her fingers began to twist. The tendons of her hand and forearm tightened painfully. Her muscles and sinews cramped and truncated along her chest and shoulders into strange, mutated shapes. Her fingers curved into vicious hooks.

It hurt so much she cried out. And as she cried, her mouth filled with blood. Through the copper taste and sharp pain, her teeth elongated, ripping open her gum tissue. Facial muscles popped and distended, forming a stubby muzzle, cracking and dislocating her jawbone. Sinuses became a screaming agony, her ears filled with a deafening roar that once was her voice.

As a teen, the first time she mutated, her mother had cradled her through it. Claude had held her twisting hands, murmuring words of encouragement and support. Connie had cried quietly for the pain all the young ones had to suffer on that first, cruel change.

Now she was alone with Amy, and as frightened as that first time. She heard her own howls of agony, hollow, echoing. Her skin coarsened and fur crawled over her, drowning her, suffocating her. And what scared her most, above her own cries, were Amy's screams.

Horrified, Amy was backing away from the mutating freak before her, eyes filled with terror and rejection. No love there. Never again would there be love there. That pain cut through Leone deeper than any cracked bone or torn ligament.

But Leone still wanted her and moved toward her, fully wolven now. The pinesap filled her nostrils, but she could still smell Amy. Scent her mate, heady and heartwarming. Her whole world. Slavering and hungry, completely bewitched with Amy's scent, and skin. Then Amy's beautiful, pale skin was in her mouth, soft and silky on her tongue. It tasted so beautiful that she bit down hard—

Leone jerked awake.

A steel gray dawn crept over the tree tops. Her back on the granite rock was cramped and chilled. Cold seeped into her bones through her naked skin. She turned her head to see Amy lying beside her, watching her, hazel eyes remote and unreadable.

"Do you always have nightmares when you change back?" Amy said.

Leone blinked at the strange question. "I don't know. I don't think so." She hesitated. "Tonight I did."

"It looked so painful, even though you were sleeping."

"It hurt in the dream."

They lay looking at each other in silence in the cold dawn. Neither seemed inclined to move.

"Amy," Leone said. "All those years ago I couldn't control it as well as I can now. And Connie was afraid I'd hurt you. Not kill or dismember," she explained awkwardly. "But maybe bite and mutate you when we made love. The wish to be with you, and in you, and all around you—that part can be so intense. And she was right. Sometimes when we were making love, I wanted to bite you so bad."

"Marie never hurt Connie like that?"

Leone shook her head. "Mom was an Alpha, and an adult. She would have had more control than a young wolf like me. And Connie didn't want to change…" Leone trailed off. They both knew Connie had little choice now. "There's a ritual, when a mate decides to join her partner as wolven. A special way it has to be done. It's important, as it's so dangerous."

"And I wasn't allowed to know any of this?"

"Not unless you were my life mate. Garoul mates know everything. I was too young and inexperienced to ask you that. Mom told me to wait until I was older. To take you as a mate then. But I wouldn't listen, so I had to be sent away to keep you safe."

Amy lay quietly watching her.

"I'm sorry, Amy. I'm sorry I lost you your home."

Amy shivered and stood. "I'm freezing. Let's go. Take my jacket." She began to peel it off even though she was trembling.

"No, keep it. My clothes are stashed over there. I always change at this rock." Leone foraged in a bush and pulled out a backpack. Quickly she threw on the clothes stuffed inside and pushed the bag back into the undergrowth.

Together they walked back silently, Amy deep in thought, Leone giving her space to process what she had heard.

"What happens when two werewolves become mates? Like Jori and Elicia?" Amy said, out of the blue.

"Mmm, it's not unusual. Patrice turned for Claude."

"Aunt Patrice?"

"Yeah. That's why they had Jolie and Andre, the twins. Werewolves always have twin cubs."

Amy came to a sudden halt. "Elicia said cubs."

"Huh?"

"Elicia said she was going to have Jori's cubs. Twins. She knew she was carrying twins. It's crazy." She shook her head and moved on again.

"Elicia's having Jori's cubs?" Leone stood rooted to the ground. "Wow. On top of her being a rogue? What a roller coaster for Jori." She quickly caught up with Amy.

"Oh, it gets better. She was part of Virgil's pack, but fell for Jori and turned against the rogues. That's why Virgil came after her last night. He wanted to kill her and her cubs."

This time Leone stopped them dead in their tracks. "What? I never scented her. Not once. Well, it was hard to, I suppose. Jori's scent was all over her. I mean, she was his mate."

They moved on again and Amy asked, "Will they be okay?"

Leone nodded. "Yeah. I think so. Jori loves her, and she's having his cubs. She'd already turned away from Virgil. The minute she mated with a Garoul she was a goner."

"Is that what happens. People become goners?" Amy asked dryly.

Leone looked over anxiously. "I didn't mean it like that. I know you'll do whatever you want."

"Since when have you ever allowed me to do what I want? You just reach in and take, Leone. You steal things. And you give nothing back. Not even honesty."

"I—"

"Don't. Just don't. I understand what happened in our teens. I'm not happy that you selfishly pursued your own wants and left us both open for eventual heartache. But I understand the reason it happened, that Marie and Connie cared about us, and rightly so. After watching what Elicia went through last night, I'm actually grateful to Connie and Marie." She shuddered. "I wouldn't wish that on anyone."

Leone walked beside her in silence, head bowed.

"What I can't forgive is your cowardly seduction this time around. We're adults, Leone. The Garouls are my second family. By keeping me in the dark you exposed me to terrible danger. You only just managed to get me away from Virgil. Connie wasn't so lucky. The only ally I've had throughout all this was actually Elicia. She put her neck on the line. Not one Garoul told me the truth about what was out there. And I told you time after time I saw something. Did you behave the same way to Connie?"

"We didn't know there was a threat until Connie was attacked. I was protecting you. The only danger you were in was when you wandered off and we didn't know where you were. And as for Connie, I didn't want to worry you until we knew how she was coping—"

"How dare you all keep that from me? She's my goddamn family. She's all I have in the world, and you took that away, too."

"Amy, it's not like that."

"It *is* like that. You brought me over to do her job. Even though you knew she'd been savagely attacked because of it. And you lied to me about her condition."

They came to a fork in the path, one way leading to Connie's cabin, the other to the compound.

"We need to part ways, Leone. And not just on this path. I'm sorry things were so hard for us when we were teenagers. At least, years later, I finally understand why. But I'll never forgive you for not telling me the truth about Connie's illness, and for your continued dishonesty with me." Amy's words were cool and clipped. "Would you ever have told me if I hadn't cracked your precious code? As far as I'm concerned, you lied your way into my bed." She took a step forward and looked Leone in the eyes. "It's not like you're the only one to ever do that, either. But when I find I'm sleeping with a cheat, I simply walk away."

She turned and left, satisfied she'd flung a final killer blow to Leone Garoul's ego. Let it pop like a soap bubble—she was through with her, through with the lot of them and their games. After she was certain Connie was doing okay, she'd pack up and go. Their precious almanac could burn in Bosch's Hell for all she cared.

❖

Leone watched her go. It was killing her to let her walk away, especially after that final slapdown, but she knew Amy needed to vent. Every word she said had a grain of truth that stung like salt in a wound. Leone had withheld the truth, but she was also madly in love with Amy and had always feared the rejection she'd ultimately brought down on her own head. And the truth was Amy didn't know everything, not even yet.

Leone felt conflicted by many things. Her wish to follow Amy home was hampered by her need to report to Marie. She was also worried how Jori and Elicia were coping. And the architect of everyone's misfortune, Virgil Bloomsy, was still on the loose. If he had any sense he'd be miles away by now, but he still had to be dealt with. Loaded down with worries, Leone turned onto the compound track.

CHAPTER TWENTY-TWO

Leaving Leone behind did not make Amy feel any better. She was very close to tears as she walked away. She was miserable and confused, and wanted Leone to say perfectly reasonable things that all made sense and took the hurt away. Except Leone hadn't any reasonable things to say. Amy had been correct on every single point—and sometimes just loving someone wasn't enough.

Gloomily, she reached the clearing before her cabin, desperately wanting a shower and a change of clothes. Then she intended on finding Marie and demanding to see Connie. She wanted a full explanation from the Garoul Alpha.

After that she was unsure what she would do. So much depended on how Connie was feeling. Amy couldn't see beyond that point.

Something was wrong. She halted on the porch steps. The closed door was battered. Lacerations ran across the entire front facing of the cabin. There was a confusion of massive muddy paw prints all over the porch floor. Cautiously, she pushed at the door. Locked? She never locked it. Only a Garoul would have the key. So someone from the family had come by and locked up her cabin. Why?

Connie's spare key was always hidden under the second step up. It was still there, wrapped in an oily cloth. Freed from its cobwebbed home, it slipped and turned effortlessly in the lock. The door swung gently open, allowing her to peep inside. The early morning light spilled over her shoulder, illuminating the main room. It was trashed. Connie's books littered every surface, torn and ripped apart. Furniture was upended, snapped like twigs. Lamps and porcelain and crockery, everything breakable lay in pieces. The beautiful watercolor paintings had been torn from the walls and shredded. Everything had been destroyed in an absolute frenzy.

Flies buzzed around the haunch of a deer. Torn and partially eaten, it lay in the middle of the polished floor, the flesh hanging from it in shreds. The air was pungent with blood and the smell of offal. Dust motes danced in the sunlight. Flies droned. The cabin had a quiet lassitude that assured Amy it was empty. The Garouls must have locked it up after Virgil defaced it.

Connie's beautiful home was in pieces. Amy's final place of refuge in the whole wide world had been destroyed. She had to fight not to sink to her knees and simply give up. What was she even fighting for? This vile vandalism was a token of all that had happened to Connie since she'd last seen her.

Virgil must have done this looking for the code keys, and as a last act of sickening revenge. Amy had been far from clever; she had told him about the keys and had ruined everything. Virgil would not be leaving Wallowa alive. He has desecrated the Garouls in every possible way. If he was still stupid enough to be in the valley, then he must be totally suicidal.

With a sad sigh Amy turned to go to Marie's when she noticed the dull gleam of the Ruger Bearcat on the mantelpiece. Its promise of security was enticing. But she was loath to enter the violence and chaos that had once been her much-loved family home. She hesitated at the doorway.

Could he still be in there? What if it was a trap? She knew she was spooking herself. Virgil wasn't there; his werewolf funk was easy to smell, even with a human nose. Nevertheless, she hurried across to the fireplace with trepidation, keeping her eyes fixed firmly on her goal and not on the destruction around her. She grabbed the revolver and on the way back out fumbled in the dresser drawer for the box of silver-tipped bullets. She scrabbled through silk scarves, and hairpins, and combs, but couldn't find it. The box was gone.

She located one hard little metal shell with her fingertips. She pulled it out and held it up to the weak morning light and it sparkled. Silver. Silver bullets. It was so obvious what Connie had been up to with the smelter tucked away in her studio. Tipping each bullet with a dab of pure silver. How could Amy have missed it? Because she was too quick to dismiss it as part of the Wicca hocus pocus Leone was indulging in. Amy slotted the lonesome little projectile into the chamber.

Poor Connie, trying everything she could think of to save herself from— A metallic click. Amy snapped alert. It came from behind her. Followed by several more clicks and rattles, like the dull jingling of coins. Slowly, she turned her head, unsure what she was hearing. Why had her body not given her the usual warning signs that danger was nearby? Where was the prickled skin, the hair on end? Where was all that when she needed it?

A drip of something wet landed on her shoulder with a small splat. She zoned in on the small pink stain seeping out across her coat fabric. Another drip landed close to it, a darker pink stain oozing out to join with the first. A heavy shadow leaned over her, close enough for saliva to drip from its jaws onto her jacket in bloody globules.

Why hadn't she sensed Virgil was there?

Amy's blood pressure fell so fast her ears buzzed and her head felt too light to form a cohesive, sensible thought. She was faint with exhaustion and soul-deep weariness with this persistent game of survival. There was no more strength or resourcefulness left in her; she'd passed her limit ages ago and was spent.

Hot breath burned across her cheek. It was stale and coppery. Stagnant with its last meal. A clawed hand reached around before her, to show a cluster of shiny bullets cupped in a furred palm. They clicked together melodiously, cheerfully tinkling. Their shiny silver points winked up at her.

Another oily thread of saliva trickled down the front of her jacket. A growl dipped into a dangerous, satisfied purr. This was not Virgil. Every one of Amy's instincts told her that. It did not make her feel any safer. In fact, she felt in considerable danger. This wolven was new to her. Hopefully, it was a Garoul and not another of Virgil's pack. How many Elicias did he have out there?

Amy turned slowly. She faced a broad, matted, silver-streaked chest. A female. It had the same softer breast tissue flattened over strong pectoral muscle she'd seen with Elicia and Leone.

It snarled, but not in a friendly manner. Its pale golden eyes seemed flatter, duller. They held none of the intelligence that shone from Leone's. Its coat was streaked in blood. Its own, from the look of it. It had fought recently and had not fared well. Its crimson muzzle curled back and its teeth gleamed, sharp and wicked. Amy blinked, transfixed. It was a thing of soul-shredding beauty.

It lunged at her with a vicious snap, missing her nose by millimeters and waking Amy out of her stupor. She stumbled back, terrified. Not a friend, then. Not a Garoul. It wasn't tall or dark enough. It had to be another rogue.

It seemed pleased she had backed off. The bullets continued to click; only now they sounded cold and menacing, like their owner.

"Amy."

The anxious call came from outside. The beast stiffened. It was Marie's voice.

"Amy? Are you in there, girl?" Claude called this time, his voice hard and urgent.

Amy locked eyes with the monster. Could she scream for help in time for it to make any difference? The beast seemed to be considering the same question. With a snarl it tilted its hand, and one by one let the bullets drop. Each landed with a sharp clatter on the floor. They rapped on the wood, loudly ripping apart the quiet of the cabin. Amy flinched, as if each and every one was an actual gunshot. Her grip on the revolver trembled. Was this a game? Could she aim and shoot before this animal pounced? The bullets rolled mockingly around her feet.

"Amy?" Marie was approaching the porch steps. The creature shrank into a crouch.

"Here," Amy called back in a strangled croak, her eyes never leaving the beast before her. "I'm not alone."

Marie's footsteps stopped.

"Connie." Marie's voice was calm and controlled. "Don't hurt her."

Shocked, Amy stared horrified at the angry creature crouched in front of her. This was Connie? Why had she not known? She had felt the connection between Leone and the hulking beast in her truck. Known it right through to her core, once she had gotten over her fear.

Hungry for a clue, she examined the snarling face before her. The gleam in this creature's eyes sharpened, becoming focused and cunning.

"Connie. You remember Amy, don't you? She draws plants, just like you. In fact, you taught her, a long, long time ago." Marie appeared at the door and carefully stepped into the room. Connie stiffened at her entrance, more alert, her body humming with excitement. Her attention was now split between Amy and Marie, wavering more toward Marie, her lover, her mate.

Marie's dark eyes settled on Amy. Silently she signaled for her to move away. Connie growled as Amy edged toward the door, and Marie immediately moved closer, claiming Connie's attention. Amy shuffled a few more paces sideways. Her boot tapped on a bullet and sent it spinning off, jingling into the others. Connie roared out, a deafening bellow. Amy closed her eyes and waited to be swallowed. She stood rooted to the spot, hunched and lost. Connie was no more than a maddened animal.

"Connie." Marie's voice was sharp and she strode farther into the depths of the cabin. "I need you over here."

Amy could see Marie's eyes already held that eerie glow she knew to be wolven. She was moving into transmutation, but in the most controlled way Amy had ever seen. Connie responded strongly to Marie's change. The tone of her growl dropped away to a harsh purr. Her whole body relaxed and she seemed to vibrate in Marie's presence. Amy knew Marie was luring Connie away to allow her to run for it. Taking full advantage, she started backing out the door.

Marie spoke gently and soothingly, and Connie twitched and

stood as if uncertain. Her teeth were bared under a snarling muzzle, her growl rumbled low and threatening. Her gaze swiveled to Amy, and for one flickering second Amy glimpsed her aunt in that bestial face. A look of love and sorrow shone out at her with such pathos she could have fallen to her shaking knees in gratitude. Connie was in there, inside this raging monster. And she was slowly emerging from her living nightmare, from Virgil's filthy infestation. Marie would see her through, with love, and determination, and her medicines. Claude would teach her to cope, as he did all the young Garouls. Connie would beat this. Connie would win, and Virgil would lose everything.

"Amy? Go with Claude. I want to stay here with Connie. Don't worry. I'll look after her," Marie said.

Amy nodded and continued her slow backward shuffle when she found herself suddenly airborne, lifted bodily by Claude and briskly carted away. He deposited her on the porch steps and darted back to lock the cabin door, leaving Marie inside.

"Will Marie be safe?" Amy said.

He nodded.

"Yeah. She's got Connie's next dose in her pocket. They'll spend some time together. Sleep a little, and Connie will revert back to her human self." Gently he guided Amy away. "Connie doesn't know what she's doing, Amy. She'll be a lot better by tomorrow, and you can talk then. I promise you."

"Did she do all that damage to her cabin herself?"

He sighed heavily. "Poor Connie. She'll be so upset. All her books and things, ruined. It's been hard on her. Virgil was such a filthy animal. She's got multiple infections on top of the shock to her system."

"He's a bastard."

Claude didn't argue. "He did nothing right. I'm guessing he attacked Elicia at some point. Probably how he gathered his followers. She's in a bad way, too. It's a wonder she ever survived. At least Connie had help from the start. Elicia was isolated, poor kid." Claude shook his head sorrowfully. "The full moon last night didn't help either of them."

GOLDENSEAL

"I went looking for Connie at the storage shack. I guessed that's where you were keeping her. When she wasn't breaking out of it."

"We knew Virgil was on the prowl, so we moved her into this cabin. Marie stayed with her. Jori needed medical help for Elicia, and Marie had to go and help. Connie wrecked the place while she was alone. If I'd known I'd have stayed with her, but—"

A distant howling interrupted him. He stood still, head cocked. Another howl followed almost immediately, then another. He turned to her.

"Virgil's been scented. Amy, will you promise me something? Will you keep going straight down this trail to Marie's cabin? I'll have to join the hunt."

"I promise."

"Is that thing loaded?" He nodded at the Bearcat dangling uselessly from her hand. She shook her head.

"Just one. The rest are…" She looked back at the cabin.

"Never mind. Just head straight to the compound."

"Wait. I have another one." She scuffled about in her jacket pocket and pulled out the silver bullet. "My lucky one."

Claude raised his eyebrows. "Whatever. But put the gun away before you shoot yourself. Okay?"

With a kindly pat on her shoulder, he turned into the forest and quickly disappeared in the undergrowth.

Amy felt unsettled after he'd gone. Another section of the Garoul riddle had fallen into place. She knew what had happened to Connie and was reassured she would recover under Marie's ministrations. Remembering Elicia's panic and pain last night made her glad the Garouls were there for Connie. But that didn't take away from the fact their goddamn code had endangered her in the first place, and that they had blatantly lied to her about Connie's condition. There were still a lot of issues Amy wanted to discuss when all this was over.

At the Silverthread she took the left fork that would take her into the compound. Amy trudged on head down, deep in thought.

But would it ever be over? She knew the code now. A secret she was obviously never meant to share. A barrier that had kept her separate from the rest of this family, and even from Connie. All her life she had been excluded and never realized it. What would happen now? Would she be ostracized completely?

The thought scared her. Earlier her anger had made her want to run away forever, but now that she had seen Connie, so lost inside the monstrosity Virgil had forced upon her, Amy couldn't bear to leave her. Connie was bound to the valley forever, learning the Garoul ways, only this time from the other side, this time as a wolven.

Amy knew she could go back to Europe and pick up where she left off, but nothing would ever be the same again. She would never stop worrying about Connie, or the next rogue pack to find the valley. There would always be some danger lurking in the shadows. The Garouls had enemies in both worlds. Humanity would treat them like lab rats, and the wolven world had its own predators, rogues who wanted to overturn the ancient werewolf clan.

Amy knew she was also kidding herself that it didn't hurt losing Leone all over again. And for the same reasons as before, lack of trust, withholding, all secrets and lies. Despite herself she found tears rolling down her cheeks. Her life felt emptier than ever. The Garoul curse had taken everything from her: Little Dip, her second family, Connie, even Leone. Everything of emotional value had been stripped away.

"My, what big tears you've got."

Virgil stepped out of the undergrowth directly in front of her. He was in human form, looking the worse for wear. Unshaven, his thin hair sticking out at all angles. Torn and disheveled, he stood naked before her with the beginnings of a soft erection.

"I find if I change back and forth frequently enough it confuses my scent trail. It won't buy me much time, but hopefully enough to disembowel you, you sniveling little bitch."

He stepped toward her. Already she could see the milky haze in his eyes. Muscles twitched and spasmed under his skin.

"It's funny, Virgil, but at this moment you are the only constant in my life," Amy said calmly. "I hate you with all my heart."

"Oh, it's mutual, my clever little whore. Now, let's play a game. I'll count to ten, and you run. It will be more fun that way." His spine was hunching over, the vertebrae popping under the stress of his slow mutation. He began to count, "One, two—"

Amy eased the revolver from her pocket, and his countdown faltered.

"Silver bullets, Virgil." Relaxed and in control, she was unconcerned with his games. She'd had enough. "I've no idea if they work on a werewolf. It might be a load of steaming movie crap, for all I know." She leveled the gun at him. "But then you're not exactly a werewolf yet, are you? You're a librarian."

And she shot him.

❖

He was easy to trail by sight and scent. He left clues everywhere—flattened undergrowth, bent twigs, small tufts of fur snagged on the denser thickets he'd pushed through. His alien smell was pungent, its stringency jarring here in her valley, her den. It raised her hackles, and she bared her teeth. Adrenaline flooded her.

Leone was puzzled at his circuitous route; the compound seemed a central pivot point but not his ultimate destination. He had his sights set on something else. She recognized the basic hunting pattern but was uncertain of his target. His movements, though stealthy, lacked finesse. His fluctuations from wolven to human must be exhausting him, though he probably thought of it as camouflage. A useless, energy-consuming ruse. She guessed he was self-taught and acting on instinct. He'd have had none of the training and discipline drummed into the Garouls from an early age.

They had expected him to run. The Garouls were everywhere looking for him. Some were patrolling the perimeter roads outside of Little Dip, some sipping horrible coffee at Norman Johnston's, others were watching Virgil's apartment or the highway, the service stations, the bus and train depots at the larger towns.

Now it seemed he hadn't left at all. Virgil still lurked in the valley on some sort of suicide mission. This was an unwelcome development. He had an all or nothing target, a must-kill, but she couldn't figure out what it was. His tracks led down to the Silverthread. Worried, she quickened her pace.

The sharp retort of gunfire echoed through the valley. Clean and crisp, a single shot rang out in the morning air. Amy! Only a human would need a gun in Little Dip. And Amy was the only human in the valley.

Leone's loping gallop ate up the ground. She flew over underbrush, swerved around trees and rocks. She became a dark, menacing shadow streaming through the forest, violent and demonic as a tornado. An electric energy burned in the air around her; the anger and anxiety in her gut made every hackle along her spine rise. She scented Amy, her mate. Hers! The filthy bastard had gone after Amy—he wanted to kill her mate.

Leone hurled herself through the forest and down to the river.

❖

Amy missed by inches. Virgil staggered in shocked relief, his sweaty face pale and uncertain. Unfazed, Amy aimed at him again.

"Oops, pulls to the right. But now that we know that, let's play a game. I'll count to ten, and you run. It will be more fun that way. One…"

He turned to flee, having no contingency plan for a victim who refused to cower and die, who actually fought back. He dove into the trees for cover—straight into the broad, furred chest of Leone Garoul.

He crawled away, anger and fear forcing him into the throes of rushed mutation. For all his presumed potency, he didn't change well or cleanly. Instead he spasmed and jerked. Ugly, undignified, inept. One swipe of her razorlike claws and she could have killed him immediately, except Leone was content to circle him, allowing him to change completely. She herded him to the water's edge, to where she wanted him to be. Always in control, always sure. It was a matter of time before he died, a time she would choose.

Amy trembled, forgotten and neglected on the dirt track. She should have run but now she was compelled to watch this macabre dance. Leone looked majestic, sleek and strong. Her slightest move rippled her blue-black coat in the morning sunlight. She flowed as liquid as prairie grass. She was fluid and dangerous. So incredibly dangerous. Snarling and snapping at his heels, she pushed an agitated and angry Virgil into the water.

He slavered back; his yellow eyes gleamed mutinous and menacing. Hatred overshadowed every move he made. He lunged, but Leone saw it coming before he'd half formulated the thought. Anger was so easy to read. She grabbed him by the throat, careful not to cut, and hurled him into the river with such speed and force Amy jumped with fright.

Leone pounded into the water after him, a seething ball of fury. She wrapped herself around him, dragging them both into the shallows. Her added height and considerable strength allowed her to hold him underwater. The extra length in her arms easily kept him down as he clung to her, scrabbling for leverage.

The water churned white and frothy around them. He surfaced once, in a panicked surge that took up nearly all his waning strength, but Leone was taller, sleeker, and stronger, and she knew how to use all three to advantage. Amy watched, her face a mask of horror, as Leone slowly forced her flailing victim back under. He frantically clawed at her exposed belly and chest. She couldn't protect her torso; it took both hands and all her power to keep him still, even as he tore at her. Her blood colored the water around them, the ruby red drifting away, diluting to nothing in the river's thick, idle swirls.

Determined, Leone pressed Virgil's shoulders against the bedrock. The life-stealing waters danced over his face. He surged again, coming up inches from the surface and the air she ruthlessly denied him. The pain as he ripped at her belly was excruciating, but it was futile. She wouldn't ease her grip.

In last-minute desperation he tried to drag her down with him, but she steeled herself, and didn't flinch. His clawing became weaker. He clutched at her, panicked, holding on to her arms as if she might save him. But she didn't.

Instead she simply pinned him down and watched through the veil of water as his blue eyes bulged with shock, and then disbelief, that this was finally his time to die. Drowned in the unforgiving Silverthread, in the valley he had dared to covet.

She watched as anger, denial, and panic flashed through him. She watched impassively as his face wavered, and fluxed, twisting back into human form. In his death throes, the body beneath her mutated back into a middle-aged, drowning man.

Still she held him under, and he in turn held her. Breath spent, lungs engorged with the cold waters of the Silverthread. He finally lay still under her hands.

"Oh my God," Amy cried out.

Rising in a cascade of blood and water, Leone dragged him out into the faster current. One last glance at his body assured her he did not look like the victim of an animal attack. She had been careful with her claws and teeth. He would be just another unfortunate victim of drowning. It wouldn't be the first time a newcomer to the area had misjudged the treacherous waters of the Silverthread. Knowing the safe swim holes was the luxury of the locals. Virgil had never been a local.

She let his body go and watched it drift downstream. The Garouls would see to it that the river took it all the way out of their valley and far into the public fishing areas to the east. In a day or two Lost Creek's ex-librarian and his terrible accident would be front-page news in the Wallowa newspapers.

Standing in the rushing waters, Leone raised her head and howled a stark guttural cry into the morning sky. Within moments it was answered from every corner of the valley. The threat was gone. The hunt over.

She waded painfully to the bank, victorious, protector of her mate and her pack. She bared her teeth and snarled with brazen glory.

Amy backed away from her, eyes like saucers, full of fear. Leone didn't want her mate to fear her. She wanted Amy to welcome her. She snapped a warning, but Amy still retreated. She snapped again out of frustration. Her mate should greet her, exalt her—she was the victor! A roar broke from her throat and Amy turned and fled.

In two bounds Leone had caught and covered her, bringing her to the ground. She lay over her, belly down, and clamped Amy's nape in her maw to hold her still, to stop her wriggling. She purred loudly, excited at this new game. Their position was a mating one. Amy's scent thrilled her.

Amy screamed, trying to twist away. Leone's weight was unbearable, and her heavy bleeding was seeping through the back of Amy's jacket. Sharp teeth were clamped onto her neck. Her spine felt as brittle as summer straw between those strong jaws. One snap and she would die; one graze and she would be like Connie.

The panting in her ear was loud and excited. Her body would shatter if Leone tried to touch her sexually. She sensed Leone was slipping further into her beast side. There was no control here. This was what Connie and Marie had worried about all those years ago.

"Don't bite me, Leone. Don't bite me." She scrabbled on the ground, trying to crawl away, trying to struggle free, trying to—

The revolver went off in her pocket.

Chapter Twenty-three

"H ave you heard from Amy?" Leone asked Connie.

"Yesterday. She's nearly done in Vancouver. She might come back for the final editorial meeting," Connie said. "Or she might just do a conference call from Canada."

"You know Amy would come back if you said the word."

"Leone. I love Amy, but I want her to return because it's the right thing for her to do. Not because I've asked her to," Connie chided her gently. "I think you're the one who needs to talk to her about coming home, more than me."

Leone's shoulders sagged. "She hates me. She won't even answer the phone when I call."

"She's busy doing your job, and she liaises with Marie now, not you. I know Amy, and she needs to think things through. It's been a hard few weeks for her, Leone. The least you can do is give her time."

Leone rose from the couch stiffly. She knew Connie was right, but her anxiety at Amy's absence grew by the day. If Amy never returned to Little Dip, Leone would be stark-staring mad in a matter of months. Now that she'd had Amy back in her life, even if it was for only a few weeks, to be separated from her again drove her to distraction. If Amy didn't have the same commitment to her, Leone didn't know what she would do.

"Leone?" Connie interrupted her panicked thoughts. "You need to rest now. Marie told me to make sure you took your medicine and had an afternoon nap. She'll be back for dinner, and you better look a lot more rested than you do now."

"Okay. I was on my way, anyhow." Slowly, Leone limped to her room. She was unsure what caused the most upset, her painful movements or the fact that Amy had been away from Little Dip for six days, fourteen hours, and twenty-six minutes...or thereabouts. And hadn't spoken to her once in all that time.

Leone stretched out on her bed and sipped her medicinal tea. Marie had removed her stitches yesterday, but her flesh still felt delicate and her stomach and chest muscles stiff and sore. She sighed at the ceiling, her heavy heart sinking through her into the mattress below, and down through the floor, all the way to hell.

Amy had left for Vancouver. The Garouls were in an uproar. The valley had been infiltrated, the family attacked—but the almanac had to go out regardless. Amy had volunteered to follow through and manage the final stages of the print production, with support from Marie.

However, Marie's input was limited. Her time was taken up with her invalids. At last Connie seemed to be pulling through. Wolven now, her body had accepted the changes thrust upon it. She would undergo the same training that Paulie and all the other adolescent Garouls had, in order to better understand and survive with her new physiology.

Paulie had been well enough to leave yesterday. His relieved parents had come and collected him. Leone, too, was on the mend, but she had always been a quick healer.

And Amy...Amy was an entirely different matter. How would she cope with the secrets she had uncovered? Leone's mood dulled as Amy's parting words echoed in her head and added to her torture.

"I don't trust you. Time after time you had the opportunity to tell me the truth, but you didn't. You left me confused and all alone in a fucking nightmare." She had been ablaze with anger and hurt. It ricocheted off her like electric bolts, singing Leone's bruised flesh.

"Did you really think I would be untouched by it all? Did you really think by fucking me you could save the day? How awfully philanthropic of you." Her eyes burned holes in Leone's soul, until it shriveled into nothing.

"You abused me, Leone. You abused my trust, and my body. And worst of all, you abused my love—for the second time. Once again your deceit has destroyed us." Amy had stood to leave, calm and composed. "I'll finish this project because I promised Connie and Marie I would. I have to go to Vancouver, and then I have a job lined up in London. I don't think we'll see each other again."

Counting the knots in the pine above her head, Leone lay wrapped in her misery. Years ago she had wallowed like this in Vancouver, gloomy and moody, like any brokenhearted teenager. But she had never truly seen it from the other side, from Amy's side.

She had abandoned Amy. Leone was the child of an Alpha; she had duties and commitments to her clan, as had all Garouls. Her mother had warned her she was too young, moving too fast in her courtship of Amy. Wolven had to pace themselves with humans, and with sexual activity. But Leone hadn't listened; she had taken what she wanted…Amy. And when her commitments to her pack began, she had to leave the valley to meet them. To do that, she had to leave Amy behind with no real explanation. She knew even at the time that her withdrawal looked like rejection. She had not chosen Amy; she had walked away. Leone really had little choice. Marie and Connie had insisted Amy was too young to have her life hobbled with the Garoul secret. That as teenagers they were both too young to be life mates. They fretted that Leone would end up physically hurting Amy. Leone surrendered to the pressure. Part of her knew the timing was wrong.

Now Leone was the abandoned one. All those years ago Amy had been kept in the dark for her own good, never truly understanding why she had been pushed aside. Because of Leone's selfish haste to start a relationship, Amy's first foray into love became a repeat pattern of the indifference and abandonment of her parents. And all because Leone hadn't been strong enough to follow through on what she knew in her very marrow. Amy was the one for her. Her bloodcall. Her forever mate.

Leone had made the same mistakes this second time around. She had withheld the truth, but taken love. Believed she was in control while Amy was under mortal threat. Arrogantly deciding what Amy needed to know, and when she needed to know it. And in doing so nearly lost her to Virgil.

She had not understood that the Amy Fortune who had left the valley all those years ago was not the woman who had returned to it. Despite her efforts, for good or bad, she was losing Amy all over again. Her life mate was slipping away.

Cocooned in her own misery, she drifted into a deep, dreamless sleep, induced by her mother's medications.

❖

"How are you feeling today?" Amy asked.

"A lot better. This is a good day. I'm feeling less itchy in my skin. And you?" Connie said.

"It's bloody freezing here. I've never been so cold." They both giggled into the phone.

"Well, you'll be back soon. Just add an extra layer. You are coming back?"

"Actually, I'm at the airport now. I finished early." Amy took a deep breath to ask the question she needed to know more than anything in the world. Instead, she said, "Connie, I'm looking at the departures board. There's a flight to London Gatwick later tonight."

"Oh?"

"And there's one for Portland leaving in the next hour."

"And?"

"Did Jori and Elicia get home all right?" Amy changed direction at the last minute. She had to circle the conversation she wanted to have with Connie.

"He called last night. He says Elicia is glowing and has a craving for salt, of all things."

Amy laughed delightedly. It was wonderful how easily Jori and Elicia had moved on with their lives, preparing a home for their twins. Nesting up for the winter. Why couldn't she move on like that? In his own way, Jori had just as big a shock as her, yet he had never lost sight of what really mattered. His love for Elicia, and his wish for them to have a future together.

"How's Leone?" It was a big question asked in a small voice, and nearly lost in the background babble of Vancouver International.

"The stitches came out yesterday. Physically she's doing very well, big, robust beast that she is." Connie spoke into a wall of silence on the other end of the line. After a moment with no response, she said, "She misses you dreadfully. I think that's what's making her ill, much more than you shooting her ever could."

Amy broke the silence with quiet sniffles.

"Amy?" Connie said. "Have you ever heard of half hearts? They're lovers born for each other, and no one else will ever fit. It's hard to be a half heart, because you never really know what's wrong with your life until the other half arrives."

"Then what happens?" Amy was curious. She dried her eyes with the back of her hand.

"Well, when you find the other half of your heart, it's often hard to accept. Because you're really admitting you felt incomplete all along. That you were only half of what you could be. Do you know what I'm trying to say, sweetheart?"

"Yes. But she lied."

"You need to talk to her. Ask her why she lied."

"I know why she lied."

"And can you forgive her?"

Amy didn't answer. Instead her gaze fixed on the departure board above her head.

"Amy?" Connie's voice echoed over her cell phone. "What are you thinking?"

"If I took the London flight I could probably upgrade."

"Will you do that? Go to London?"

Amy hesitated. "No."

"Does that mean you'll fly to Portland?"

"I bought the ticket yesterday."

❖

Leone woke into a twilight room. Disoriented at first, she realized she had slept away the entire afternoon into the early winter evening. Her nostrils twitched; a small herb sachet rested on her pillow bedside her head. She pressed it to her nose: lavender, rosemary, and something else, maybe myrtle? It was drawn with a green thread tied in intricate knots. It was like the love charm she'd made for Amy. Her heart lurched at the unexpected thought. *I haven't opened my eyes two minutes and already I'm in hell.*

She sat up and swung her legs out of bed. It was then she saw the green thread around her ankle. Cautiously she touched it. It was the same pattern of knots as the herb sachet. These were love charms.

Barefoot, she padded to the bedroom door and peeped out. The fire blazed away merrily, haloing a head of blond corkscrew curls. Amy sat curled on the couch, head bent over a book, lost in her own world. The tang of scullcap floated high in the rafters. Leone's heart soared.

Amy glanced up and pinned Leone to the spot with a cool, clear stare.

"Are you going to come in, or just stand there letting all the heat out?" she said.

Startled, Leone took a step into the room, and then hesitated. "You're back."

"So it would seem. Unless there's a spell in here for astral projection." She held up another Wiccan Wheel spell book. "Who does these? They're beautiful."

Hesitantly, Leone approached. "It's a Garoul imprint. Connie and I started it. It's doing really well. There's been a groundswell in magical interest since the millennium."

Amy closed the book and set it aside. Leone was unsure if her connection with it had somehow soured Amy's joy. She was prepared to blame herself for anything and everything, her misery and self-loathing ran so deeply.

"How are you feeling?" Amy said.

"Okay. I got the stitches out. There'll be scars, but I'm fine."

Amy nodded at this, seeming satisfied.

Before the silence could stretch too far, Leone blurted, "How did things go in Vancouver?"

"Easy, really." Amy uncoiled from the couch and stretched. Her top rode up and firelight danced on an inch of creamy belly. "Like clockwork. I've already spoken to Marie and Connie. They can fill you in."

"Where are they?" Leone realized her mother and Connie were absent.

"They went over to Connie's for tonight. They're going to clean the cabin up a little. Connie says she's ready to face it." Amy sighed. "Poor Connie, she loved that cabin, yet she destroyed it and all her beautiful things in it. She must have hated herself so much at the time."

"Connie's adjusting fine now that the initial rage has gone. She's one strong woman to survive a rogue attack and come through it. Elicia, too."

"I'm so angry they had to go through it at all. But then I'm angry about a lot of things these days."

"Oh." Leone felt very uncertain about this information.

"Marie left soup in the kitchen for supper. I'm going to turn on the stove and heat it. Do you want some?"

"Yes, please."

Amy nodded to the couch. "Sit. I won't be a minute."

Leone squeezed into a corner, sitting bolt upright.

When Amy returned she noted the stricken look on Leone's face, her stiff posture and awkward body language. She snuggled into the opposite corner of the couch, drew her knees up to her chin, and stared at Leone's rigid profile.

"Why did you lie to me?" she murmured. Leone started, turning her head to meet her squarely.

"I thought I was protecting you. We didn't know who had attacked Connie, and we needed her work completed for the almanac. I was to look after you until we found the rogue wolf. Sometimes rogues come sniffing around an established den but they soon clear off. We thought Connie fell victim to one of those. No one realized it was a concerted attempt to capture our code."

"So you offered round-the-clock protection and slept with me. And to make me sleep with you, you pursued me with spells, and charms, and witchcraft?" She indicated the green cord around Leone's ankle.

Leone's face scorched.

"Okay, so I took the opportunity to try to woo you back. Connie showed me some spells…and I was desperate. I'd do anything to correct my teenage mistake."

"It wasn't a teenage mistake, Leone. Your mother was right. We had to split up. You would have harmed me. I never realized how right she was until you lunged for me after Virgil was…after he was…" She cleared her throat. She still had problems with his death but accepted it was the fate he had consistently, and persistently, brought upon himself. "If the gun hadn't gone off, you would have really hurt me, whether you intended to or not."

"I thought you were leaving me, and the wolf side was never going to let you go. It's what Marie warned me of when we were young. Now I understand the power she was talking about. Amy, there's a part of me that will always see you as my mate. I don't think I can bear losing you again."

Amy nodded. She was beginning to understand how this worked for the wolven side of Leone, but there were still questions.

"How can I be your mate? You didn't trust me with your great secret. Yet you slept with me and dragged up all that old emotion. Were you ever going to tell me the truth? Or was I always going to be on the outside forever?"

"I wanted to tell you. I loved you. I wanted to ask you to stay. But I couldn't until you and the code were safe." She turned to fully face Amy on the couch. "From the first day you arrived, I wanted to be with you. You can't deny that. You know that. You saw it."

Amy nodded. It had been apparent from very early on that Leone still had feelings for her.

"I was trying to win you, and protect you. And you made it so goddamn difficult," Leone said.

"I had no assurances you weren't going to use me up like before. And once I found out there was a code, I knew I was being used in some way. I just couldn't figure out how. And by the time I did, it was far too late for me to trust you, or any of the Garouls. You should have come clean from the start."

They were sitting opposite each other now. Arms wrapped around knees, curled in their respective corners.

"I can only tell the Garoul secret to my mate, and I didn't have time to win back your love. If you hadn't been replacing Connie, you would never have found out about the code. If you'd just come for a visit, I could have wooed and won you. And then told you the truth. But until I claimed you as my mate, there was no way I could let you know."

It was a weird, circular logic, but Amy could see the dilemma. It was laughable. If she'd let herself easily fall back in love with Leone, she'd have been told about the code almost from the start. But instead she had resisted because of their history, and found the code all by herself. All that had done was seed even more distrust between them.

"Leone, are the Garouls the only werewolf family, is everyone else a rogue wolf? Like Virgil, or Elicia? Turned after an attack."

"Usually humans don't survive an attack. And if they do, the shock of mutation on their system normally kills them soon after. Virgil and Elicia are rare, but not unique. There are rogue werewolves out there, but not as many as the movies would make you think. The majority are born into a clan like the Garouls. There are many ancient families all over the world." She plucked nervously at the cord around her ankle until Amy reached over and slapped her hand.

"Stop that."

"What is it for? You've got one, too." Leone pointed at Amy's bare feet. Amy handed her the spell book.

"Look under Charms."

It was a spell called Wander less.

A binding and a span for each year parted.
A triple knot to hold your lover close.
Bind left foot and journey's never started.
The thread will break when spell holds fast.

"Oh, Amy. You don't need magic for that."

"How can I be sure you won't hurt me? If you become a wolf and want to…mate?" This was the heart of the matter for Amy. Though she knew beyond all doubt that Leone wanted her, for Amy it had to be more than just being claimed.

She wanted to be loved, and furthermore, loved forever. She wanted to come home and to be held there, with care and comfort, and never have to go away again. The world was a cold, calculating place, but she could survive in it, and had done so easily. But she was always alone, scattered and incomplete. A half heart.

Now, in this valley of utter madness, of werewolves, and potions, and spell casting, she had discovered the ability to love again. She had traveled the world over, but here was where all the love in her life was held.

"If you were my mate that wouldn't happen. I would always be in human form when we made love. I would never hurt you. I chased you at the river because I thought you were leaving me. I was always nervous you might not accept me once you found out what I was."

"Now I know, and I want to understand how it might be for us."

"My sex drive will be stronger, and some nights I'll want you over and over. I never really get enough of you…ever. But I'll never be wolven. I'd end up hurting you."

"What about Connie and Marie?"

"What about them?"

"I saw scratches on Marie."

"From Connie. A wolven mating is more…active."

"Oh." Amy blushed. "Have many Garoul mates crossed over

to the wolven side? I know Connie had to, and Patrice wanted to for Claude. But any others?"

"It's dangerous. I'd never ask you to. It's something you have to want."

Amy mulled this over. "Has a Garoul ever entered a…a life bond with any of the other wolven families?"

Leone shook her head. "I've never heard tell of it. Not to say it didn't happen in old Europe." She shrugged.

"Leone. Tell me what the code actually does?"

"But you broke it."

"Only a line or two. What I mean is, what information does it contain that's worth getting killed for? Is it a treasure map? Does it bestow some great supernatural power?"

Leone laughed, "No. It's a sort of rulebook and survival guide all rolled into one. Some of the recipes and infusions help with wounds and transmutation. There's medical advice, pack etiquette, and general news. It tells of our origins and the history of our pack. And most importantly, everything you'd need to know to pass in the human world. It's used to educate and inform. No gold, no magic powers, just good old-fashioned knowledge. It's just an ancient handbook."

"So new code is hidden every year in the almanacs."

"Yes. Since the Middle Ages, when we started to disperse from southern France. The almanacs were how the Garouls kept in touch, then and now. We have other, more modern methods now. We own Ambereye, a software development house, where we embed information in computer programs, for instance."

"Wow. Who's it for? Who reads it?"

"We do. All of us, from all over. The software is in games for the kids to play and learn about their heritage. Mom is the Alpha and it's her job to maintain our historical records and information gathering, and to pass it on to the next generation. I'm in training to take over her role as her firstborn daughter. The Garouls are matriarchal, so command passes down the maternal line to females only."

"So you'll always be tied to Little Dip," Amy said.

"Yes. I will spend most of my life here. If I had a mate I would want her to share the valley with me." She looked over at Amy. "Could you do that? After all the traveling you've done, places you've been, would Little Dip ever be enough?"

"Leone, this place has always been home. I've struggled all these years to stay away. This is where I want to be, because the people I love are here."

"They are?"

"They are."

Leone thought this over. "Are the people you love in this room?"

"They are."

Leone made a play of looking around her. "There's only me in this room."

"There is."

Leone gave the brightest smile and reached for Amy, pulling them prone on the couch. She winced and wriggled into the cushions for comfort.

"You're still sore." Amy eased her weight off Leone, concerned she was hurting her.

"Not much. Maybe you could kiss me better. Somebody shot me, don't ya know."

"Somebody grazed you in a firearm accident that you initiated. Where's my lucky bullet, by the way?"

"Paulie dug it out of a tree. If you kiss me better it could be my lucky bullet, too."

In response Amy pushed Leone flat and carefully straddled her waist. Gently, she opened the buttons of Leone's shirt and laid bare the bright red scars that crisscrossed her breasts and stomach.

"Oh, Leone. It looks so painful."

"Nah. I'm healing really well. Look, the bastard nearly got a nipple." Leone pointed in outrage.

"Poor baby. Maybe I should kiss it all better." Delicately Amy dropped butterfly kisses along each and every scar line. Beginning at Leone's belly, she worked her way up to the crinkled nipple. She nuzzled it into a hardened nub, caressing it with her tongue. Breaking away with a playful nose rub on the pouting tip, she said, "Is that enough medicine?"

Leone looked up at her in consternation. The game had ended much too soon.

"What about this one?" She pointed to her other nipple.

"It wasn't injured."

"But it was scared. It needs reassurance."

"You are such a chancer, Garoul." But Amy dropped her head and drew the tip into her mouth, gently sucking it to a firm point. She teased until Leone squirmed under her.

"You have the most beautiful body I've ever seen," Amy whispered into the scars.

Leone awkwardly drew her into her arms. They lay face-to-face.

"You seen many naked women, then?" Leone tried to sound casual.

"Some. A few." Amy realized she was being asked about her former sex life.

"Oh."

"It's been seven years, Leone. We've both had our share of lovers. Don't tell me you're jealous."

"No, no. I'm not. I was just wondering. It was a stupid question."

"It's okay."

They lay looking into each other's eyes.

"Was there ever anyone special for you?" Now Amy was curious.

"No," Leone reassured her quickly. "Never. No one."

"No one?" Amy found it hard to believe this woman had not been snapped up a hundred times over. Was Oregon myopic?

"No one."

"What. You were just a player? Big Stud Runamok?"

Leone laughed at the moniker. "I'm only amok for you. There's been no one. No one at all." She swallowed anxiously. Her eyes locked with Amy's. "No one. Just you…Only you."

Leone lay there, totally exposed. Her breath stilled. She looked into the depths of Amy Fortune's soul, trying to read it. Would she be any less for her confession?

There were many ways to say, "I love you," to say, "There has only ever been you," or "I will wait for you forever"…and Leone had said it the only way she knew how. Year after year, alone and waiting. Cradling her half a heart, until now, when the missing half had at last returned. Her wait was finally over.

Amy was mute, stricken at the magnitude of these two little words. No one.

Leone had waited for her all this time—and no one. All the pain, rejection and humiliation she had carried for years—and no one? Two words. Five letters. Five stupid little letters. No one. All this time…

"Does that make me someone?" she whispered.

❖

Hours later, Amy's eyes eventually drooped. She had been loved and adored, her body satisfied to the edge of distraction. Her heart was full and content. And now she begged Leone for sleep.

Leone lay beside her and watched until she knew Amy was in deep slumber. Only then did she slip away from their bed and walked naked out onto the porch. The night breeze was sharp and chill, and it thrilled her heated skin.

The full moon was coming around again, ripening in its cycle to the point when it would pour preternatural energy down upon this planet. Then all the dark creatures of the night would honor their golden, lunar goddess.

Leone's blood stirred and her flesh tightened. Energy flowed through her like quicksilver. She would hunt tonight, the first time since her kill. Since ridding the valley of rogues.

She left the shadows of the porch and moved to the central clearing. There she stood and looked to the stars, and the heavy crescent moon. Silently she thanked her lunar mother for her wolven heart, for her loving family, and for Amy Fortune, her one true mate.

Then she flung back her head and howled her heart out.

About the Author

Gill McKnight currently lives in Greece alongside snakes, scorpions, and spiders bigger than her head. When not scribbling in a notebook or pecking away at her laptop, Gill tries to learn Greek and survive riding on her rattly, secondhand scooter. She has secret fantasies about growing lavender and hanging straight shelves in a crooked house.

Books Available From Bold Strokes Books

The Seduction of Moxie by Colette Moody. When 1930s Broadway actress Violet London meets speakeasy singer Moxie Valette, she is instantly attracted and her Hollywood trip takes an unexpected turn. (978-1-60282-114-9)

Goldenseal by Gill McKnight. When Amy Fortune returns to her childhood home, she discovers something sinister in the air— but is former lover Leone Garoul stalking her or protecting her? (978-1-60282-115-6)

Romantic Interludes 2: Secrets edited by Radclyffe and Stacia Seaman. An anthology of sensual lesbian love stories: passion, surprises, and secret desires. (978-1-60282-116-3)

Femme Noir by Clara Nipper. Nora Delaney meets her match in Max Abbott, a sex-crazed dame who may or may not have the information Nora needs to solve a murder—but can she contain her lust for Max long enough to find out? (978-1-60282-117-0)

The Reluctant Daughter by Lesléa Newman. Heartwarming, heartbreaking, and ultimately triumphant—the story every daughter recognizes of the lifelong struggle for our mothers to really see us. (978-1-60282-118-7)

Erosistible by Gill McKnight. When Win Martin arrives at a luxurious Greek hotel for a much-anticipated week of sun and sex with her new girlfriend, she is stunned to find her ex-girlfriend, Benny, is the proprietor. Aeros Ebook. (978-1-60282-134-7)

Looking Glass Lives by Felice Picano. Cousins Roger and Alistair become lifelong friends and discover their sexuality amidst the backdrop of twentieth-century gay culture. (978-1-60282-089-0)

Breaking the Ice by Kim Baldwin. Nothing is easy about life above the Arctic Circle—except, perhaps, falling in love. At least that's what pilot Bryson Faulkner hopes when she meets Karla Edwards. (978-1-60282-087-6)

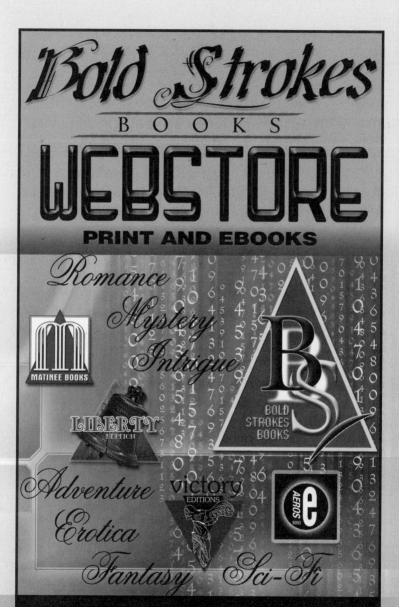